RECLAMATION IN ICE

A VAMPIRE ICE AGE
BOOK TWO

SUSAN PERSON

PERSIV
PUBLISHING

For those who have supported me on this challenging but exciting journey

RECLAMATION IN ICE

CHAPTER 1

JOSIE

Redemption. *Was it just an illusion?* My hope of it hinged on reclaiming our world from the ice age my father inflicted on the world a century ago. The months since I defeated him in the blood rite ticked by with minimal progress on any of the major tasks.

I closed one eye and peered into the microscope. "Damn." I jerked my rubber gloves off and chunked them toward the trashcan.

"You'll figure it out, Josie. We get closer every time," Natasha said, her tone sincere.

"Thanks," I said. "Even when we get it right, we'll still have to figure out how to manufacture the synthetic blood."

"The taste isn't that bad," Natasha sat the cup of fake blood down without tasting it. "It's going to happen"

"It's the only thing that will keep both the humans and vampires around for a while," I said. Vampires, including myself, needed blood, and the humans donated. It wasn't enough though. There were too many of us and too few of them. A few vampires turned Rogue and were lost to animal-

1

istic madness when a vampire consumes enough vampire blood. *And there would be more if I didn't figure out this fucking formula.*

"Maybe you just need more help." Natasha touched my arm.

"Where?" I sounded as frustrated as I felt.

"What about Agata? She passed the computer training with ease and would make a great assistant."

Help was exactly what I needed, but I couldn't ask Agata as much as I would love to see her and have another person I trusted implicitly here.

"Her family wants to stay at the Southern Compound. I can't ask her to abandon them to be my assistant. Especially here in what feels like the actual place humans are referring to with the saying when Hell freezes over."

The sympathy dropped from her tone. "Don't be so stubborn. She'd do it for you," Natasha said.

"And I'd hate myself for asking her," I said. "But you're right. I do need some help."

Most of the scientists disappeared when we took over the Southern Compound, and I assumed they were with my father. *Wherever he is.* He'd disappeared after I revived him when the blood rite ended his existence. The longer he stayed away, the more I feared what nightmare he'd bring when he returned. *And would our people be ready for another battle?*

"I'm going to my office," I said.

Natasha patted my arm. "I should check on Em anyway."

Two guards flanked me as I left the lab for the walk to my office. They were an ever presence since the victory. Fewer people made eye contact or smiled with them at my side. I suffocated from the constant sentries, even when they were outside the door of my office.

I entered the newly remodeled, well upcycled, space and closed the door. A present from the wonderful vampires and humans for our victory against my father. Their show of gratitude and faith spurred me on each day to look for answers.

Vin's scent mixed with mine in the air, and I ran my hand over the edge of the desk. *Something about the desks.* I smiled, remembering the events of the day before on this one. He knew every inch of my body and showed me often. A sigh slipped from my lips at the thought of his touch. I let go of the thought and dropped into the chair to comb through more of Mother's old books.

One drew me over and over again, almost like when Mother tapped me on the shoulder to read when I was little. I flipped through the pages of the book as if new words would appear.

The door to my office flew open. Vin peered into the room. His eyes wide and his dark hair uncharacteristically tousled. "We found him, Josie."

I jumped up from the desk chair. "My father?"

"Yes." He closed the door behind him and came closer.

Tears sprung to my eyes. *He would finally pay for his crimes. I'd make sure of it.*

"And Livia's daughter?" *Gods, please let Luna be okay.* When Father kidnapped her daughter, he thought he had some claim to her because of his experiments on Livia. Luna was one of only three vampire children born in the last hundred years. As a mother to one of those three, it crushed me inside to think what Livia must be feeling.

He shook his head.

"No sign of her?" My heart beat faster. Panic at what my father might have done to her. Experiments he could have done to her. *No, we're not going down that path. We don't know anything.*

"No reports have included her, but he could have her hidden," Vin said, his tone solemn.

"Let's go get him." I walked towards the door. "I'll let Livia know."

"She'll want to go." Vin's voice lowered.

Livia wasn't in any shape to fight. She barely existed. I wouldn't deny her a chance to be there if we found Luna. "It's her daughter and her choice. I'd do the same."

Vin thrust his hand out in front of me. "Her strength hasn't returned. She'll be a liability."

I took his hand between mine and pressed it to my cheek. "If it were me and our child, I'd rip anyone's head off that stood in my way."

"You've been spending too much time with Natasha." Vin kissed my temple and opened the door for me. "See you soon."

I sped down the hallway and scented the air for Livia. Her aroma led me to the same chair by the same window she eventually ended up in every day since she was released from the doctor's care six months ago. I held a hand out toward the guard for them to remain at a distance. Livia's hair needed brushing, and she was thin, even by vampire standards. All our strength didn't come from blood, but it helped. Livia hadn't consumed much at all over the last few months, and it showed in how her cheekbones protruded out. She rarely spoke to anyone except me or Natasha.

"Livia?" I called her name, but she didn't move. I rested my hand on her shoulder.

4

She jerked away. My father had done a number on her when he kidnapped her. I'd ceased to carry the hate for her I once had when I saw how broken she was. I didn't trust her, but I didn't hate her either.

"Sorry, Josie. I mean Empress."

"No need to apologize or call me Empress."

I sat on the wide wood window seal and clasped my hands, looking up at her face.

Livia wiped the pink trail of tears away.

"We found him, Liv," I said, my voice low. "We found Ezra."

Her eyes widened, and she sat up straight in the chair. "And Luna?"

I wished I could tell her, yes, but that wasn't the case. Guilt dug into my gut worse than any thirst I'd ever had. "No sign of her, but he's probably hiding her."

She recoiled back into the chair.

"We're going after him, Livia." I propped myself up on the window ledge in front of her and waited for it to register with her.

Her face hardened. Her gaze, trained out the window, never wavered. "I'm going with you."

Good. She has fight left in her. She'll need it for this journey.

"I suspected you would." *If it were me, even old magic couldn't keep me away.*

Livia's grief was palpable wherever she went. My wish was that we could give her a happy answer. Either way, we would give her closure.

"We'll leave soon, so go see Killian for preparations."

"He won't want me there." Livia squeezed her eyes together.

"It's not his decision." I rested my hand on her knee.

She opened her eyes, fresh pools of pink gathered in them. "Thank you."

"No thanks needed. Go prep," I said. "I'll meet you soon."

My next stop took me to the wing of secure apartments we occupied. The guards took up their stance at the end of the hallway with the ones posted there. I found Natasha in her and Killian's suite.

She opened the door with one hand and held Emilia's hand with the other. Em took her first steps months ago. While her growth rate was still fast, it was slowing. We hoped the genetic engineering my father did wasn't a death sentence for this sweet girl.

"Hey," Natasha said. "Come in."

"She is walking so good now."

"A year ago, I didn't even consider a child, and now, I can't imagine not having one."

"Are you thinking more are in the cards?"

"I'd love to have more. Killian would too, but I'm not sure it can happen without Ezra's engineering." She handed Emilia to the nanny.

"We found him," I said.

"I heard. Killian told me." Natasha sighed. "I'm in, Josie. If he had Emilia, I..." Her mouth twisted to the side.

"I know. I feel the same way."

"We can't let him get away this time," Natasha said.

"We won't," I said.

"So what's the plan?"

"Just the four of us plus Livia. In and out. We secure Luna and terminate Ezra. He's lived enough lifetimes and destroyed even more."

Before the doomed mission my father sent me on last year,

the thought of anyone killing him seemed impossible. *Shouldn't I feel sad? I only feel numb.* Maybe I'd subconsciously chosen to not process it. I blocked out my relationship with him as much as I could. I let a little bit in, and an ache of loss nested in my chest. My loss needed to wait, and I wanted to do what most vampires did when they didn't want to deal with pain or human-like feelings and turn off the emotions around them. I didn't want to know the pain of losing another parent, and the guilt of it ate at me in a way I'd never experienced. *Would Mother agree with my decision?*

Natasha's voice drew me out of my thoughts. "You couldn't do it during the blood rite. Are you sure you can now?"

The old magic lived in fables for me until that moment. It followed me around as a failure even though no one else said it was but me.

"No, ancient magic saved me from the decision. That's why I wanted to talk to you, Natasha." I paused.

Even through all his treachery, I dreaded this outcome. A small piece of me was sad it came to this. He did it though. There was no going back from what I asked of her, and it wasn't the first time I'd asked her to do something dangerous. Many former subjects of my father wanted the opportunity, but I needed it to be someone who would do it swiftly. It wasn't fair of me to ask, but fair and vampires rarely occupied the same space. "If I'm unable to end my father, will you step in and finish him in my place?"

"Gladly," she said, without hesitation.

And no doubts existed in my mind that she would keep her word. Relief flowed over me and then shame at the plan. Shame for what I'd asked of my friend. Shame for the way I conspired to end my only living parent.

"Vin has an aversion to killing anything, and Killian's loyalty was to my father for so long--"

"You don't have to explain, Josie. I don't have the history, and I hate what he has done to the world. The decision is easy for me." Her resolution stronger than mine raised my confidence in our success.

I hugged her. "Thank you, Natasha." I let go. "We've come a long way in a short time. I never thought we'd be friends when Calidora introduced you as Vin's fiancée."

Natasha's lips curled. "It's hard to believe she is his mother, but I didn't see anyone after I saw Killian. Don't get me wrong. I would have gone through with it to save my neck, but I never wanted him."

She and I had more in common than I'd been willing to see when we first met. Leaders manipulated us into situations for their gain. My father with me, and Vin's mother with her. The blood I'd had for breakfast worked its way up my throat. I swallowed hard against it. I'd be a better leader than my father and Vin's mother to all our people.

"You were a pawn like so many in the game Calidora and my father created."

"How close are you to completing your mother's formula for reversing their damage to the climate?" Natasha changed subjects to something more neutral or more important as she'd argued with me several times.

"Close, but not close enough. I'm much closer to that than figuring out the growth rate for Emilia but not as close as we are with the synthetic blood."

"I meant it earlier when I said you're spreading yourself too thin again."

"You sound like Vin." We need answers to all three, and I

didn't want to let anyone down. If I didn't figure out the growth rate for Emilia, Natasha could lose her daughter. If I didn't develop synthetic blood, more vampires would turn Rogue. If I didn't solve the equation to reverse the ice age, we'd all perish, and it would be bad.

"Well, we both care about you." She shrugged and tilted her head to the side. "He might care a little bit more."

I laughed and rolled my eyes. "He better."

"When are you going to let him put a ring on it? I know he's been driving Killian nuts about it."

"The timing seems off, and weddings are really more a human thing."

"But it's important to him, Josie."

I nodded. "It is, and I'll talk to him after we take care of my father." When I told Vin I'd marry him, we'd been facing death by Rogues. The worst possible death a vampire could face. With so much to do, I'd felt selfish even considering a wedding.

"Fair," Natasha said. "When are we leaving?"

"In the morning. I'd rather travel by day so we can avoid Rogues."

"Those red-eyed vampire-eating bastards creep me out."

"Me, too." I glanced at Natasha's daughter. She played with the nanny, oblivious to our discussion. "Are you sure you want to leave Emilia?"

"I never want to leave her, but Luna deserves to be with her mom too." Pink tears welled in her eyes.

My eyes burned, and I imagined they looked the same as Natasha's.

I walked towards the door. "Pack light. We're traveling on foot."

"No tundras?"

"They make too much noise. We can travel faster than they move anyway."

"True." Natasha sighed. "I guess I won't wear those cute boots I found in the building we dug out of the ice and snow."

"Probably a wise decision. See you at sunrise."

"Ugh." She glanced at the window. "See you in a couple of hours."

I covered the short distance to mine and Vin's suites and opened the door to our main apartment. Adam ran to me and hugged my leg. He looked so much like Vin with his thick dark hair, but Vin said he looked like me. I picked him up and snuggled him. Gratitude gripped my heart. I hated the thought of being any distance from Adam, but Livia couldn't hold Luna like this. Adam would understand when he was older. "Hey, little man."

"Mama," he said.

My sweet boy. His first words. My useless heart swelled. "Did you just say--"

"Mama," he said, his confidence increasing.

Tears pricked the corner of my eyes and down my face. "Yes, I'm Mama."

He bounced in my arms. "Dada," he said.

I giggled. "No, he's not here. I'm Mama."

"Dada." Adam flopped over to the side.

"You're distracted, Josephine."

I turned towards the sound of his voice. Vin leaned against the doorframe, a broad smile on his face. His fingers ran through the dark mass of hair. He needed a haircut.

"You are just jealous he said Mama first, Vincent." I dragged out his name.

"Dada." Adam stretched his hands out to him.

Vin took him and Adam patted his face. "Dada."

"He clearly has a favorite, and it's not me." I wrapped an arm around Vin and cradled Adam's little cheek in my hand.

"Mama," he said and reached out for me.

"His favorite is whoever is feeding him. Our son has quite the appetite."

I laughed. "It's true. He does like to eat."

"Are you hungry, little man?" I asked.

"Mama!" Adam yelled and dove into my arms.

"Once again, I am right," Vin said.

"Whatever."

We walked toward the kitchen together. The ever-present guards were a few steps behind us.

"He'll probably be making complete sentences by the time we get back."

"Maybe he'll solve the formula for reversing the ice age."

"Our little Einstein just might," I said.

"Dada." Adam leaned back and looked at Vin upside down.

"Any progress today?" Vin took Adam.

I poured a blood bag into Adam's sippy cup and handed it to him. He tilted it up and drank.

"A little. I wish Mother was here to explain her notes." No matter how deep in research she was on a topic, she always made time to talk to me or help me like when I struggled with calculus. She told me the importance of math in science and spent hours making sure I comprehended the theories.

"She'd be proud of you, Josie."

Would she? She wanted to see an end to the division between created and born vampires, and we had made strides here at the compound in Dallas. Lots of little factions who supported keeping them separated had cropped up while staying in the shadows. I wasn't sure we had the numbers for another battle since I ousted my father.

"Down." Adam pushed against Vin's chest.

Adam ran around the kitchen at baby vampire speed. It would be some time before he could keep up with Vin and me. Speed was the only way Vin and I kept Adam from getting into things he shouldn't. And Adam maximized every opportunity to explore. It was both joyous and terrifying.

"We should power up for the trip." Vin handed me a blood bag and a glass.

"Thanks." I sat the glass on the counter and squished on the bag. I stared at the red liquid.

"Do you want me to warm it up for you?"

I smiled. "No, I was thinking about the synthetic blood formula," I said. "Trying to figure out what we are missing there. I feel like we are so close and at the same time so far away from figuring the ice age out, the right formula for synthetic blood, Emilia's rapid aging, and everything else. If Mother was here, she'd already have it solved."

Mother epitomized grace and patience. If she was here, she would tell me to do the same. Except, the clock ticked against us for survival.

Vin wrapped his arms around me and pulled me into an embrace. I rested my head in the crook of his neck. He laid his head against the top of mine.

"Who's to say? You have limited tools, and it's remarkable how far you've come working on all of this at the same time. I'm not sure anyone could have done it better."

"I love you, even when you are consoling my ego."

He chuckled. "I'm not. I'm just reassuring my lover and mother of my child how amazing she is."

I giggled into his chest. "Mission accomplished."

"Speaking of missions --"

"We should get our gear together." I finished, my tone somber in recognition of our next tasks.

"I was actually thinking we need to get little man to bed, so we can have some alone time." Vin kissed the top of my head.

On cue, Adam put one hand on Vin's and one on mine. He pushed, trying to pry us apart. "No!"

CHAPTER 2

VIN

I scooped Adam up. "Time for bed." I ruffled his hair.

"No." He head-butted me and connected with my nose I rubbed the bridge. *Fucking hell that hurt.* His solid connection was like a sparring partner versus a toddler.

"That's not nice, Adam." I gave him a stern look.

His lower lip jutted out and pale pink tears pooled in the corners of his eyes.

"You didn't mean to hurt Daddy. Did you, Adam?" Josie leaned over and kissed his forehead.

"Mama!" He reached for her.

"No, Mommy has to go put her pajamas on too." I wagged my eyebrows at her.

She laughed. "I don't have pajamas unless Adam is letting me borrow some."

"No," Adam said.

"Mommy is going to take a shower," she said. "It might be the last one I get for a few days."

"I'll join you after I get our little man in bed," I said, wagging my eyebrows at her.

Josie kissed Adam on the cheek. "Night night." She winked and leaned up to kiss me.

I pressed my lips to hers. We were luckier than most. *Love. A child. If I could just get her to the altar, it'd be perfect.*

"Sing Itsy Bitsy Spider to him. It works like a charm," she said and left Adam and me in the kitchen.

I watched the guards take up their positions behind her. It should bring me comfort for them to be with her, but it made her unhappy. My happiness was tied to hers.

Adam bounced his sippy cup off my cheek.

"Done?"

He chunked the cup toward the sink. It landed with precision.

"Nice shot," I said. "But don't tell your Mommy."

I carried him to our apartments and into his bedroom. He cooperated as I dressed him for bedtime like he knew we had a heavy day coming and cut us some slack. Josie had many difficult duties since we came to the Northern Compound, but this mission would be the most challenging of them all. She'd been raised by her father, and I remembered her tears at the end of the Blood Rite when she thought his existence had ended by her hands. Regardless of her anger towards him, she would feel the loss. I would support her and lift her up in every way possible to see her through it.

Adam held his hands out for the stuffed dog. I handed the little brown and white plush toy to him. He tucked it under his arm and reached for me.

"I love you, son," I said. This little guy made the decades of waiting for Josie worth it. I didn't think children would be in my future or a family like this, and there was no price too high to protect their future. Regardless of the ice covering the planet, Josie and Adam were my world.

Adam curled up on his side, and I kissed the top of his head. His eyes closed.

I turned the light out and shut his door. The little vampire could sleep better than most humans.

Steam billowed out of the bathroom. We didn't need hot water, but the haze it cast over Josie's body looked like a dream. *I'm a damn lucky vampire.* Fang Shui agreed, and I slipped in behind her.

She leaned back against me. The decades I'd waited to hold her and show her how much I loved her rolled away with the water drops. When she was near, my world felt whole, like she and I had never been apart. My body, my mind, my heart, and my immortality belonged to her.

I wrapped my hands around her and rested them on her stomach, letting the water run over us. We'd come a long way since I'd almost died in the tundra at the start of our mission. She'd taken control, and once we learned the truth, she became the leader the world needed. Her body bore the weight of our parents' treachery and climbed a mountain to make it right. There was only one thing that could break the pervasive tension she carried.

I tilted my head down and pressed my lips against her neck. A soft moan escaped her lips. My hand dipped down. Her head tilted back against me.

"Don't be gentle this time," she said. "I need to feel everything."

Fuck she was hot. Fang Shui liked when she expressed what she wanted and hardened against her back.

I circled my fingers at her center and plunged two fingers deep inside her.

"Gods," she said. One of her hands pressed against the wall of the shower. The other reached around and grasped my shaft.

I growled in her ear and moved my hand to hardened nipples.

"Now, Vin. I need it." Her voice raspy, she turned in my arms.

My hands went to her hips and around to lift her up. She wrapped her legs around me, and I pressed her back into the wall.

"I love you, Josephine," I whispered in her ear.

"Don't call me Josephine." She put her hands on either side of my face and forced me to look her in the eyes.

"My Josie." I sunk deep into her.

She moaned. "Always," she said in a breathy tone. That one word nearly sent me over the edge. I wanted every part of her. Needed her closer.

I found my rhythm and pushed deeper.

"Vin," she gasped out. She clenched around me, and I could tell she was close.

My release close, I bit down on her shoulder.

Her neck arched, and she met me at the pinnacle. Her muscles contracted.

"Fuck..." I filled her with my warmth.

She rested her forehead against my chin. "I love you." She found my lips.

"How did we go decades without that?" I whispered against her cheek. Josie was unlike any woman or vampire, and she had no idea how special she was. I'd spend every second I had to show her.

"Stupidity," she laughed. Her body completely relaxed, she rested against me.

I kissed the top of her head. "Let's get dried off and go to bed."

"It's not like we are going to sleep," she said.

"You're right." I turned the water off. "I'm going to spend the rest of the night convincing you why you should marry me."

She laughed, but her shoulders stiffened. Each time I brought up the topic of marriage Josie redirected the conversation. She said it was a human tradition, and we had bigger problems. I wanted to show her it was more than that. It would be my pledge to her for our undead lives. I didn't want to add to the stress she had. I'd waited decades. I could wait a little longer.

"We only have a few hours." She squeezed her hair with a towel. Her eyes met mine in the mirror, and she bit down on her lower lip. "Promise me one of us will come back."

My heart splintered at her plea. *She never shows her fear. Josie.* I wrapped her up in my arms. "We're both coming back, Josie. Adam needs both of us."

Gods, let me be right. Please let us both return to raise our son.

CHAPTER 3

JOSIE

The sunrise bathed our path in pink and orange hues. Light glinted off the snow. The Rogues' sensitivity to the sun would keep them in the shadows today. *A good omen for the mission.*

"I guess that view was worth missing some beauty sleep." Natasha drudged past me, her black backpack slung over both shoulders. We each had one packed with blood, poison, and various tools.

"Like you need beauty sleep," I said.

"Maybe not, but they do." She tilted her head toward Vin and Killian.

They surveyed our route about twenty yards in front of us. The morning sun highlighted Vin's dark hair in coppery tones and cast a warm glow over his pale skin. He looked like a god, and I imagined what the glow would look like over his entire body. I shook the thoughts from my head.

"If you don't take that back, you will sleep alone," Killian said over his shoulder.

"I doubt it. You can't keep your hands off me."

"Too much, Natasha, too much," I said, through my giggles.

Livia walked several steps behind us. I waited for her to catch up.

"I'm good on my own," she said. "I worked like that for years."

"But you don't have to anymore," I said. I hoped she could keep up when we went to full speed. The element of surprise could be our only advantage, and we'd lose that if we took a slower pace. Father would smell us coming if we moved too slowly. Vin and Killian did the last-minute checks on our path.

"I don't know why you're helping me," Livia said, her voice too low for the others to hear.

Help was something I struggled to ask for many times myself, but that wasn't what she meant. "I'm not my father, Livia. He was wrong for what he did to you. He did things out of selfishness and power lust. I want to make that right."

"But I did bad things too," she said.

"As did I. As Natasha did. We were manipulated, but we have a chance to be more and do more. We have children who deserve a better place than what Ezra and Calidora created."

"Do you really believe we can make a difference?"

"I do." We already had. Not as much as I wanted to, but we made progress.

"Then I need to tell you something."

The blood I drank before we left gurgled in my stomach.

"I overheard some of the born vampires talking," she said, her tone bitter.

"About what?" I rolled my neck against the tightening.

"There is a group of born that want to keep the division intact."

"Yes, we are aware. We've broken up a few pockets of them already," I said.

"Did you know the created vampires are planning to go after them?"

Damn it. This can't be happening now.

"Without our support or the approval of the council?" I'd only formed the council the last few months, so everyone was still getting their bearings. We struggled every meeting to get born and created to agree on the simplest of proposals. Unification was the goal, and I believed in our ability to achieve it. If the born attacked the created, the humans would be next, and our society would go right back to what my father established.

"They don't think the council is doing enough."

No way am I letting this faction destroy what we worked so hard to build. My anger spiked hard, and I bit my lip to bring myself back to center. "It takes time, and that is something vampires have plenty of. Do you know when the born plan to attack them?"

"In the next few days. They heard the leader of the dissenters will be near the compound, and they plan to take him out," she said in a worried tone.

"Damn it. You could have mentioned that before we left." It was like the universe plotted against us.

Livia's hand shook and she wrapped them around her waist. "I --" Her voice was weak.

"Sorry, Livia. I know it's been hard on you." She had been deep in the absence of Luna and trust wasn't going to come easy to her.

I kicked the top layer of snow, and it rained down on us. "Stop," I called out to the rest of the group.

Vin darted to my side and took a defensive stance. "Are you okay?"

Natasha and Killian joined us.

"No, I'm not. Livia, can you tell them what you told me?"

She recapped the details as she had with me. I hated hearing it even more a second time.

"The council hasn't been in place long enough to have the maturity to deal with this," I said.

"Do you want to go back?" Vin asked, his tone empathetic.

"Yes, and no. We might never get another chance at Ezra like this, but everything we've built could collapse if I don't return." I didn't want to divide our team, but there wasn't another viable option.

"You want to split up," Killian said, a statement, not a question.

"I don't think that's a good idea," Vin said, his voice a mixture of concern and defiance.

"I'm not sure we have a choice." I looked at Natasha. Her head tilted to the side in thought.

"No time like the present for the council to figure shit out," Natasha said. "I say we stick together."

The people at our compound and the surrounding area needed their leader. They needed the head of the government. This mission could carry on without me.

"I think you four should keep moving forward. I'll go back and settle the disruption. Then I'll catch up."

"It's not a good idea," Vin said. "You shouldn't travel alone."

"I agree with Vin," Killian said.

"I'm with the boys," Natasha said. "That's the majority."

My only move left was to play the Empress card. "Unfortunately, this isn't a majority rules situation. I'm the leader, and I need to be there." The rank card wasn't my first choice, and I wouldn't have done it if there was an alternative. *How could any of them argue with that? Except they will, and someone needs to press forward on the mission while I fix the dissension.*

"I'm against it," Vin said.

"We'll all go back then," Killian said.

Livia shook next to me. Panic must have taken over for her. *What mother wouldn't be in this situation?*

"You two go with, Josie," Natasha said. "Livia and I will continue on. The three of you can meet us at a designated location. We'll scout out the area and be ready to move when you arrive."

Natasha's plan made sense. Good sense. Too good to disagree.

Killian opened his mouth and closed it. He probably wanted to argue as I did.

Vin's eyes narrowed on Killian. "Are you good with that decision?"

Killian's gaze locked on Livia. "Natasha can take care of herself. She's strong." The implication he didn't say out loud is what I was thinking. Livia's strength hadn't returned in full yet. Natasha was a badass, but she wouldn't be able to defend them both against a hoard of Rogues. "Can I talk to you for a second?" Killian said to Natasha.

She nodded, and they sped off out of earshot.

"If this is a trick, Livia, you will be held accountable," Vin said.

His concern was valid based on Livia's past actions, but she was a shell of the spy she once was. A mother eaten away by the absent space her child should fill was what stood here with us.

Livia shook harder, and I put my arm around her as a shield. "Livia just wants to bring Luna home, and we will make that happen." Her body steadied.

"It's what she's willing to do that concerns me," Vin said, his voice bitter.

"She's willing to do what any mother would do," I snapped back, but I centered myself. "I get it. I do, but she's a citizen who needs our help today." I didn't like this adjustment to our plan any more than Vin did.

He stayed silent, but his eyes softened on me.

Killian and Natasha returned. "All set," Natasha said. "Let's go, Livia."

"See you soon sexy." Killian kissed Natasha's cheek.

"Count on handsome." Natasha grabbed his ass.

Natasha and Livia marched on through the snow, and Killian, Vin, and I turned back to the compound. The uneasiness of the decision unsettled me. Either direction felt wrong to me.

We hadn't ventured more than 20 or 30 miles when Livia shared what she had overheard, and made it to the compound in no time. Everything seemed normal. Most vampires were asleep while the human residents bustled about on their tasks.

"Wake the council members and ask them to meet in the chamber in ten minutes," I said to one of my aids. The stillness in the compound almost made me think Livia's intel was wrong or misleading.

With Vin and Killian at my side, my confidence strengthened, but I missed Natasha. I'd come to value her input as an advisor. She played Devil's advocate and wasn't afraid to challenge me, but she offered passionate support when I needed a voice. We'd become friends and colleagues out of the worst circumstances. *If we could do it, then this council can make it happen for the born and created, and they had to include humans too.* That was an even tougher subject. I had to unify the vampires first. Then mix the humans in next. In the interim, I was the buffer between them, a responsibility I held at the top of my list.

I entered the chamber, my head high and eyes fixed, portraying conviction for our cause. Inside, my nerves jittered around as to what the council would decide and whether I would have to intervene. The council members were seated at the table, and I took my seat at the head of the table. Vin sat on my right, and Killian stood behind me. Natasha's chair on my left sat empty. I shared with them the information Livia had imparted on us. My biggest fear was this would divide them and the people further instead of finding a way to cement our unification. At least half of them shifted uncomfortably in their chairs, and I wondered if they played a part or were concerned about the test at hand.

"We need to deal with this swiftly," I said, with more poise and composure than I felt. "We can't allow our people to sacrifice themselves, but it is an opportunity to capture the leader we can't ignore."

"Why not let them do it?" Julius, a created vampire, asked.

Not the first reaction I wanted, but I expected it.

"Would you support borns attacking created?" Darius, a born vampire, jumped from his seat.

"Of course not," Julius answered.

I slammed my hand on the table. "This is the exact problem we are trying to resolve. We cannot unify and provide equity to all our people if we are divided in here."

Quiet disseminated over the room. Even for someone who

grew up with attention constantly on her, it made me uncomfortable. I refused to let it show on the outside. What happened next would make or break our movement, and I chose my words carefully.

"If you are not committed to making this work for a better future, to end the ice age, and restore our world and build a society where we are not dictated what we should be by how we entered this world, then you should resign yourself from the council now." My voice stayed calm, but I trembled on the inside. If everyone walked out, we would fail.

"Empress, I support you and defer to your guidance," Darius said and took his seat. He had a hot-headed temper, but he made it around to reason... most of the time. It did me good to see his allegiance. He spent time among the people listening and understanding them, others would follow his lead.

Vin remained silent. He often did in these meetings. He reserved his opinion for rare occasions except to vote.

One by one the others chimed in agreement.

Julius, the last to respond, sat like a statue for a long pause. "Empress, I'm not convinced we can achieve your vision with this group, but you have my respect and support."

I'd take it. Julius was the first created vampire to express interest in joining the council and others looked up to him as a leader. I'd work on getting him to see we could be this change.

"Thank you all. Now, let's go through intelligence and see how credible this threat is."

"I don't think it's credible based on the latest information. My opinion is they wanted to distract us from something else." Darius read a report from our scouts. "I spoke directly to the office who drafted this, and he pointed out several suspicious inconsistencies... like information was being planted." Darius passed it down to me.

I glanced through it, and I tended to agree with Darius.

"May I?" Killian asked.

I handed it to him.

He flipped through the report, reading at vampire speed.

"It does appear to be inconsistent." Killian stiffened and passed the information to Vin.

"Interesting this information surfaced immediately after certain other intel came to us," Vin said.

They were right. This information was planted.

"My thoughts as well." Killian cut his eyes to me. "Someone wanted us distracted and confused."

"Empress, what other information are they referring to?" Julius asked.

"A high-priority mission that was kept to a need-to-know basis," I said. My stomach sank. Natasha and Livia were out there alone, and we didn't know what the hell was going on.

"Are we not your trusted advisors?" Julius asked.

"We were working on securing a high-value target," I said, fully aware of how personal it would seem if I mentioned my father's name. And it was deeply personal. I wanted him to pay. I fiddled with the papers. The time to keep secrets was over. My advisors deserved to know the truth whether my integrity came into question or not. "It was my father, Ezra."

"And what would be the point of capturing him now?" Darius asked.

I glanced at Vin and fought back tears. It was one thing to admit to my friends and Vin that I planned to kill my own father, but it was entirely different to admit it to the council.

Vin took my hand and squeezed. I blinked back the tears and steadied my inner self.

"It wasn't a mission to capture him," I said.

"Then what were you going to do?" Julius asked, confusion in his tone.

I looked him in the eyes. "We were going to end him."

The air in the room became stale and heavy. No one spoke, and all eyes waited for me. *What else do I say?*

"He might be the only chance for us to repopulate," Mara said. Her only child went Rogue a few years ago.

"He's not, and we outnumber the humans now. That's not sustainable. I'm close to creating the synthetic blood and reversing the ice age." Their faith in my father disappointed me, but I expected some residual nostalgic loyalty to the past... and him.

"I can't support you killing Ezra," Darius said. "We should bring him back to face his crimes."

The council all spoke at once.

I raised my voice above the buzz. "With all due respect to you, I will not allow my father to escape again."

"I thought you wanted something different for us, Empress," Julius said. "Did you mean only when it suited you? Don't get me wrong. I want to see Ezra ended, but I want justice here for all to see. We should send the troops to collect him if you know where he is."

"Ezra would never let a group of troops, even our best, sneak up on him," Killian said.

"You are not part of this council," Darius said, his tone dismissive.

"No, but he knows things about my father that most of the people in this room don't," I said. "And I trust him."

"But not us?" Mara asked in a resentful tone.

"No, I trust you too. Ezra will never come back to face retribution though, and there's no way anyone else will be able to get close enough except me."

If they don't agree, I'll stand in direct opposition to the council I created. My hope of building an equal playing field for vampires and humans will die here. The people could end up seeing me in a similar light as Ezra.

"You are right, Empress," Darius said.

"I agree," Mara said.

"Agreed," Julius said.

The rest of the council agreed. Relief washed over me, and if I'd been human, I would have sighed. It didn't matter if they agreed or not, but it did give me hope that they saw reason.

"So, can this council continue to function for a few days while I deal with my father? Can you all get along and push forward on our task? Can you protect our people? All of our people while I am gone?"

"Yes, we can." Mara stood up.

"Yes, Empress." Julius mirrored Mara's actions.

Darius studied me. I met his gaze full-on. He stood up. "Yes, Empress."

The remaining council members did the same.

"Don't fail me," I said and left the room. My confidence was shaken in them and myself, but I still had faith we would succeed. Humans and vampires would survive.

Vin and Killian kept pace with me down the hall. "Give me five minutes to change, and we can leave. We should catch up with Natasha and Livia before nightfall."

"Josie..." Killian's voice trailed off.

I stopped and rested my hand on his shoulder. "I'm sure we're all thinking this same thing, Killian."

"It's a trap," Vin said.

"Let's just get to them as fast as we can," I said. "Go peak in on Emilia and meet us at our room."

Killian nodded and sped off.

CHAPTER 4

JOSIE

Adam slept soundly in his bed. He looked bigger in the few short hours we'd been apart. His hair waved like Vin's.

"He looks like you," Vin perched his chin on my shoulder.

"No, he looks exactly like you," I said. Adam grew so fast. I missed the baby snuggles. "We'll have to try for another one when this is over."

"Before or after I get you to marry me?"

"We can see which happens first," I said. "I do want to marry you, Vin, and grow our family. My father is never going to let us be happy though. We have to deal with him swiftly and finally."

He kissed my temple. "I know," he said. "I know. We'll get him. My hope is that we don't lose you in the process."

I leaned in against him. "What do you mean? I'm yours. I've been yours since I picked you up at the gates of this compound a hundred years ago."

"If you kill Ezra, I'm worried the best part of you might die with him."

I closed my eyes and held the tears in. Vin voiced what I'd been afraid to allow myself to think. I wanted to be here and present for him and Adam, for our family. It felt like I'd been anything but that and couldn't be with my father out there.

"I'm afraid part of me will die too," I said, my voice low and thick with tears. "I don't even know if I'll be able to do it. I showed him mercy once."

Vin tapped into a piece of my desperation around this mission.

"Natasha agreed to end Ezra if I fail."

"She agreed to that? Killian or I --"

"No, it's not fair to burden either of you. Natasha understands my reason and shares the choice."

"If that is what you think is best, I'll support you in it, Josie." He wrapped me tightly in his arms.

A knock at the door made us both jump. "Killian," Vin said.

I stepped out of the safety of Vin's arms and opened the door.

"No time to waste," Killian said.

The sun was already past the peak of the day. We left in the full force of our speed toward the agreed meeting spot. If Father harmed either of them... *No, I'm not even going to think that way. They are fine. Natasha and Livia are waiting on us.* The realist in me knew there was a good possibility Father had them, and my hatred for him shot into my fingertips. I curled my fingers into my hand but stopped before the nails drew blood.

We stopped a few miles away. The sunset colors faded into darkness. Rogues would venture out soon.

"Vin, let's see those tracker skills work," Killian said. He didn't rib Vin. His tone was all business.

Vin inhaled deeply and closed his eyes. He opened them. "It's only Natasha and Livia. No one else, not even a Rogue, for miles."

Killian nodded. "Let's ease in all the same."

"You don't trust my tracking skills, Killian?"

"Just being cautious, tracker ass." Killian gave him a tight smile and patted Vin on the shoulder.

"Let's go boys." I marched forward.

Killian dashed past me. Vin matched my pace.

We zigzagged our way to a short distance from the old safe house. Killian whistled and paused to listen.

Natasha returned the end of the tune. The tension in more shoulders eased.

The door cracked open and Natasha stepped out. Killian rushed to her and wrapped his arms around her. He lifted her, and she kissed his forehead.

Vin and I followed them inside. Livia slept on an old couch. She didn't even flinch from the rustling noises we made coming in from the snow. Natasha had a small fire going in the fireplace. We didn't need the warmth or the light, but it did seem more comfortable with it. I suspected she did it to put Livia at ease and cover our scent. It wasn't total protection, but it would make it a little harder for a vampire who wasn't a tracker to know it was us.

"This place is filthy," Natasha said. Her nose wrinkled. "I've been afraid to sit down, but it didn't faze sleeping beauty over there."

"No, I imagine she's been in worse," I said.

"Any sign of trouble?" Killian asked, his arms still around Natasha.

"No, nothing. Not even an animal."

"That seems odd, but we are pretty far north," I said. Big-game species were a frequent site near here.

"I didn't smell any animals either," Vin said.

"I guess they may have sought better conditions or died off in this area," I said. "We settled in the southern area for a reason."

"Because the humans couldn't survive here. We followed our food source," Vin said.

"Still. Don't you think it's odd?" Natasha said. "There are lots of animals around Dallas now. Populations have adapted."

"I would think that after 100 years, there would be some return, but it still gets well below freezing here. We hover around freezing, so that's more adaptable."

"Maybe," Natasha said. "Did you squash the rebellion?" Natasha raised an eyebrow at me.

"We are the rebellion, Natasha," I said.

Vin and Killian ventured deeper into the safe house.

"I already checked it out dudes," she said to them and turned to me. "Not anymore. You are the Empress and the leader. You are the government," she said.

"I look forward to the day I can renounce that title and let the council lead without me," I said. "I'd rather focus solely on our research. I'd probably already have the answers." Tears threatened, and I didn't even know what I was crying for.

"That group is always going to need a leader, Josie," Natasha said. "They are too stuck in their ways to move forward without a guiding hand."

"I hope you are wrong," I said. I believed in the council and the new government we established.

"I'm usually right," she said. "Maybe you need like an

Assistant Empress or Vice-Empress or something like that. Then you that would free up your time."

I considered it. She sat at my side during council meetings and offered input. A title could be the next step in developing the government. "Hmm... I like that idea, Natasha."

"See. I'm always right." She smiled.

"I'd still have to find the person." I studied her.

"Oh, not me. No one is going to want one of Calidora's ex-subjects in that position."

"We're all the ex-subject of someone either Ezra or Calidora. It doesn't matter," I said.

Vin looked back in our direction at the mention of his mother. We hadn't talked about Calidora much being so consumed with Ezra's whereabouts and getting Livia's daughter home. She and Ezra had conspired on the project that released this ice age on the world. She'd have to pay too...eventually.

"It doesn't matter to you, Josie, but it does matter to others," she said. "I did some horrific things under Calidora's orders."

"We've all done bad things under orders. You are not alone in that pool of sin."

"Except for Vin. He's truly good. So much better than the rest of us."

I smiled. "He is. I wonder all the time what I did to deserve him."

"You saved him, Josie, and you love him. That's what you did."

"He saved me too. I'm not sure he even understands how he saved me. I don't know if I would have ever stood up to my father or initiated this rebellion without him and his high moral code." And even beyond that, he was there after I lost my mother. I loved him with every ounce of my vampire blood and every piece of my existence.

Natasha laughed. "Yep. He's special, my friend," she said. "But so is my sexy man. Killian?" She called out to him, and he arrived in less time than a human could blink.

"Are you ok?"

"As long as you are here." She wrapped her arms around him.

Vin was on his heels and sidled up to me and slid his arm around my waist. "You've been hanging out with Killian too much."

"I'm way smoother than him," Killian said.

"Definitely." Natasha kissed him like no one else was in the room.

"Huh hmmm," Vin said. "Maybe you too should chill for one night."

"If you didn't keep Killian out on all these search missions..." Natasha's voice trailed off.

I mashed my lips together to keep my thoughts inside. Natasha had my back, and it wouldn't be fair to lash out at her. "That would be my fault. I'm the one that sanctioned the trips to find my father."

"Maybe we should go through the plan for the morning," Vin said.

"Good idea, tracker ass," Killian said.

"Thanks, Killer." Vin punched Killian in the arm. He pulled the maps out and walked toward the kitchen. Natasha and Killian followed him.

I glanced over at Livia. Vampires didn't normally sleep this long, but she rarely ate and her strength was nonexistent. I pulled a blood bag out of my backpack and sat it on the coffee table in front of her.

The others reviewed entry points into what we suspected was Ezra's home base now.

"This point is optimal, but we have more coverage from this point," Killian marked the points on the map.

"What about this one?" I pointed to one that had plenty of cover.

Killian grimaced. "It would probably give us the best chance at surprise, but we would need to repel down this old mountain that's feet thick with ice from an old dam that burst."

"I've never been afraid of a little repelling action," Natasha said, her eyes lit up.

"It was one of the few things I beat Killian at in training when we were kids." I smiled and turned to Vin.

He shook his head. "If it wasn't Ezra we were after, I'd say let's race to the bottom. I'm pretty damn good myself."

"This is a challenge we will settle when we get back to the compound," Killian said.

We all laughed. This was the most normal we had been since ousting my father.

"We better power up tonight. Father is known for his elaborate traps, especially when it comes to preserving himself." Ezra would have an evil but elegant game ready for us.

"I'm sure there will be plenty of Rogues waiting for us between us and him," Natasha said.

Rogues didn't scare me on remotely the same level as my father.

"I brought poison grenades for us. They're like the flash grenades only they have the poison I made when we moved on the Southern Compound. The weapons specialist had the idea to put a concentrated formula in them."

"Have you tested them?" Killian asked.

"Don't you trust my poison-making skills?"

"I want to know that we will not be ended by these grenades."

"She packed gas masks for us," Vin said.

"Of course she did." Natasha smiled. "I don't know how you do it all, Josie. I really don't." She shook her head still smiling.

"No sleep. It's not like we need that much anyway." At the mention of sleep, I looked over my shoulder toward the couch. Livia was gone. My unneeded heart pounded in overdrive.

"Where did Livia go?"

"Livia?" Natasha called out. "Livia where are you?"

I stepped into the room. "The blood bag I left for her is gone."

"I'll check upstairs," Vin said.

Killian nodded. "If she's outside, she'll be easy prey for the Rogues."

"Easy might be pushing it, but she would be at risk," I said.

"The sat phone you gave me is gone, Killian," Natasha said. "She played us. I'm going to kick her --"

"We don't know that. Let's not jump to conclusions. She hates Ezra too," I said. Livia was a mother consumed with guilt and loss for her child. Most parents would give up their souls in a lesser situation.

"Let's just find her before she gives our location away or draws in Rogues," Vin said.

"Out in the fucking snow we go," Natasha said.

No moonlight hampered our ability to see any signs. Our eyes were better than humans, but even vampires couldn't see perfectly in pitch-black conditions. The only upside is the Rogues would have trouble seeing us too.

"I think there are some tracks over here," Natasha said.

I followed the sound of her voice, and Killian and Vin were already there.

Vin inhaled. "It's her." He sucked in the scents around us again. "She's not alone."

"How many?" Killian asked.

"Just one."

My throat dried, and I swallowed hard. "Do you recognize the other?"

Vin inhaled and shook his head. "No, I'm not familiar with her accomplice, but it is a vampire."

"Rogue?" Killian asked.

Vin squatted down to examine the tracks. "No, the scent of death isn't in the air."

Natasha snorted.

I shoved my elbow into her arm "Ezra has supporters. It's probably one of them." I reserved my conclusions on her actions until we had more of the facts.

"I think this was her plan all along," Natasha rubbed her bicep. "She's damaged and crazed from her daughter's kidnapping. Her thoughts have been jumbled since she showed up at the gates."

"Let's not pursue her. She made her choice." I turned back for the safe house. Livia wasn't a threat. She could have left the safety of the compound anytime. She just didn't know where to go.

"You want to go back to the compound?" Vin asked in a surprised tone.

I walked through the middle of the group. "No, we're still going after my father. I'm not worried about Livia though." They fell in step beside me.

"What if she gives us away? She could have heard the plan," Natasha said, her voice worried.

"We were going to have to fight our way in anyway. We've come this far. Let's finish it," I said with complete conviction.

Vin entwined his fingers with mine. "Josie, I want to tell you we should go home, but I don't think we'll ever get this close to Ezra again."

"Agree," Killian said.

"Let's leave predawn. The timing change might give us a little advantage," I said.

"Predawn it is." Natasha kicked snow out in front of us. "I'm ready to get out of these wet boots. Vampire or not wet feet still suck."

I glanced up to the moonless sky. These three had fought a hoard of Rogues more than once with me, stood by me against my father even when I released him, and supported me as we built a new government. But we were parents now. Two children waited at the Northern Compound for their mommies and daddies to come home. My resolve strengthened in my heart. I'd make sure we all made it back to our little ones.

Killian and Vin locked down the safe house while Natasha and I went through the supplies to make sure it was divided evenly for the four of us. We wouldn't take the backpacks, so anything we took had to fit in the pockets or on the clips of the tactical suits. The lightweight suits were built with a thin mesh to prevent Rogue fangs from making contact. Not a guarantee but better than nothing.

"Everything is secure," Vin said. "No one is getting in here without our knowledge."

I coiled up the four repelling ropes and laid them out on the table. "Thank you." I slipped my arm around his waist and leaned my head against his chest.

Vin made anywhere feel like home, and I needed a moment of safety before we walked into Gods' know what.

"Why don't you get some rest?" He laid his cheek against the top of my head.

Whether the events of the day or the thought of ending my father, it drained me. "I could nap."

"Good night," Natasha said. She and Killian disappeared upstairs.

Vin took my hand and led me to the couch. He dropped down and pulled me into his arms. "You know it's ok to let it out sometimes."

"I will. Just not right now. I don't think I could put myself together in time if I did." *In time to kill my father.* I closed my eyes and let sleep take me.

CHATPER 5

JOSIE

I peered over the steep cliff. It was at least a hundred and fifty feet down. The ropes would get us close, and it's not like a drop of another twenty feet or so would hurt us.

"Everyone buckled in?" Killian asked.

"Your hands were all over me," Natasha said. "I'm looking forward to returning that favor." Natasha smiled and backed to the edge.

Vin performed one last check on my gear, and I checked his.

"Good?" he asked.

"I'm great." Except I'm going to kill my father. My resolve weakened the closer I came to the task, but Natasha was my backup if I failed this time.

"Let's do this," Vin said and back to the edge.

I positioned myself next to him.

"On one," Vin said. "Three...two... one..."

I pushed off and fought the urge to shout in pleasure.

Vin held up his fingers for the countdown as we moved down

the ice face. Our silent movements reset and synchronized each time. I glanced down. Sharp daggers of ice jutted up from the bottom, but there were a couple of flat landing spots. Killian had done a good job of lining each one of us up with a smooth patch. The silence disrupted by a scuffle above. Ice pellets rained down on us. Our presence had been noticed. *Damn it.*

Rogues scurried back and forth at the edge. Natasha's rope jerked.

"Fuck," she said. The rope shook again and Natasha dropped about a foot. She took an axe and dug into the frozen wall.

I focused between the showers of ice. Not good. We need to move fast. "They're cutting the rope."

"Get down as quick as possible," Killian said and went into action.

I reached for Vin, but my desperate hand couldn't quite reach him. My leg muscles tightened in preparation.

"Go," Vin said.

He and I raced to the bottom. My feet touched ground, and I unbuckled my harness while moving into position under my friends. If one of them happen to slip, I was prepared to break their fall. I kept my eyes up on Killian and Natasha.

Killian swung back and forth until he got close to Natasha. He reached out and took her hand. "Cut," he said.

She grabbed a knife from her pocket and made a clean slice. Her other hand firmly in Killian's, she dangled like a rag doll. Killian descended slowly, making sure Natasha had her grip. He readjusted until she had a secure hold around him. Then he slipped them down the rope at lightning speed. They landed with a thud, and their rope pooled at their feet. I stared at the rope and back at them in disbelief.

"That was close," Natasha said. "Too close." She gave the ice spike behind her a back kick. It shattered into a million pieces.

"So much for an element of surprise," I said in a rush. "Who's ready to go kill my father?"

"Me." Natasha bounced up on the balls of her feet.

Vin and Killian both gave her side-eye.

She looked at Killian. "What? You didn't think I was going to let you have all the fun. Did you?"

"I still think we should consider bringing him back as the council wanted, but I know I'm overruled by this crowd," Vin said, his tone even.

"Let's go find Ezra," I said.

We headed to the air duct to slip inside.

"This suddenly doesn't feel like the best choice," I said, staring down the narrow shaft. It reminded me of a coffin. A very long coffin.

"I'll go first," Killian said. He jumped in before anyone could protest.

Is no one else nervous?

"Next," Natasha said. Holding her hands above her head like it was an amusement park ride.

"Josie?" Vin held out his hand to help me into the chute. I didn't need the help, but I took his hand anyway. It offered reassurance, and I needed that en masse.

"Anything?" I whispered to Killian.

He gave one left-to-right shake. *Strange.*

Vin landed on his feet next to me. He inhaled. His head

cocked, and he inhaled again. "Ezra and I'm not sure what the other smell is. Not human or vampire."

"What do you mean?"

"I've never smelled it before."

"Other vampires?" Killian asked.

"Maybe," Vin paused and tasted the air again. "Not Rogue. If there are vampires, whatever that is covers them."

"Knowing my father, he probably has figured out a way to mask his scent to keep a tracker from locating him," I said. "If we follow it, we probably get close to him."

"I don't know, Josie," he said. "It smells...different."

"Masks on," Killian said. "Just in case."

We positioned the gas masks and checked each other to make sure they were secure. We each took a poison grenade from our belts, even Vin. Anyone left with Ezra was willing to die for him or they wouldn't be here. We had to be ready for that type of fight.

We kept at human speed down the hall and cleared any rooms as we went.

"What was this place?" Natasha asked. "It smells like chemicals and death."

"That's your breath in the mask," Vin said.

I mashed my lips closed to keep from laughing.

"Well, look at Vin thinking he's got a sense of humor," Natasha said. "I'd be impressed if it was actually funny."

Killian chuckled. "Sshh," he chastised.

I caught wafts of the same odor Natasha did. It reminded me of some of the laboratory rooms in the Southern compound. The ones where Ezra's scientists performed experiments. I stopped in my tracks.

"Everyone stop," I said. My gaze shifted to one of the

rooms. I stepped through the door and the scent assaulted me. "Experiments were happening here too."

Killian ran a finger through the dust on the table. "It's been some time since anyone has been in this room."

"That odor is overpowering everything here," Vin said.

"No incentive to get rid of it if it offers cover," Natasha said.

"If my father was experimenting at the Southern compound, and Vin's mother at the underground compound. Who was here?" I looked to Killian.

"I don't know, Josie," he said. "As far as I know, this area was abandoned shortly after the ice age began."

"I thought so too," I said. "So, were they already preparing for this? Did they know what would happen?"

"And where did they go?" Vin asked.

"Maybe they joined with Ezra or Calidora," Natasha said.

"Maybe," I said. I wasn't convinced. This was once a large operation. I noticed a tarp over a table and pulled it off. "What the..."

"Is that a dead Rogue?" Natasha asked, disgusted.

She'd barely decomposed. Her skin was a greyish color and shriveled some, but her body was whole. "She doesn't look fully Rogue though." I moved closer to examine her. "They must have been looking for a way to turn her back."

"Or turn her into one," Vin said. "Rogues were a superstition before the ice age."

I met his eyes. Even through the goggle vision of the mask, I saw the realization there. Rogues were part of the plan.

"Why? What was the point of turning some of us into those things?" Natasha asked.

"Control." Vin, Killian, and I said in unison.

"Hmmm," Natasha said. "They already had control. We were just blind to it."

"Remember when we moved on the Southern Compound? The Rogues had focus. There is something about them we've missed all this time."

"That they report to your father?" Vin asked.

"Something like that, but why?"

"His experiments were relentless. It could be anything." I bent closer to look at an insignia on the Rogue's uniform, and it was a uniform. "Recognize this?" I pointed to the patch.

Killian and Vin stepped for a closer look. Natasha leaned forward but didn't come closer.

"It's the old military symbol, like my tattoo," Vin said. "And the symbol on the Rogues Killian ended."

I nodded. "Yes, the ones when we first traveled to the Dallas Compound. I wonder if this Rogue is branded like them."

"Let's not find out," Natasha said. "We've been here too long as it is."

"You're right," Killian said.

"Of course, I am," she said. "And I can't stand what this mask is doing to my hair."

I had more questions about the activities in this lab, but we needed to get to Ezra before he and his cronies found us.

"Let's go," I said. "But I want to come back when our business is done."

"Provided an army of Rogues aren't chasing us to avenge Ezra," Natasha said.

"That would not be a good ending," Killian said. "I refuse to die at the hands of Rogues."

"I'd prefer none of us meet our end. If there was an army,

they would have already been on us at this point." My gut said the Rogues probably didn't like this place any more than we did, which meant it wasn't good or a place we wanted to be for long.

We went back to clearing the rooms in the hall.

"This place is larger than it looks," I said.

"It will be another hundred years before we find Ezra like this. We should split up," Natasha said.

"That's not a good idea," Vin said.

"Agree. That would make us vulnerable," Killian said.

"Then can we at least move at vampire speed versus this painfully human pace," she said.

"Fine," I said.

"Watch for sensors," Killian said. "We don't want to trip any traps."

"I don't think we have to worry about that. This feels like one big trap," I said.

We sped deeper into the building and paused for Vin to check the air.

"We're getting closer. Ezra's scent is stronger and so is that other strange odor," Vin said.

"Anyone else have that sinking feeling?" Natasha asked.

"I've had it since the Rogues ambushed us on the rappel down," I said.

"Same," Natasha said. "But it's getting worse."

"The feeling or the bad scientist aroma?" Vin asked.

"Both," she said.

Killian held up a fist, and we froze like statues. He pointed to his ear.

I listened, letting my sense of sound take over. A child's muffled whimper of a cry. My eyes flew open. *Livia's daughter.*

48

I tapped Vin's shoulder, and he looked at me. "Is it Luna?" I asked, my voice so low I wasn't sure he could hear me.

He shrugged. "The other scent is too strong. I can't tell." He whispered back.

Killian peaked around the corner. "It's clear."

I followed the sounds down the corridor. The whines grew louder. Movement on the other end of the passageway caught my eye. We split into a side hall, Killian and Vin on one side and Natasha and I on the other.

Bam! The noise echoed down the hall and reverberated as a metal door slammed into something else, probably a wall.

I peered around the corner. The figure was gone and so was the door. It could be a Rogue, but I'd never seen one play like this. I tilted my head in that direction and moved forward, sticking to the walls.

The child's cries turned into laughter and rippled down the hall. Chills ran up my arms. My heart couldn't take another Rogue child. *Please no.*

When we made it to the room, there was light. Bright light to mimic sunshine.

On the floor sat Livia cradling Luna in her lap. I smiled. Luna was safe. I stood still taking the site in before me. Mother and daughter reunited and happy. My hand covered my heart. I didn't want to be the one to ruin the moment, but we needed to move.

Livia didn't look up. "They're gone, Josie," she said, her tone ambivalent. "Ezra and his team left. He promised Luna would be unharmed if I gave him enough warning to escape."

I took a step, and fingers sank into my shoulder, guiding me to a stop.

Vin shook his head. He sniffed the scent in the air. His head tilted toward the doorway.

I nodded that I understood. It didn't take a tracker's sense of smell being this close to figure out what the smell was.

"Stay with Livia," I said to Natasha and Killian.

Killian opened his mouth.

"Just do as I ask," I said.

In the hallway, Vin led me to the far corner. "The scent is coming from Luna."

"What do you mean?" I was sure of the answer, but I needed to hear it out loud.

"She smells like Ezra and something else. Something..." he paused. "Odd. It's not natural."

"Wouldn't you recognize it though?" He was the most skilled tracker. Part of his training was to identify scents with minimal interaction.

He considered it. "I saw her for seconds before the doctor kidnapped her, so it's possible I don't remember."

"But you think something has changed with her?"

"Yes," he said, his tone bitter.

My mouth filled with venom, ready to attack. "That my father did something to her?"

"Exactly."

It never ended with my father. His treachery grew with every act, and as if it wasn't enough that he'd manipulated Livia and Natasha's pregnancies, he'd done something to Luna. It dinged my confidence. "Will it ever end with him? Will we ever catch him, Vin?"

He held out his arms, and I sank into them, wrapping my arms around his waist. His hands rubbed my back, and he kissed the top of my head. "We will."

I composed myself and reaffirmed my resolve. "We need to tell the others," I said. "Tell Livia. Although, as a mother, I'm guessing she already knows."

"Let's see if we can find out how much of a head start he has on us from her."

"At least we know why it was so easy getting in here." I rolled my eyes safe in the knowledge no one could see me with my head buried against Vin's chest.

We returned to the room. Livia held Luna close as a mother would.

"Livia, we think Ezra did something to Luna," I said.

"No, he told me she was safe. Look at her. She looks fine," Livia said, unconcerned. She believed the lies, and one thing my father did well was lie.

Her denial was understandably strong.

"When did Ezra leave?"

"Last night. They locked me in a cell with a time-release on it to give them sufficient time."

"What is their destination?" Killian asked.

Livia looked up and said in disbelief, "Do you think they would tell me?"

"I sure as hell wouldn't," Natasha said.

I elbowed her hard.

"What? I wouldn't." She rubbed her side.

"Let's head back, Livia. It's not safe here."

"It's as safe here as it is there," she said.

"It's not." I squatted down in front of her. She must have been at a level of desperation I never have to want to keep her daughter here. "This is not a healthy place to keep a child."

"And you think the Dallas compound is?" Her eyes darted

around. "There isn't anywhere that is safe for me or Luna." She wrapped her arms tight around the toddler.

I noticed Luna had something in her small hands. "Hey, Luna. Do you have a little dolly?"

Luna smiled and held it up.

My mouth fell open, and I looked over my shoulder.

CHAPTER 6

JOSIE

The doll had a uniform like the dead Rogue we found, right down to the insignia on the chest. It wasn't the sign of an old military initiative. The symbol represented an active cell and Ezra was a part of it.

"Livia, do you know anything about that symbol?" I touched the insignia on the doll's uniform.

"It's the Unified Army," she said.

"The Unified Army?" Natasha said. "What is that?"

"It was formed in secret, even before they released the ice age," she said. "Ezra commissioned trials on humans and vampires, and those that survived were branded. Those who didn't were put in the incinerators and cremated."

"What do you mean branded?" Vin asked.

"They were marked with the insignia."

I closed my eyes and ran my tongue across my fangs. Venom filled my mouth, and I swallowed it.

"Were only those who were experimented marked?" I asked.

"I believe so, yes," Livia said.

"Do you know or not?" Vin yelled.

I almost lost my balance. It wasn't like Vin to raise his voice.

"I don't know for sure," she said. "Why does it matter? The branded are all Rogue anyway."

No, they are not.

"At least I know why I was one of his favorites," Vin said, under his breath.

Livia didn't seem to notice. Either that or she chose to ignore it.

"When did they stop making these Unified Army soldiers?" Killian asked.

"They were all made here, so whenever this place shut down." Livia shrugged. "Maybe fifty years ago."

"Was Ezra trying to make more? Is that why he was here?" Vin asked, his tone bitter.

"I don't know. They didn't exactly give me all their dirty details," she said.

"Let's go back to Dallas," I said. "There's nothing left for us here." I was disappointed we missed a chance at my father again, but the council needed my attention at home. Maybe it was for the best.

"There might be answers," Vin said. I met his gaze. The desperation in his eyes tore out my heart.

"We'll stay a day," I said. The compound wasn't my idea of a safe place to stay, but the vampire who waited nearly a century for me needed answers about his past. Giving him a day to explore ground zero was a small risk. None of us were familiar with the layout other than from maps. The advantage would not be ours if we were caught off guard, but we had Killian's expertise and Vin's tracking skills. Plus, my father was on the run for a reason. The tension in my shoulders relaxed. Ezra wasn't coming back here.

"I'll stay one more night, but then I need to get back to my daughter," Natasha said. She crossed her arms over her chest.

I nodded. "I'd like to go back to where the dead Rogue was, but I can do that on my own. Natasha, are you good staying with Livia?"

"I don't need a babysitter," Livia said, her tone defiant. "I'm not going anywhere."

Natasha rolled her eyes so far back that only the whites were visible. "Yes, I can babysit the traitor."

"She was trying to save her daughter. Go easy on her." I touched Natasha's arm. She gave me one quick nod.

"You two go see what you can find out about the Unified Army. We can all meet back here in two hours?"

"Killian should go with you," Vin said.

"We've already cleared that area, and I'll set the perimeter with sensors. The slightest sign of anything that doesn't seem right and my boots will be on the ground back here. I patted his chest and stood on my tip-toes to kiss his cheek. "I'll be fine, and I think you could use a second set of eyes." I love you, Vin."

He pressed my hand to his chest. "Thank you."

"Know that whatever you find changes nothing. We're still hitting that chapel whenever you want."

A small smile crossed his lips. "I'm holding you to that."

"It's a date." I smiled back and took off down the hall. Tears threatened my eyes, and I wiped at the corners. The nagging pit in my stomach grew with every step I took away from Vin. He needed answers. He'd wanted these answers since he got most of his memory back. Calidora messed with his head in a way I wasn't sure I could fix. She couldn't have been more different from my kind mother. I'd love Vin through it.

THE LAB where the Rogue's body was had a generator. After a little coaxing, I was able to fire it up. The systems came online, but many of the files were corrupted which I expected. It took some time to repair them. The tasks burned through the first hour of my time, and I'd left my comm in the bag with Natasha. *I'm sure Vin will have something to say about that.* With only an hour left to research, I scanned the restored files as fast as I could.

"What?" I reread the paragraph.

Subjects showed a high level of compliance when their blood was removed, mixed with the desired leader, and returned to the subject's body. The desired leader must be of significant age. The older the vampire, the more likely the closer it is to the original, which results in less mutation from the original. Best results were obtained when the subject was still human while this process was performed. Only those viable subjects would survive the turn.

I looked at the Rogue's body. The woman had been human when this happened. The scientists murdered her for this experiment, and it pissed me off. She was someone's family. I checked her body for any tags that might have indicated her subject number. The number on the cuff of a sleeve looked similar to a prisoner number on a prison uniform. The database hadn't been fully restored yet, but I typed the number into the search box.

She was ex-military, a wounded veteran, and volunteered for this experiment. Her file was full of accolades. Her injuries resulted from a failed highly secret mission. She sacrificed herself to ensure the other members of the unit survived. Valor defined her.

I identified with this woman. I'd been willing to fight to my end to right the wrongs my father laid on all the people, born, bitten or human, left in the world. Vin shared this burden with me for his mother's role. I wiped my face with my hands, surprised to find them damp. Humans volunteered for this torture. *Why? Why would anyone choose to become Rogue? What had they promised them to make it worth it? Did they not see the results of other experiments?*

The file shared her partial turn to Rogue and eventual death. It horrified me. The scientists did attempt to save her, but from what I read, it sounded like they only prolonged her agony. In their final attempt, they injected her with poison to slow the progression. She was here for them to dissect her remains, but the file ended there with little of the examination completed or documented. They had taken fingernails and blood samples. *But what had they found? And who were the "leaders' these Rogues were tied to? What happened if the leader ended?*

"Josie?" Vin's voice came from behind me.

I spun around on the stool. "Hi," I said, glad to see him. He would help me sort through the notes.

"Find anything?"

"Just more questions," I said. "You? Where's Killian?"

"He's with Natasha and Livia," Vin said. "You got the computers running in here without me?" He gave a weak smile.

"I did," I said, not missing he was distracted. "What's wrong?"

"You forgot your mini." He held up the device.

"I know. I'm sorry it was stupid of me."

He walked over and planted a long kiss on top of my head. "I was one of the experiments." His word hung in the air around me.

My stomach dropped. "Wh-what? But you're a born vampire? Calidora proved it to us."

I wrapped my fingers around the seat of the stool to hold myself steady.

"Yes, and they experimented on born soldiers who--"

"Volunteered," I finished the sentence for him. "But you didn't turn Rogue."

"No," he said. "They drained me multiple times, bringing me to the brink of my end. It's how they were able to tattoo me."

Blood gurgled in my stomach as anger grew for what he went through.

"But it didn't work," I said, more for my confirmation than his. "Even if you volunteered, why would they choose such a high-born vampire like you? I mean Calidora's only son seems like an illogical choice."

"My mother volunteered me." He sighed.

That Bitch. No, bitch was too nice for her. I pulled him tight to me. "So, she's always been cruel. But her only son?"

"They wanted to make me the leader of the Rogues."

I pushed back so I could see his face. His eyes were tinted pink and his forehead wrinkled, I saw betrayal and pain on his face, and it ripped my unneeded heart apart.

"Do you think you can control them?" I asked, keeping my voice soft.

"There were several chosen," he said. "After a hundred

years, there is no way for me to know which ones were meant to be mine versus the others."

"Have you tried to reach out to them?" If he could control them, we'd have additional forces to stand against my father and his mother.

He shook his head, "No, I wouldn't even know how to try."

"You've never reached out to Adam when he's not with you? Just to see if he's ok?" With Calidora's mind tricks and not having created any vampires himself, maybe he'd never learned the technique.

"No, have you?" He grimaced. His thoughts were probably of the horrible experience when his mother used the sire bond to call him.

"Yes, frequently," I said. "It's a different touch than the call of a sire. Reaching out is more like a whisper on the wind or a gentle knock at the door, and it's the only way I'm able to stay sane being this far away from our son."

"Does Natasha do that Emilia?"

"I've never asked. It's almost an instinct for me to do it, so I would assume it is for her."

"Killian's never mentioned he does it." Vin untangled himself from me and leaned against the counter. Stress creased his face.

"Do you want to try with Adam first? You'll need to be calm," I said.

"I don't want to hurt him," he said.

"And you won't." I stood and took his hand in mine. "Close your eyes."

He studied me with a leery look. His eyes closed.

"Think of your son and your connection. I usually picture

myself as a butterfly fluttering over him. Remember those? How gentle they were?"

"I feel him," he whispered. "His heartbeat. His happiness. His safety." Pink tears leaked from the corner of his eyes.

"Yes," I agreed, my tears flowing down. "Now, gently, back away and return here."

His eyes fluttered open. "That was amazing."

"It is special," I said.

"Does he know when we check on him? It doesn't hurt him like when..." Vin's voice trailed off.

My throat dried at the memory of the day we left on our mission from the Southern Compound to the Northern Compound. Calidora almost ended Vin that night. She summoned him with such ferocity. Torture led her actions. She meant to anger him to search. To awaken his memories, but it didn't work, not completely.

"No, this act of love doesn't hurt. It hurts when the recipient is defiant or the parent is forcefully summoning their child."

"Does Ezra ever reach out to you?" He nudged some papers around on the workstation.

"Not since the day of the Blood Rite. I think it severed the connection in some way," I said. A part of me missed it, and the other part of me relished that he didn't or couldn't.

"My father never has," Vin said.

"He might not be here anymore, Vin." So many vampires were gone or turned Rogue, and Calidora could have killed him. I wouldn't be surprised if she had.

He nodded and wiped the tears from his face. "Let's try for Rogues."

"Are you sure you are ready for that? You can't go in like a butterfly. You'll have to be forceful and strong, like a lion making a kill, given their state of mind."

"Let's do it," he said.

"Picture yourself diving into a Rogue's head. Be confident to find the answer."

Vin didn't close his eyes this time. They were wide open and darted back in forth like he was searching. If he could latch onto a piece of information from one of them, it might give us a new advantage.

"Focus," I said. "Find one and focus"

"Aagh." He grabbed his head and stumbled to the side. "It's chaos."

"Can you make sense of any of it?"

His eyes closed. "Let me try again."

Blood trickled from his nose. "Vin, I think you should stop."

"I've connected to one. He doesn't understand what is going on. He's confused. So much confusion." Blood ran in a trail over his lip and down his chin to his neck. "Pain. He feels pain."

I grabbed his arm. Getting lost in another vampire's emotions was dangerous. This call was about command and not compassion, and he was on the wrong side of it. "Break the connection, Vin."

"Do they all feel this pain?"

"Break the connection," I said.

"I can't," he whispered.

I slammed the heel of my palm into his chest.

His eyes flew open. "Damn." He rubbed where my hand had struck. "That hurt."

"Sometimes a little pain helps sever a connection," I said, my voice full of relief.

"Thanks," he said. "I think."

"Could you glean anything from the Rogue?"

"Not really. The thoughts were so chaotic, and the deeper I dove the worse it seemed to get."

"Not that surprising I guess." I hoped he could reach them in some way like a hive mentality, but that didn't appear to be the case.

"How would anyone control that insanity?"

"Practice." I shrugged. "I've never been in a Rogue's mind, but I can't imagine there is much to latch onto."

"The confusion was so powerful. I wonder if they are all that confused."

"They lose their minds. The chaos is probably a symptom of their insanity."

He nodded. "We better get back to the others."

"Maybe wipe the blood off your face first," I said.

He pulled the hem of his shirt off and cleared it.

NATASHA MET us at the door. "Livia refuses to leave. She's afraid she and Luna will be targeted at the Dallas Compound."

The threat was everywhere around us whether here or there, but I understood her point. It's not like anyone welcomed her there or consoled her when Luna was taken except for Natasha and me. I wanted to do more research, and I was sure Vin wouldn't pass up the opportunity either.

"Let's stay the night here then," I said. "We can work on her plus do a little more research. If she doesn't want to leave in the morning, we can tackle that problem then."

"I'm not sure how we are going to convince her." Natasha cut her eyes toward the room where Livia and Luna were.

"Is our protection not enough? My protection?" This compound stressed me out, and it showed. *I'll have a heart-to-heart with Livia in the morning.*

"You can't be with her every minute, Josie. You have duties, and the council needs you. There are times when the four of us do not have the bandwidth to cover her."

"True. Her fear is indicative of the bigger problem I tried to address with the council when we went back."

"They are stuck in their ways. I hate those meetings," she said.

"Then why did you agree to be on the council?"

"You need me." She smiled. "I'm the only one from outside. I feel like my voice needs to be there."

"Good point. I want to add humans, but I don't think they are ready."

"They'll never be ready unless you push them, Jos."

At some point, humans had to be included, or our society could never move forward and learn from the errors of the form leaders, like my father.

"You're right," I said. "I should have forced it from the beginning."

Vin and Killian joined us.

Vin kissed my temple. "We're going a couple of halls over to check records. There's a room we saw that shows signs of recent use, so we might be able to find out if they did anything to Luna."

I'd end anyone who harmed that little girl. Maybe there was a chance to reverse it if they did experiment on her.

"Ok. Natasha and I can check for blood stores. If they were working from here, they had to have some food. I'm sure we're all getting hungry after today."

"Think she'll be ok by herself?" Killian inclined his head toward Livia.

"She's not by herself. She has her daughter," I said. "And she thinks she's safer here than anywhere else."

"I saw a few rooms with potential," I said.

Natasha and I hurried down the hall and ducked into a room that had several refrigerated units.

"Josie, I want to tell you something, but I don't want you to freak out," Natasha said when we were out of earshot of the others.

"What is it?" I slowed my pace to match hers.

She came to a stop and faced me. "Vin's been different since we've been here, and Killian told me what they found."

"That they experimented on him? Yes, he told me," I said, my voice full of the impatience I had for the conversation. I didn't want to rehash it. "What's your point, Natasha?"

"Did he tell you what they were trying to do?"

"Yes, and we tested it by trying to reach out to some Rogues."

Natasha's eyes widened. "Did it work?"

"Yes, he reached one, but he couldn't control it. The Rogue's mind was all over the place."

"Sounds like their experiments were a failure," Natasha said, her tone relieved.

"Yes, at least a hundred years ago anyway," I said.

"This is another level of fucked up from your dad."

"It wasn't my father. At least not on his own," I said. "I'm sure he had involvement, but this feels bigger than his reach was at the time."

"That we know of," she said. "Gross." The unit Natasha opened had random organs in it, but no blood stores.

"I need to get back to the compound to make sure the council is maintaining our wishes, but there is so much to learn here. I don't even know where to focus our efforts anymore. Between here, the Dallas Compound, the Southern Compound, the immediate needs, and tracking my father again."

The betrayal of my father to the world, to me, and to my mother stung each time I mentioned him.

Natasha opened another door to an empty cooler. "Maybe it's time to let Ezra go. At least for now. We have Luna back. I mean I'm still happy to end him for you, but how much of a threat could he be?"

"Enough that his name still creates fear so palpable among the people that you can taste it." I opened the last cold unit to find it empty. We made our way down the hall checking each room for signs there could be a blood depot.

"Focus is important and spreading it this thin makes you and us vulnerable."

"It's true. We don't have enough hands to cover everything we need to," I said. All the tasks for survival alone ticked off in my head. *How do I focus our efforts in the right place?*

"So, what does your gut say?"

Without hesitation, the answer came to me. "Focus on ending the ice age, because we can help rebuild the human populations from there."

"Do you not think they are too far gone to recover?"

"For our sake and theirs, I hope not. The numbers say we haven't hit the tipping point yet, but we are close." Every minute we didn't work towards reversing the ice age was a risk.

"Then that should be the number one priority," Natasha said. "Damn everything else. You can't do it all yourself, Josie."

She was right. The weight of it settled over me. "Even without sleep, there are not enough hours in the day. I'll redirect the efforts when we get back to Dallas."

Natasha laughed. "Vin must be happy you gave in and called it Dallas. He was so adamant about it."

"I know," I said. "His passion is one of the reasons I love him." I stopped at a door with a familiar symbol. "This room looks like it could be a blood storage."

"Let's check it out."

CHAPTER 7

JOSIE

Natasha and I finished our rounds with little to show for our efforts. We found Vin and Killian combing through the paperwork and computer files. Natasha went straight to Killian's side.

"Find anything good?" He draped his arm around her waist.

"Not in the least," she dropped our small pack on the table. "Unless you consider disgusting body parts good."

"We did find some blood. Just not fresh blood." I stood behind Vin and leaned over his shoulder. "What have you uncovered this time?"

"Ezra mixed his blood with Luna's."

I closed my eyes. He experimented with her. My father wanted to turn her into one of the Rogue leaders like they tried to with ...Vin. "He really is a monster. No wonder Livia didn't want to leave. She didn't want to be anywhere near my father. Probably afraid he would try to control Luna or use her to control Rogues. At least here they are isolated for now."

"Bastard," Natasha said. "What will happen to her?"

"It doesn't look like venom was part of it, so we're not sure," Vin said.

"Time isn't on her side if she is turning Rogue though," Killian said.

"If he didn't mix any venom, she shouldn't become Rogue," I said. *Why wouldn't he use venom? What was he doing?* "The odor you scented earlier, Vin?"

He nodded. "Yes, it was her."

"Livia must be losing her mind," Natasha said, her tone compassionate but concerned. "She will be inconsolable. Her hope was tied to rescuing Luna."

"Can we reverse it?" I asked, "Is there anything we can do about it?"

Vin pressed his hand over mine. "There isn't anything in the documents that indicated they cared about being able to reverse it."

"We need to figure it out," I said. "Vin, they drained you and never turned you. Maybe if we did that to Luna."

"We're not sure what Ezra did beyond mixing his blood with hers," he said. "It could kill her."

"She's going to die anyway," I said, tears welling in my eyes. Luna's little body would last long in the brutal transition to Rogue, but if Ezra didn't use venom, she shouldn't turn. *Shouldn't. What did he do?* The only thing I knew for sure was if it involved my father it was bad.

"We don't know that," Natasha said.

I flipped through some of the pages of the journal and met Natasha's gaze. "Do we wait and see or do we try to do something? Because if it was Adam, I'd kill myself to save him."

"We should talk to Livia about this," Vin said.

"I'm here," a voice said from behind me.

I turned around to see Livia standing at the door. She stood tall with her jaw set.

"I'm not as fragile as you all seem to think," she said.

"Where is Luna?" Natasha asked.

"Sleeping," she said. "My daughter will not turn."

"Livia, her blood is mixed with Ezra's," I said. "Vin has smelled it, and we found the scientists' notes on it."

"But no venom," she said. "There needs to be venom as a catalyst. If his venom entered her body now, then there would be an issue."

"So, we wait here to see if she turns?" Killian asked, his tone frustrated

Wait and see was dangerous, but we didn't know what we were dealing with either.

"She'd already show signs if she was," Livia said. "And I know you want to go back to Dallas."

"Yes, and I know you are concerned with your safety," I said.

"There is no safety there for me or my daughter. I don't want Luna growing up in a place where her mother is despised and hated."

She had a point. While Luna would be welcomed as a child, Livia's acceptance would be challenged every day.

"What do you want to do, Livia?" I asked.

"I want to head to my home. My first home. I don't know if there is anyone there, but it's worth the trip to see."

"Where is home?" Natasha asked.

"New York City," Livia said.

It was a horrible idea. The area was abandoned and had been for decades, almost since the onset of the ice age. I couldn't offer her more protection in Dallas, and I wouldn't control her like my father.

"New York City has been overrun by Rogues for years," Killian said. "The last expedition there was more than two decades ago."

"We'll go as far as we can," she said.

"If that is what you wish Livia, we will not stop you. I will not stop you," I said.

"It is what I want," she said, her tone grateful. "Thank you for taking me in when I didn't deserve it and thank you for helping me find Luna."

"Will you stay here until morning?" I asked, sure she wouldn't but offering anyway.

"I'm not afraid of the dark, and neither is Luna. We'll leave as soon as she's awake."

"I wish you well then." I hugged her, surprising myself as much as I guess it surprised her.

She tentatively hugged me back before squeezing tighter. "Thank you," she whispered. "Thank you for being like your mother and not your father."

Her words meant more than I could voice. "Thank you for seeing her in me."

I fought back tears. Tears for the journey Livia would face, and thankful tears that I wouldn't be the horrible abomination my father is. I might not be as kind as my mother was, but I would never let myself fall to the madness my father has.

"Ezra ended her because she threatened his vision," Livia said. "Don't forget that. He is desperate, and his child or not, he will do the same to you."

I nodded. It still hurt, but it was an answer I already knew. He'd had opportunity and hadn't, but that was before the Rite.

His supporters grew in strength the longer the new council spun on our most important topics. *All the more reason to get back and guide them.*

All those years I wanted excitement, adventure, and to prove my worth. Now, I had the chance and felt more like a failure each new day.

"Let's stocked up for your trip." I handed her about a dozen blood bags Natasha and I had found. "They're old but still work."

"You need to keep some," she said, pushing the last of them back at me.

"We'll stop at the safe house for the rest of our gear. We've got some there. You could come get some of those as well."

"No, I'm anxious to get on the road. I'm hoping my family is still there."

A dull ache spread through my chest. So few families remained intact and many were gone completely whether Rogue or ended. The thought seemed fleeting, but I hoped for her and Luna she would find them well.

"Do you ever hear from your parents? Do they ever reach out?" I asked.

"No," she said. "I know it's not likely they are, but I have to try."

"If it was my mother, I'd do the same," I said. "You will always have a place in Dallas if you need it."

"Your mother would be proud, Josie. She always saw the good in people. You are good like her. Hang on to that."

"I'm not even in the same stratosphere as her, but I'll work the rest of my days to live up to her legacy."

Livia touched my hand. "I know you will, and give yourself

some credit, you are more like her than you allow yourself to see."

Luna pattered down the hall towards us. She looked bigger.

"She's still growing fast," I said. *How much has Emilia grown since we left?* The work on their growth patterns needed to resume.

"She is, but it will slow down. She's strong. She'll be fine."

"Mommy," she said, sounding like a miniature adult.

"I'm here, sweetheart."

Luna ran to her and wrapped her arms around Livia's legs.

"Are you ready to go?" Livia knelt down to Luna's level.

Luna nodded. "Running fast fun." She giggled.

"Yes, it is," Livia said. "Can we leave the doll here?" Livia put a hand on it.

"No," Luna said. She jerked it away and held it tight to her.

"I think you are in the terrible toddler stage?" I wondered. "Isn't that what they called it?"

"Close," Natasha laughed. "It's the terrible twos."

Livia giggled. "Guess the ugly doll is going to NYC."

"Seems so," Natasha said. "I'd remove that insignia if you can though."

"Right," Livia said. "I'm not sure anyone there would know what it is though."

"You never know." Natasha wrinkled her nose. "I'm jealous you're getting away from this awful smell before we are. I'll probably never get it washed off me or out of my hair."

Livia took Luna's hand. "Stay true to your mission, Josie." She placed her free hand on my shoulder and squeezed it.

"Make good decisions," I said.

I patted Luna on the top of her head. "Mind your mommy, Luna."

"No," Luna proclaimed defiantly.

I smiled. *Terrible twos.* Two toddlers waited for us at the compound, and I was ready to get back to them.

Livia nodded at each of us and walked down the hall.

CHAPTER 8

JOSIE

Vin stopped us a few miles or so away from the safe house. He picked up on an unusual scent. We snaked our way closer at a painful human pace. Worry nagged at me until venom oozed into my mouth. I swallowed them both down.

"Still getting stronger?" I asked.

"Yes," Vin said, his attention laser-focused on our path. "It's him and something else, like when we were in the facility."

He never did anything without intent. Father planned for this, and we were his pawns. My vision tinged red with anger. This would be the last time he manipulated me or my family.

"So, it's Luna?" Natasha asked.

"No," he said. "It's Ezra, but I'm not sure what is with him."

"You mean who," she corrected him.

"I mean what."

I cut my gaze over to him. "I'm out of plans. Killian?"

"There are three ways in and out of the safe house. The subterranean would be best, but I suspect it is occupied by Rogues right now."

"Yes, there is a Rogue scent in the air, but I can't tell from where with the other," Vin said.

"Then the front door or the back door are the other options," he said.

"Do we just let them have it and move on then?" Natasha asked. "The sun is bright today, so the Rogues couldn't follow until dark."

I let him walk away from the Rite, and I owned my mistake. This was the time to fix it before he got enough power to do more damage.

"If Ezra is in there," I said. "How can we pass up this second chance?" I looked to my side at Vin.

"We can't," he said. He breathed in and gagged. "Whatever is with him is sour and putrid."

I inched toward the building. With each step I made, the scent increased exponentially to me.

"How are you taking that smell?" I asked Vin. "Plus the smoke smell."

"I'm not inhaling anymore."

"Good idea," I said. "Natasha? Killian? Tell me I wasn't the only one still breathing the stench?"

Natasha giggled. "Did our serious Empress just make a funny?"

"I was the only one, wasn't I?"

"Sorry, Josie. It burned my nostrils."

"I stopped when we went on the move," Killian said.

"Great. So, I'm an idiot," I said.

The group chuckled under their breath in unison.

"It's nice to know you're not so damn perfect," Natasha said.

"Is that what you think?" I asked. "I'm not sure I could be further from perfect."

"Maybe show that imperfection a little more often," Natasha said.

"You are perfect," Vin said. "For me."

"Barf, tracker ass," Killian said.

"Says the vampire who can't keep his hands off --"

"Let's not go there," I said. "I'll make sure I advertise my imperfections more if Killian and Natasha stop making out in front of us."

"Not a chance," Natasha said. "Let the rest of the world think you're perfect then. I know the truth now."

I giggled. "Thanks, Natasha."

"You know you love me," she said.

I glanced her way. "I do love you like a fighter loves to take a punch."

"That is so wrong, Josie." She feigned pain and laughed.

"It's why you love me, Natasha." I laughed.

"You got me," she said. "If we weren't about to end your father, I'd dunk you in the snow for that."

Quiet fell over us. The reminder of the task ahead sobered me.

We were about a hundred yards from the house with plans to go to the back door, but the front door opened instead.

My father stepped out. His face sunken in like a starved vampire, and his skin was grey instead of the translucent appearance it once was. Being on the run had taken a toll on him.

I dug my nails into my hand as a reminder to stay present and control my actions.

"Come inside," he said. "It's a bit chilly out here."

What did he mean? We didn't feel the cold. Did he mean our presence? Our mission. It wasn't that long ago he sent me on a doomed assignment.

I moved into the open. He clearly knew we were here and expected us. There was no point in hiding.

"There is my daughter," he said, his voice welcoming. "I'm happy to see you."

The others positioned themselves around me. I glanced at each of them, lingering on Vin. They were ready to stand and fight if it came to it. My father was never this happy to see me. He wanted or needed something from me.

"And your friends guarding their Empress," he said. "Come on. I have a fire going."

"That explains the smokiness," Natasha said. "I didn't have Ezra pegged for the fire type."

"He's not," I said.

"I don't like it," Vin said.

"It smells of a trap," Killian said.

"I'm not letting him escape again," I said, thinking about the words Livia whispered to me. *Am I kind like my mother or a monster like my father? Could I end him for good?* For the evil he'd done that cost humans lives and vampire existence, especially my mother's, I could. "Let's go."

My father stood aside and held out an arm to invite us in.

"Where are the Rogues?" Killian asked.

"In the basement," he said.

He had dark shadows under his eyes, and his hair looked lighter. He looked thin and sick. Why had he let himself get this way? He still had resources. The blood in Chicago wasn't a fine meal, but it was edible. Yet, he'd not eaten it. If he tainted it and I sent it with Livia. *No, that cannot be it.*

I walked past him and looked him up and down. He didn't try any of the usual intimidation posturings he did when he was emperor. Instead, his shoulders sagged like a tired human.

"Ezra, you look like shit." Natasha echoed my own thoughts.

"Ever observant, Natasha," he said. "Nothing escapes you."

"Have a seat at the table," he said.

We waited for him to sit, and none of us took the seat on either side of him. I narrowed my eyes at him and remained silent as I waited for his request.

"You can't catch what I have," he said.

"You know why we're here, Ezra," I said.

"Ezra?" He studied me. "Have I fallen so far from your pedestal that you cannot call me father any longer?"

"There is nowhere left for you to fall. I'm sitting across the table from the vampire who ordered the ending of my mother." Tears burn in my eyes, and I ran my tongue across a fang to draw venom. I suppressed as much emotion as I could with him. He deserved my anger and nothing else.

He nodded. "It's true, but I can say I'm not the vampire I was then."

"None of us are," Killian said.

"Ah, Killian. You were always more loyal to Josephine than to me. Do you have that same loyalty for Natasha? Who would you choose if you could save only one?"

"You're head games will not work on us, Father." I drug the word out, but I couldn't punch it with the disdain I felt. Ezra looked like death. He looked like he had died every day since the Rite ceremony. In his current state, he appeared to be an easy kill.

"I'm not playing games, my dear daughter," he said. "Killian will always choose his Empress over his love. Loyalty is his grace and his glory."

"Fuck you," Natasha said. She was on her feet and around the table.

I pushed back my chair, ready to defend her. Killian was there though.

He leaped the table and grabbed her. "Natasha, I love you. You are the mother of my child."

Ezra focused on me with a smirk across his face. "How is my grandchild? Is Adam growing?"

Vin and I exchanged a look. Fury engulfed me when he said my son's name. Vin's jaw tightened. Ezra wasn't there when we named our son, so he had to have someone inside the compound to know. I'd assumed there would be spies among us, but it still distressed me.

"Yes, I know his name, and the rapid growth you are seeing in Emilia. Luna experienced it. Adam is growing at a slower but still accelerated rate."

"Keep my daughter's name out of your disgusting mouth," Natasha screamed.

"Calm down, Natasha," I said.

"She's quite the hot head," Ezra said.

Natasha fought Killian, but he held her strong.

"Maybe take her outside for a minute," Vin said.

I met Natasha's eyes and held her gaze. Splitting our small group up wasn't a good idea with Ezra in front of us. It would make us vulnerable, and I needed her to be there in case I couldn't finish my task.

She stilled. "I'm good, Killian. Let me go."

"Are you sure?" He whispered in her ear.

She rolled her eyes. "Yes, I'm a vampire. We can turn our emotions off. Remember?"

He let her go.

Natasha took her seat.

"You smell like death," Vin said.

I hadn't inhaled since we talked about the stink in the air. I opened up my senses. My body responded with an involuntary gag. The rotting smell like a thousand dead humans in various states of decomposition.

"One of your experiments gone wrong?" I cut off the breathing motion.

"Not quite," he said. "Old magic did this."

"You're dabbling in magic now?" I asked. "Wasn't the lesson of the Rite enough?"

He stared at me. His eyes didn't waver.

The Rite.

"I see recognition in your face," he said. "Yes, the Rite is the source of my new cologne."

"It gave you bad body odor?" Natasha asked.

"It's turning me into something else," he said, his voice anxious.

I leaned forward and studied him. Most of the physical changes he had could be faked if he refused to consume blood, but the odor couldn't. I sniffed the air and regretted it. He wasn't lying. Changes occurred to his makeup.

"What?" Vin asked.

"I have a guess, but I don't know. This magic predates even me."

"But the Rogues still serve you?" Vin asked. "So you are still vampire?"

"They do obey me, yes. I'm not much of a vampire

anymore though. My senses are still strong, but I cannot stomach human blood any longer."

No blood equated to a weak vampire. An ultimate death would come quick in his state. What in the Rite would have blocked his ability to eat? Punishment for his loss maybe?

"Why are you telling us this?" I asked.

"I want your venom," he said.

"My venom?" Vampire venom exchange could be dangerous, even turning a vampire Rogue. He valued his mind too much to go Rogue.

"Yes, your venom."

No, should be my answer, but I wanted to know more. "And what would you do with my venom?"

"You need to inject it into me."

"Why?" I asked. He doled out tiny pieces of information, and I began to feel like one of the kids asking a million questions. Either he didn't know what was happening to him, or I'd missed an important clue.

"To prolong my life long enough to help you end the ice age. I know you haven't figured out the missing piece to your mother's formula."

Prolong his life...

An end to his existence was my goal, but he was right about the missing piece in Mother's formula. I hadn't solved the equation. He was one of the brightest minds in the vampire world but also one of the most psychotic. Nothing in me wanted to help him, but I did need collaboration in the lab. Knowledge and assistance only someone like him could provide.

"I don't trust him," Natasha said.

"Neither do I," I said. "So convince us why we should.

Wouldn't it turn you Rogue? Why would a vampire need help to extend his life?"

"Something in the Rite, when I died and came back, changed me. At first, human blood irritated my stomach. Then I could no longer keep it down. I switched to animal blood, and now, I'm experiencing the same reaction."

"So you're sick?"

"I'm dying," he said. "A slow miserable death like you all wished."

I leaned back in the chair and studied him, still skeptical if he was telling the truth. "How do you know you are dying?"

"Look at me," he said. "Smell me."

It was hard to argue with. It added up and made sense.

"Why help us now? Just because you're dying?"

"I don't want to leave you with the mess I created."

It was hard to swallow that he had any regrets. He'd never shown any remorse before today.

"What makes you think Josie hasn't already figured it out?" Vin asked.

"If Josephine knew how to reverse the ice age, it would have been done by now." He turned to me. His face was dispassionate like he had shut off his emotions. "It's a fine line, isn't it? Knowing how to thaw so much ice and snow without flooding the coastal cities or entire islands?"

Despite wanting to deny him, my curiosity compelled me to answer. "It is. The slower we do it, the more water can evaporate into the natural cycle."

"Too slow, and it does no good."

I nodded. "Yes."

"And what if you had the exact formula your mother

developed and could control the rate of temperature climb and water evaporation."

My interest peaked at the level of understanding he had, but it battled with my guilt for considering his offer. "That would be optimal. We wouldn't have to worry that a town missed the message."

"Because the human population is on the precipice of crossing the line to inevitable extinction."

"True," I said. "Why are you making me go through this?"

"So that you understand you need me," he said as if it were a fact.

"There are a lot of people in this room I need," I paused. "But you are not one of them." I moved to scoot my chair back, but Vin placed and hand on my knee to stop me.

My friends were looking at me for the next move. If I walked out of here, was I walking away from our only chance left to save the world?

CHAPTER 9

JOSIE

Natasha and Killian stayed with my father while Vin and I stepped away. I needed to get my bearings.

"If I take Ezra back to the compound, the council and everyone else are going to expect a trial and execution." I paced back and forth in the snow, whispering to Vin. "And how do we know we can trust anything out of his mouth?"

"He certainly seems to be dying," Vin said.

"Yes, it's hard to deny when he smells like a pile of rotting corpses on top of another pile of rotting corpses."

Vin put his hands on either of my arms and looked me in the eyes. "It is your decision, and I feel comfortable in saying, we will respect it and keep the secret if you choose to not take him back."

'I don't want you to keep secrets for me. It shouldn't be that way," I said. If I kill him here, the threat is gone, but I wouldn't be able to tell the people. If I did, they would see me as his daughter forever, and it could drive a further divide between the people. I didn't want to be that kind of empress.

"Leaders always have secrets, Josie. It doesn't make you a bad leader to have them."

"Everything in me says he's telling the truth, but there's always a twist with him," I said. "Always." I looked high at the sun. "We'll need to leave before the sun drops much further if we want to be home before dark."

The only choice for the situation was to take him back. If he could provide any assistance to reverse the ice age, and I suspected he could, then I had to take him back.

Vin gently took my chin and brought it back to look at him. "Don't overthink it. You know the right thing to do."

"We're taking him back," I said. "How are we going to sneak him on the compound? And what do we do about the Rogues in the basement here?"

"I don't want to kill them," Vin said, his tone flat.

"It's the humane thing to do," I said. The Rogues only understood chaos. I'm surprised he hadn't changed his stance from being in one's mind. A Rogue would never know peace unless we gave it to them.

"Is it? I'm still not convinced."

"Killian can do it."

"Can we just leave them?"

"They will get out at night. If we leave, they will kill other vampires." I said, keeping my voice soft.

"So will all the other Rogues we don't know about."

I nodded. "You know they will never get better."

"It doesn't mean we need to end them."

I assumed the attempt to reach out to one made him feel more connected to them. I could give him this because he was right. There were plenty of other Rogues out there doing the same thing. Ending these wouldn't make a huge difference. "Yes, we can leave them."

"Thank you." He wrapped me up in his arms.

"Don't thank me yet," I said. "You have to tell Killian we are leaving the Rogues here."

KILLIAN AND NATASHA entered with Ezra concealed through the gate where humans tended to congregate. The hope was it would cover some of Ezra's smell since there were so many different odors there. Vin and I entered the front gate, and I instructed one of the guards to have the council meet me in the chamber.

I confined Ezra to my lab area. There was a small exam room with a single bed and filtration. I could at least control his access from there and hopefully some of his scent. His smell would lead any curious vampires to the lab, so I had to tell the council, and I dreaded it. Would they understand my reasoning Would they support me?

"I'm locking you in for now, but I'll be back after I meet with the council."

Even with the confinement and filtration in place, I could smell Ezra. It would be all over this wing of the compound, but not many had access to my lab area. I could at least get to the council first before the rumors started. Distrust crept in as I thought of the knowledge Ezra had. Was someone on my council the one feeding him information? Would they try to let him out? I'd never had a reason to not trust a council member before, and I needed to know if I could trust them now.

I pushed open the doors with a show of strength, and they slammed against the wall. The two guards on the outside scurried to close them behind me and Vin. The shock on the council members' faces comforted me a little. Maybe it wasn't one of them that betrayed our efforts.

Vin pulled my chair back for me. "Calm down," he whispered in my ear.

My heart thudded. He might not have known, but he gave me strength.

"We found my father," I said.

"So Ezra is gone?" Darius asked his tone even.

"No," I said.

"He got away?" Julius asked, sounding frustrated.

"We brought him back here," I said.

"Finally justice," Julius said.

"He will remain confined to my lab for now," I said.

The council spoke all at once in a dull roar.

I held up my hand. "He has information we need, and that is all I can say at the moment."

"We deserve to know more," Darius said.

"You do, but there is someone among us that is not loyal to our cause. Until that vampire is found, I will not share any other information." If it made the traitorous vampire uncomfortable, maybe they would make a mistake.

"Do not isolate yourself the way Ezra did, Empress," Mara said.

"I will not," I said. It stung being compared to my father, but it didn't break my conviction in my decision. "But I will not jeopardize our future with the knowledge someone seeks to destroy what we are building. The future is too important."

"How do you plan to flush out the traitor?" Darius asked.

"I'll leave that to you all to figure out. When you work together to identify the vampire, you can present your findings to me. We'll decide together on the next course of action," I said. The situation forced them to figure it out together, and they would have to decide whether they could trust each other. They needed to do this to bond as much as I needed the answer.

"We will not fail you, Empress," Mara said.

"Thank you, Mara," I said. Her support should be rewarded. "You are appointed the lead of this investigation."

She nodded.

I stood and exited the chamber. Anxiety built in me, but anticipation grew as I moved toward my chambers to get cleaned up and see Adam before returning to the lab.

The situation would make or break us in so many ways, but if we couldn't work together, it didn't matter if we solved the ice age.

Vin grabbed my elbow and slowed my pace. "That was quite an entrance, but you can let go of that energy now."

"You're right," I said. The stress wafted away from Vin's touch. "We're in a longer venture here. I'm ready to get answers though."

"It will happen."

"Thanks for believing in me," I said. "It's not the easiest job sometimes."

"Easier than you think."

AFTER CHECKING IN ON ADAM, I returned to the lab. If Ezra had the right information, we couldn't waste any time. I punched in the code and the keypad. The door slid open.

I leaned against the open door. "Should I thank you for the locks on the exam rooms here?"

"Some things didn't need to roam our halls," Ezra said, his tone amused.

"I've set up this area for you to work and will supervise you most of the time. If I need to step away, Vin, Killian, or Natasha will be here. Plus a guard rotation will be with you at all times. Experiments will only occur under my supervision."

"You've thought of everything," he said. "You do realize we will need to collaborate."

"Of course," I said. It made me sick to my stomach, but I needed him at this point.

"I will take some venom now," he said, taking a seat on a stool.

"How do you know this will prolong your life?" I asked.

He stared at me. His eyes dared me to break first.

"You've already done it," I said. Realization sank in. "With Luna?" I gripped the counter. "You milked venom from a baby vampire." The disgust rolled off of me.

"It's pure but less potent at that age." He shrugged.

"And you mixed your DNA with hers, so you knew it would match. That's why you waited for me." Of course, it didn't have anything to do with regret. He needed me.

And I could use that.

"Don't worry. It's not a permanent solution. I'll still die."

"Not soon enough," I said. I pulled the syringe out of my pocket and jabbed it hard into his neck.

"Aagh." He flinched. "Your mother would have been gentler."

Every time he brought her up, hate grew in me for him.

"Do you think so?" I paused. "Maybe she would have filled it with poison." I smiled and cocked my head to the side.

A bubble of dark red blood mounded up where I retracted the needle. He covered it with his hand.

I hoped he wondered if I had filled the syringe with poison. It gave me some satisfaction.

"You might be more like me than I thought," he mumbled under his breath.

"Just enough to make me wise to your actions," I said. "Where do you want to start on the formula? Do you want to review what we found of Mother's version?"

"Yes, that's a good start," he said. "But I already know the missing piece. You might have even figured it out yourself."

"What is it?" I asked, waiting on whatever artifice was going to come out of his mouth.

"You're Mother," he said. "She was gifted with formulas. Poison or reversing an ice age. It didn't matter."

"If you --"

"Let me finish." He pushed himself up off the stool like an elderly human with stiff joints. "Her private lab is where she kept everything."

"Her what?" I'd never seen a private lab. *Was he after freedom?*

"It's off the atrium garden," he said. "Where you gathered the ingredients for the poison gas you used to take over the Southern Compound."

"You forced my hand on that and sent me on a mission

where you expected me to die," I said. "I'd say you deserved it and more."

"Nevertheless, there is a hidden door to a lab that was hers alone. Her quiet place. The place she retreated when the world was too much." His voice sounded distant, and it almost convinced me he missed her.

"I've walked the entire garden and never saw a door," I said.

"That's the point," he said. "She wanted to be undisturbed there."

So much for confining him to the lab. How am I going to get him across the mansion without everyone knowing he's here?

CHAPTER 10

JOSIE

K illian parked the green plastic rolling can inside the door of the atrium. "Is there anything else I can do for you, Empress?"

"No, go spend time with Natasha and Emilia," I said. "Thank you."

He closed the door behind him.

The lid flipped open. "I can't believe you made me ride in a trash receptacle." Ezra climbed out of the bin.

"It covered your horrible odor well enough," I said.

"There had to be other options," he said.

"Probably."

"I think you have been around that Natasha too much."

"Where's the door?"

"This way," he led me across the garden to a paneled wall. The beautiful garden scenes were still intact on it. A sign of the care the compound had from Mother's followers while we were in the south. This was a special place to her, and I'd walk in those steps. My heart swelled in my chest.

He laid his hands over a painted flesh-colored rose.

The panel groaned and creaked. Despite the protests, it slid to the side and exposed the hidden lab.

"Her secret within the garden," I whispered.

"Yes." Ezra walked in, and I followed him.

Smaller than the lab I worked in, it was equipped in unique ways. It shouldn't have surprised me as much as it did that the most sophisticated and elegant equipment would be here. Ezra wouldn't have denied her no matter if he opposed her views. It made my lab look like it was stone age equipment.

"Her best-kept secrets are locked in there." Ezra pointed to a large safe at the end of the lab.

"And you know how to open it?"

He shook his head, "No. We'll have to figure it out." Ezra ran his hands around the edges.

"There's no dust or frost damage in here," I said. "Everything looks so well preserved."

"It's climate controlled and filtrated," he said. "As long as it has power."

I took in this personal space. A piece of my mother I never knew. Her handwriting *-covered notes left on the workspace as if she'd return for them. A picture of me, her, and my father sat on the desk by the computer. She loved her family, and there was a time when I'd felt that love. I picked it up and ran my fingers over her beautiful face.

"Do you remember the day this was taken?" Ezra asked, his voice soft.

"It was my birthday," I said. I wanted to wear a tutu and she had a much more appropriate dress picked out. "We argued about what I would wear."

"And she won," he said, his voice still soft. "She was stronger than you gave her credit."

I sat the picture down. My hands shook, and I folded them against my waist. "You killed her just the same."

"You want to hate me for her ending, but it was Calidora who had her killed," he said, his tone full of regret.

"Vin's mother? Why?" *And why would he divulge this now? To deflect blame?*

"She didn't trust your mother to comply."

If this is true, I'll end her. "She was right not to expect compliance from Mother. You should have protected her. It doesn't reduce your culpability in it."

"No, it doesn't," he said. "You're right." He ran a finger over Mother's face. "She deserved more than I could give her. She deserved a better end." His voice was soft and sad at the memory of my mother. Remorse did live in him.

"She did." I almost wanted to forgive. Nearly a hundred years of pain from losing my mother and knowing his role in it made it impossible.

"You haven't completed the bonding ceremony with Vin."

"He wants a wedding like the humans do," I said, not sure why I told him. I didn't want him to know anything about our relationship, but it rolled out of me. Some part of me still looked for his approval, and I wanted to erase that part of me. "I'm not sure a humanlike marriage is for me."

"Don't let what you think happened with your mother and I jade your experience with Vin," he said.

"Don't pretend to be a father now," I said. My stomach ached like he'd driven a dagger into it. "I know your interest in Vin relates to the experiments done on him at the Chicago facility."

"I'm sure you are mistaken," he said. "I do care for you, Josephine, and Vin has always been good, like your mother. He's a good match."

"Do you really think I would take any advice from you?" I shook my head and looked up at the ceiling. "Let's do an inventory of supplies we think we need and make this our base of operations."

VIN. *I needed to see Vin.* I dropped Ezra off in the exam room and headed straight for our apartments.

I opened the door. Vin looked up from the couch, papers spread all around him.

He smiled at me. "I didn't expect you this early. Adam is outside with Emilia and Natasha."

I leveled my smile on him and wagged my eyebrows. "Want to go spar?"

He stood up and unbuttoned his dress shirt. "Only if it means a shower afterward."

"Are you planning on working up a sweat?" I asked.

"Abso-fucking-lutely."

"Good," I said. "I am too." I kicked my shoes off and unbuttoned my shirt.

We both pulled on workout clothes and headed to the gym.

"I'm going to drop your ass on the mat," Vin said.

I turned my head and smiled at him. "Really? You think so?"

He chuckled.

"I've missed that," Vin said. "Being connected to you."

I ran my hand across his bare chest. "I've missed this closeness too."

"You seemed pretty determined when you hit the door. Did you just look up from your work and think of me?"

"Something like that," I said, my hand stilled over his unneeded heart. As much as I hated to admit it, Ezra was right about how good Vin was.

"Hey, come back to me," he said. "Where did you go?"

"Ezra said something to me earlier about my mother." I buried my head into his neck. I didn't want to have this conversation. Not now.

He pulled his head back. His fingers went under my chin and tilted my face towards him. He pressed his lips lightly to mine.

"This was great, and I'm not complaining," he paused. "But don't let Ezra get in your head and don't use the intimacy between us to avoid dealing with your past."

"I wasn't --"

"I know you weren't intending to do it, but you did. Remember what happened last time we didn't talk things out? We broke up for decades," he said. "I don't ever want that to happen again."

"Neither do I," I said. Vin's ability to make me see mistakes without any malice. "Feel free to remind me of my communication failures in real time."

"They're not failures. They are learning opportunities for both of us. The only failure would be if we both stopped caring," he said.

I kissed his cheek. "You are so patient and understanding."

"And that worries you why?"

"Because Ezra pointed out how much you are like my mother," I said.

"And that's a bad thing?"

"It reminds me that I'm not," I said. And I wanted to be like her.

"I didn't know your mother, Josie, but I do know you are not like your father if that is what you are worried about."

"But I am, Vin," I said. "I am more like him than my mother. I've always known I would never be as kind as her. My father's ruthlessness lives in me."

"Not even close. You spared Livia. More than once. You gave Livia her freedom. That's one example of a dozen and something Ezra would have never done."

"Vin, I'm not good like you. I've killed, and I'm prepared to end my father." I'd done some good deeds as he listed, but my bad outweighed the good, like Ezra.

"Give yourself some credit, Josie. Most of our time here has been lived in a prison Ezra and a few arrogant leaders created. It's been nothing short of war."

Tears threatened to overflow my eyes. I dabbed at them. "I want to believe."

"Then do," he said. "You are a great Empress, who plans to hand that power over to the council, and beyond that, you are the most amazing mother to Adam."

I don't think I'd ever be good at accepting compliments, but his words lifted my spirits. "And what about partner to my handsome man?"

"He thinks you're amazing too, especially when you talk to him like this." He pulled open the drawer to the nightstand. "That reminds me. I found this when we were out exploring some of the old buildings today." He opened a little black velvet sack and empty the contents into his hand.

I gasped at the enormous diamond. "Vin--"

He slid out of bed and onto his knee in all his naked gloriousness. Bare on the outside and inside.

"Josie, I know the human marriage ceremony is a little extreme for vampires, but I am declaring my undead love for you. May it never die. Will you accept this ring as a token of my love and commitment to you?"

"Vin..." My voice broke. Tears spilled out of my eyes. "Of course, I do."

He slid the ring on my finger and took my face between his hands. His lips pressed firmly against mine, and I felt something I rarely felt. Safe. He pulled back and looked into my eyes. His eyes crinkled at the corners. This was the happiest I recalled seeing him. His thumbs brushed the tears from my cheeks.

"When we are done with Ezra, I promise you I will give you the humanlike ceremony you want."

"Don't do it for me, Josie."

"I'm not," I said. "Not just for you but for us."

He kissed me again, more urgently this time, and slid back into the bed beside me. This I could do for him. There was no need to deny him or myself this happiness. When everything with Ezra was done, I should be able to hand the nation over to the council. Freedom to be me and just live, as much as vampires do, with Vin and Adam was what I wanted. For once, I felt my dream within reach.

CHAPTER 11

JOSIE

My first task today was to update the hand scanner on the lab door to read my palm. It took longer than expected and Ezra had to help. We focused on opposite sides of the lab, reading through Mother's research.

A leather-bound book sat under a folder I hadn't noticed earlier. I opened it and found my mother's writing. It was my mother's journal. I gasped. Her life in her own words. Nothing could be more valuable to me than to have a piece of her, and maybe the missing piece to the ice age will be in here. I laid my hand on the page as if I could absorb her knowledge and experiences from it. It'd been almost a hundred years since she left us, but her thoughts were here to revisit.

"What did you find?" Ezra asked.

"Nothing." I covered the journal with the file not ready to share this special find with him.

"Come look at this. I think it's relevant." He motioned me to his side of the lab.

I peered at the computer screen, but my thoughts were on the journal.

"She had success on a small scale with this formula," he said.

"But it looks like when she modeled it on a broader scale, she couldn't find the right catalyst for that massive size." A smaller scale might have worked back then, but it would take a large activity with the current place in the ice age. Time was too short for small movements.

"No, but it is somewhere to start," he said. "She lists the catalysts she tried."

"We can see what new ones to try or if we can combine some she used," I said. It was something to try.

"Exactly. The answer is here, Josephine. We can figure it out." He smiled, the first genuine smile I remembered seeing on his face since Mother was murdered.

I smiled back but composed myself. He didn't deserve smiles.

"This one looks promising." He pointed to one on the screen. "It went farther in the modeling than any of the others."

"Ok. Let's start running models with that one. It combines easily with others, so we can run several modes simultaneously." The results were encouraging and more than I'd had on my own.

"I'll start setting them up, and you can review them before we start the model."

"Let me know when you are ready." I hoped the shock at how collaborative he was being wasn't written on my face.

He went straight to setting up the model.

I backed away to the desk and retrieved the journal from under the folder. I perused the pages but couldn't control the urge to go to the last entry. *Would it be the ice age solution?* Fear of what it might say didn't stop me.

The words stared back at me, and I needed time to process it.

Mother dabbled in the old magick. The magick that the Vampire Rite was bound in. She'd been prepared to use it against Father if needed. How had she kept it a secret and how did she know what to do?

"Your mother was older than me," Ezra said from over my shoulder.

I startled and slammed the journal shut. If the answer had been there, I'd have to disclose it, but I'd wanted a little time with it on my own.

"She knew many things we will never know," he said. Lamentation filled his voice.

"And you still let her meet her end," I said. The fact he allowed her death with that knowledge made it even worse to me. I wanted to slap him, but I reigned in my temper.

I twisted on the chair to face him.

His face creased with remorse, but he didn't push any further. "The model is ready for your approval."

I nodded and went to the computer.

"It looks fine," I said. "No issues that I see." He'd done a good job, but he was a scientist at heart like Mother.

I glanced over my shoulder to see Ezra seated in front of the open journal. His head rested in his hands, and his shoulders shook.

It angered me to share this piece of Mother with him. *Did I have that right though when our very existence hinged on our ability to reverse the ice age?*

The daughter in me wanted to go to him because the loss was renewed when I looked at the pages, but the Empress born from his terrible actions gave me pause. I gave in to the part of me that was still his child and crossed the room to him.

I placed a hand on his shoulder.

His hand covered mine. "What did I do Josephine?"

I didn't answer, and I'm not sure he wanted me to. I wanted to kill him and comfort him at the same time. The conflict in me could tear me apart if I didn't get it resolved. I took a humanlike breath and let it out like they do to see if that helped. *It did somewhat.*

"Do you think I will join her when I die?"

"The humans say we have no soul and only those with souls reach an afterlife," I said. "But they know no more than we do, so I think it's possible." More likely he would just cease to be, but he was a fraction of who he was as Emperor. As angry and disgusted as I was by his past actions, I couldn't drive the knife deeper into his wounds. It wouldn't make me any better than him if I did.

He patted my hand and wiped his face. "Did you see the run time on the model?"

"Yes," I said. "Twenty-four hours seems like a long time, but it is pretty complex."

"I'll hit start, and then you can take me to my room," he said.

I don't know what came over me, but I heard my mother's voice in my head telling me to forgive. *I'm hallucinating. That has to be it.* Words came out of my mouth in a voice I didn't recognize. "How would you like to meet your grandson?"

It felt like I was granting his dying wish, and maybe I was.

His face lit up. "I'd like that very much," he said. Fresh tears formed in his eyes but didn't spill over. "Thank you, Josephine." He struggled to get out of the chair.

"Do you need more venom?" I asked.

"Yes," he said. "I tried to go as long as possible without asking."

"You didn't ask." I pulled a syringe from my pocket. "Shall I use the vein in your neck again?"

"It would be best." He pulled the collar of his shirt aside.

My fingers trembled, careful not to jab him in the same manner I did last time. I removed the needle from his neck.

"Done," I said.

He rolled his shoulders and neck. "Thank you."

"ADAM?" I called when we entered the apartments.

He padded across the floor towards me with his arms out. My heart swelled in my chest. "Mommy."

"Are we done with mama already? Am I mommy now?" I scooped him up in my arms and spun him around.

He giggled.

I hugged him to me. "I love you."

"Wuv you," he said.

"I want you to meet someone." I turned him to face Ezra. "This is your grandfather."

Adam looked between Ezra and me.

Ezra's eyes reddened and filled with clear tears. Not pink like ours. Another sign of his loss of vampire characteristics.

"He's my father."

Adam looked back at Ezra and reached for him.

"Hello, Adam." he touched a finger to Adam's nose. He

smiled and tickled Adam under the chin. Adam giggled and squirmed. "Is it ok if I hold him?"

Forgive. It came through so clear in my head.

I nodded and handed Adam to him, but I was ready to fight for my son if needed.

"You are bigger than your mother was at your age," he said. "And you look like your father."

I laughed. "Vin and I debate often who he looks like, and I've stood firm that he looks just like Vin."

"He does," Ezra said.

The door opened and Vin stood there. His eyes narrowed in on Ezra. On Adam in Ezra's arms.

"It's ok," I said. "Come on in."

"I'm not sure it is." Vin took Adam from Ezra. His movements were smooth, but anger boiled underneath.

Adam cried and reached back for his grandfather.

"He's fine," I said. "Close the door."

Vin pushed the door shut with his foot. "Have you lost your mind?"

"Let's talk about it later." If Vin had been this angry before, I hadn't seen it.

Adam wailed for Ezra.

"You're upsetting your son. Just let them be for today," I said.

Vin put Adam on the floor and he beelined for Ezra.

"Play," Adam said. He put his tiny hand in Ezra's and pulled him toward his pile of toys on the floor.

"Yes, future Emperor," Ezra said.

An ick formed in my gut. I wanted to dismantle the monarchy and restore the government to the people. If I got it right, Adam would never inherit this title. He'd run for public office if that was the path he chose.

Vin stood over them and watched every movement. "We don't talk to him about titles."

"It's never too young," Ezra said. "Josephine knew her potential responsibility from the beginning."

"Actually, we plan to turn the nation over to the council eventually," I said. The changes I'd made weren't a secret. He had to have seen the movement toward an equal society.

Ezra glanced over his shoulder but resumed playing with Adam. "The nation will always need a leader, Josephine. They need one person to love or hate, whatever the circumstances bring."

"Something you and Vin agree on," I said. "The ice might melt from that alone."

Vin glared at me.

The look on his face pained me. I shrugged, not knowing if he was mad at me or Ezra or the whole situation. I suspected the latter though.

"You." Adam placed a truck in front of Ezra. He picked up another one for himself. Vin found a box full of toys in the old nursery during the cleanup. Adam had finished his doll phase and was going through a truck phase now. The little truck Adam chose looked like one of the old de-icer trucks humans used before the ice age went too far. The delivery mechanism...

I bent down and held out my hand. "Can mommy see?"

He handed the toy to me and smiled.

"Thank you. You are such a good boy." I studied the little toy. It was surprisingly realistic, right down to the delivery system depiction. In the end, it didn't work. The humans couldn't stop what was to come. They didn't know it was caused by vampires. They didn't even know we existed then. Would they have done anything differently then had they known? I handed the toy back to my son.

"Tank you," Adam said.

I rubbed his hair and stood back up.

Ezra played with Adam as a grandfather would. I noticed his skin took on a grey tone. My venom didn't rejuvenate him as much as the first time, similar to how he couldn't consume blood. If this was his last hoorah, we were nearing the end. He wouldn't be with us much longer. With Adam so young, I wondered if he would remember Ezra.

We needed to find the answers to Mother's formula before my father met his end.

Vin fumed over them as they played, like a volcano ready to erupt. I'd been impulsive, and that wasn't like me. He was right to be angry.

"Adam, I think that's enough play for today," I said. "Go to daddy to get ready for bed."

"Oh," he said, his little voice sounding disappointed. He hopped up and wrapped his arms around Ezra's neck. "Wuv you."

My sweet little boy.

Ezra's eyes glistened and closed. He hugged Adam back.

"Nigh night," Adam said and waved to Ezra. He ran full speed to Vin.

"You need another haircut." I brushed the hair out of his eyes. "I'm going to walk your grandfather back to his room. Then I'll be back to tuck you in." I kissed the top of his head.

"No," he said.

"I'll be back soon," I promised and kissed his outstretched hand.

"Ok," he said. His mood resolved in a moment. If only adults were appeased so easily.

I glanced at Vin's face. He didn't meet my eyes.

Ezra and I walked back to his room in silence. The guards cleared the hallway ahead of us. I tortured myself wondering what the discussion with Vin would be like when I got back to our rooms. I should have talked to Vin first, but that voice in my head pressured me. *How could I tell him that?* I'd have to take his anger and apologize.

When we reached the room, Ezra paused at the door. "Thank you," he said. "Thank you for letting me meet him before ..." his voice broke and trailed off. He cleared his throat. "I hope Vin isn't too hard on you for it."

Ezra changed, and it wasn't all physical. "I'll deal with, Vin," I said.

"I have no doubt you will," he smiled. "You're the best of us, Josephine."

I couldn't accept his compliment. I didn't believe the words. "There are many vampires better than me," I said.

"No, I mean the best of your mother and me." He smiled and laid a hand on the side of my face. It had a little warmth to it. "You represent the best qualities from both of us. Not that I had that many to pass along, but your mother certainly did. You are the exact combination of us needed to lead your people now."

He'd never be one for compliments, and I wasn't sure how to respond. The daughter I once was longed for this kind of approval, and it hit a hidden place inside me. The Empress wanted to reject it, and Josie was stuck somewhere in the middle of those two opposing feelings.

"Close your mouth and say thank you, Josephine," he said.

I snapped my mouth closed. "Thank you, Ez... Father."

He smiled. "I'm tired and want to rest."

"Of course," I said. "I'll see you in a few hours."

"Good night," he said.

"Rest well." I closed the door and locked him in. A pang of guilt struck me, but I wasn't sure I could say exactly which of my actions I felt guilty for. *Maybe all of them. My whole selfish life.*

CHAPTER 12

JOSIE

I paused with my hand over the doorknob to mine and Vin's room. The urge to take in a breath like a human was real. I smoothed down my hair and clothes, even though they didn't need it. My fingers wrapped around the brass handle and twisted.

Vin sat on the couch in the sitting area. He sat upright with one ankle over the opposite knee. It made him look larger.

"Hey," I said.

"Hey," he said. "Come sit. We need to talk." He was too calm for my liking.

Dread built in my stomach. Or maybe it was hunger. I hadn't eaten in a couple of days. *No, definitely dread. I hated disappointing Vin, and I had a strong feeling I had.*

I nodded and sat on the end where I could turn to face him.

"I--"

"No, I want to talk first," he said.

I sat in silence, waiting for whatever verbal punishment he delivered.

His face softened though. "I don't disagree with you letting Ezra meet Adam," he said.

"You don't?"

"Let me finish," he said. "But you should have spoken with me first before bringing him to our personal space. It should have been a conversation between us on how, when, and where the meeting would take place."

The sting of my mistake multiplied with how understanding he was.

"You're right, Vin. I was impulsive and selfish," I said. "It hit me when we made a breakthrough, and Ezra was at a vulnerable moment. I wasn't intentionally excluding you from the decision." I held back the voice telling me to forgive. I imagined it from working so hard.

"But you did, and this is a partnership," he said. "Raising our son takes both of us communicating on the decisions for him."

"You are right. I'm not arguing at all," I said. "You looked so angry earlier. I expected this conversation to go differently."

I relaxed into the cushions.

He took my hand and kissed it. "I love you, Josie. Even when I'm angry, I still love you."

"I love you too." I slid across the couch and let him envelop me in his arms.

A rapid knock at the door made us both jump.

I sat up. *Ezra? I didn't think it would happen this soon.*

Vin answered the door.

Killian stepped inside. "There is a pack of Rogues sighted a couple of miles away."

"The ones that were with Ezra at the safe house," I said. It was my decision that allowed them to be here.

"We don't know, but it's a larger group than we have encountered here. We need to move everyone into a safe space."

"No one should be outside at this hour anyway," I said.

"The humans were having a bonfire celebration for what would have been the Spring Solstice," Vin said.

I jumped to my feet, and Vin was at my side. The humans would be a banquet for the Rogues. We had to get them into the safety of the compound.

"We need to get them indoors," I said. "The Rogues will smell them by now."

"I'll notify the guards," Killian said.

"I'll take Adam to the nanny and meet you down there," Vin said.

"Natasha is doing the same," Killian said.

"We should have repaired the wall sooner," I said, cursing under my breath. It wasn't a priority with everything else, but it should have been. "Can we reinforce that temporary structure? Do we have time?"

"Our efforts would be better spent securing the doors," Killian said. "I've instructed soldiers to block from the outside. You should go back inside."

"Not a chance," I said. I made the decision that put us here, and I should bear the consequences.

Vin and Natasha joined us.

"They are close," Vin said. "Their scent is all over the air."

"Can you tell how many?"

He inhaled. "Twenty to thirty."

"We should be able to take them with our soldiers," Killian said. "I recommend the Empress move to the back."

"I will not hide," I said.

"It's not hiding," he said. "Our Empress should not be on the front line."

"He's right," Vin said.

I looked at Natasha and pleaded for backup. "I'm agreeing with the boys on this one," she said. "I'll go with you though."

"I'd appreciate it if you didn't pull what you did last time," Vin said.

"I guess you've forgotten how much ass we kicked," Natasha said.

"Not forgotten," Killian said. "Today is not the day for heroics though."

I nodded and gave Vin a quick kiss.

Heroics might be exactly what we needed, not just today but every day.

"Did you have to agree with them?" I asked Natasha.

"You know I'm honest to a fault," she said.

"And the kids are safe?"

"Yes, tucked away in the panic room with the nannies."

"I'm glad we got that room online," I said.

We took up a place in front of the main entrance at the back. Guards flanked us.

"Do you see them?" I asked Natasha, pacing back and forth.

"Right there in the front," she said. "Where else would they be?"

We waited. And waited. My adrenaline waned.

"Shouldn't they be here by now?"

"Seems so." Natasha stood on her tiptoes to look over the soldiers.

I did the same.

Vin was coming toward us. He frowned and looked distant.

"They are outside the wall, and they just stopped," he said. "We don't know why."

In all our Rogue encounters, they attacked without pause. "They aren't moving at all?"

"No," he said. "It's almost like they are frozen in place."

"Controlled," the three of us said in unison.

"Ezra," I said. Anger exploded inside me. If this was his plan all along, I'd serve him up to the people for punishment. "I'll go talk to him. Bring him out here if needed."

"I'll go with her," Natasha said.

Vin's forehead creased. "Killian and I will keep the front line ready just in case."

THE DOOR OPENED and Ezra didn't move. His slumber was deep. His lids and breath were heavy.

I touched his arm and shook lightly.

His eyes opened, red and restless. He hadn't commanded the Rogues. His body was too weak, and he'd been asleep. I almost had a pang of guilt for thinking he was behind the Rogue appearance.

"Do you need more venom?" I asked.

"I'm not sure it will work, but we can try."

"Natasha, do you mind grabbing a syringe? They are in the top drawer of the hutch by the desk."

Natasha rifled through the drawer.

"There is a pack of Rogues outside the wall," I said. "Did you call for them?"

"No," he said. "I've been asleep."

His eyes widened. His shock seemed genuine.

"Could you have called for them in your sleep?"

"Here," Natasha passed me the syringe.

I pulled the plunger out and milked the venom from my fangs.

"Maybe they sense how close I am to the end," he said, confusion in his voice.

"Neck?" I asked.

He pulled his collar aside.

I inserted the needle into his vein.

He winced.

A vampire would barely notice a prick from a needle this size, but a human would have pain from it.

"You felt that?"

"I feel everything now," he said.

I suspected what might be happening to him from the Rite, but this solidified what I'd been assuming.

"Ezra, I don't think you're just losing your immortality. I think you're turning human."

"I'm sure of it," he said. "And bound to a human lifespan along with it."

I helped him up off the bed. "Why didn't you tell me?"

"It wouldn't have mattered, Josephine. My end was coming either way."

"The Rite did this," I said. His death would be on my hands no matter what now. "Old magick."

"This was no one else's doing but my own. I'm to blame for

this and everything else that has happened over the last one hundred years."

Forgive echoed in my head again. He'd taken responsibility, and that earned him a fraction of forgiveness. He needed to do more to make up for the last century.

"Do you think you can stop the Rogues?"

"If I have enough vampire sense left in me, but we won't know until we get closer to them. Can you help me get out there?"

"Natasha, can you support his other side?"

Natasha and I assisted him on the trek outside and to the front line. The guards offered help, but we could handle his slight weight. I ignored the gasps as we passed through the crowd. I'd prided myself on being transparent with them, and seeing Ezra was the opposite.

"Tell them to go," Vin said.

"That won't be enough." Ezra walked through the broken place in the wall.

The Rogues shifted when he approached them, like a pack of animals about to be fed. I glanced around the group. If he told them to attack, we had the numbers for this size pack, but there would be losses.

His words were soft but forceful. "Do not harm anyone on the inside of the wall. Tear each other apart. Don't stop until there is nothing left. If you survive the night, then stand in the sun."

The sounds were awful. Ripped flesh. Broken bones. Screams and shrieks.

I covered my ears. Others nearby followed my lead. It did little to block out the noises.

Ezra crossed the threshold of the wall. He dropped to his

knees. Blood spattered from his mouth onto the white ground covering. It took a toll on him to come out here. Not only did he do it anyway, but he also made sure the Rogues wouldn't come back here.

I went to him and squatted down. My anger was replaced with regret for the time we didn't have. "What do you need?"

"Rest," he said.

"I've got him," Killian said. He picked Ezra up in his arms.

Ezra flopped around. I tucked his arms into his lap. "Don't take him to the exam room. Take him to the vacant room on our hall."

"Yes, Empress," Killian said, his formality meant for the crowd around us and not me.

"What is wrong with him?" Darius asked.

"Later, Darius," I said.

"But--"

"Now is not the time, Darius." Vin stepped between us and parted the crowd, so we could follow Killian.

CHAPTER 13

JOSIE

Natasha pulled the furniture cover off the couch. Killian placed Ezra there. This could be it for him, and I'd do what I could to ease his transition if it was.

"Can you grab some towels and water from the bathroom?" I asked Natasha.

"Of course," she said.

"Ezra, do you need more venom?" I asked. "What can we do for you?"

"It's almost time," he said. "I'm almost completely human now." Blood trickled out his lips with each word. "Then it will be over."

He confirmed my observations. This man wasn't the same one I hated, and I struggled to maintain any of the old anger I'd carried.

"Are you sure? There's nothing else we can do?"

Natasha returned with wet washcloths and dry towels. I blotted the blood from his face.

"Not unless you can turn me back to a vampire," he said.

Maybe I could. He's more human than vampire now... likely all human. I needed him for the ice age reversal, and I'd been hearing a message to forgive.

"What if I bit you?" I asked. "Like I was creating a vampire and injected my venom? Would you go Roque or turn vampire?" If he turned Rogue, he would have to be ended, and there could be other Rogues under his control. *Would they come attack if I that happened? Or would it be like the pain a created vampire experiences when their sire dies?* Occam's Razor would suggest the latter.

"It's old magick, Josephine. We have no way of knowing," he said.

"The risk is high for you," Vin said. "You could turn Rogue if you consumed his blood."

"He's almost fully human, so I would say that risk is low." He was my father, my responsibility, and I couldn't finish the ice age formula without him. If he died, we were lost.

"It's still a risk," Killian said. "A price our Empress shouldn't pay."

"I'll do it," Natasha said.

I massaged my browbone. Natasha had a family now. I couldn't let her do it. "No, I'm the one who invoked the Vampire Rite, and if not me, then no one should."

"You heard my vote, but I respect this is your father," she said.

Ezra slipped into unconsciousness. I had to do it. I needed him. We all needed him whether anyone else admitted it or not.

I bit his neck, venom ready, but his blood tasted bitter. I gagged and pulled away, spitting it out on the floor. My venom bubbled at the top of the puncture marks.

His body jerked and a bloodline of goo oozed from the

open wound. Each created vampire experienced the transformation with some difference, but it was similar enough, I knew this wasn't normal. I pressed a towel to the wound.

He opened his eyes for a moment. Then they shut. He started breathing. It was shallow, but they were breaths. He seemed to stabilize, and his color improved a small amount. He looked human not vampire, but he didn't cease to exist. I sat back on the floor.

"I don't think it was enough to work," I said. "Maybe I should try again."

"No, Josie," Vin said, his tone consoling. "You shouldn't." He sat beside me on the edge of the couch. "Whatever happens now is up to him."

"You need some rest too," Natasha said. "Why don't you go lay down and I'll come get you if anything changes."

"No, I want to stay with him." I watched his chest rise and fall. It was strange seeing him take human breaths. "Can you go check on the kids?" I asked Natasha. "And Killian, we should monitor for activity around the compound just in case."

"I'll increase patrols to make sure there isn't a threat from Rogues," Killian said, his voice softer than usual.

Natasha squeezed my shoulder, and they left.

I missed the strength their presence gave me, but the space gave me the freedom to be in the moment with my father.

Vin scooted closer to me, and I leaned into him. The support was something I didn't realize I needed until that moment.

"He's going to die, isn't he?" My stomach tightened and a weight settled across my chest.

"I believe so," Vin said.

"Just when he turned into the father I needed him to be," I said. He wasn't the cold heartless emperor anymore. He'd shown compassion and wanted to right his wrongs. He bonded with Adam. He knew he was going to die and still aided in what might save the world.

"At least he got there," Vin said. "That's something to be thankful for."

"It is," I said. "I'm grateful for the few days we had."

"He's not done yet, Josie. Maybe you'll have a few more days."

"I hope so. Maybe he'll hang on long enough for me to find a solution to the old magick causing it."

"Old magick? The Rite?"

"Yes," I said. "Mother dabbled in it too. Ezra said she was older than him and knew about it. Maybe there is something in her lab we could use."

"Old magick can be dangerous, Josie. We were trained to avoid it."

"Look at Ezra now. Who knew that Rite would do this? There has to be something to counter it." I moved from the floor to the couch next to him.

"I'm sure there is, but there isn't anyone left that knows it."

"That we know of," I said. His mother popped into my head. Calidora was old. She might be familiar with old magick. *Dare I ask him?* "What about your--"

"No, we are not asking Calidora," he said.

"But--"

"No, Josie," he said. "We're not bringing her into our lives. Period." Vin stood up.

I almost slid off the couch.

"I don't want her anywhere near our son." He paced back and forth.

"You know where she is," I said. "Don't you?"

He stopped in front of me. "Yes."

It hurt he kept it from me, but I'd withheld things from him. I couldn't judge given I'd done the same. "Have you been keeping tabs on her?"

"To make sure she didn't show up here unexpectedly. To protect our family and our life here."

I met his gaze and saw the love I was desperate for whenever he was near. His actions were out of pure love.

Ezra stirred.

I took his hand in mine. His hand was warmer than a vampire's but colder than a human's.

His eyes opened. "Josephine, I think the time is near."

"I'm going to check on the cleanup outside the wall, but I'll be back soon. That will give you two some time alone." Vin pressed his lips to my temple.

"Thank you," I said.

I sat with Ezra all night. Vin returned and stayed until it was morning. He only left to be there when Adam woke up and to feed him breakfast.

Ezra sat up on his own. His color looked better, but his breathing was still labored.

I rested my hand on his arm. "Your color looks better. Do you want to try some human food? They brought some dried meat and fresh fruit and vegetables from the greenhouse."

He shook his head. "The model should be done running. Let's go to the lab."

"Are you sure you feel like making the trip?"

"Yes," he said. "As long as you don't put me in a trash receptacle again."

I laughed. "I think we can avoid those dramatics this time."

He stood and refused my help. "Then let's go see how close we got."

We walked at a slow human pace. Heads turned in the hallway. I leveled them with stares.

"I deserve the hatred in their eyes," he said, his tone solemn. He didn't look down and met their gazes instead.

"It's bewilderment and curiosity," I said. "And maybe a little hatred mixed in."

Ezra laughed. "I deserve it, Josephine. All of it."

"Maybe you did once. Even a few days ago, but you aren't the same person." His first thought when he woke up was to check the model...of finishing the work required to save the world.

"No, and it's thanks to you."

"And the fact you are dying," I said.

"That realization certainly changed my perspective," he said in sincerity.

We entered the lab, and the computer beeped indicating the model had completed.

I looked through the data. *No way.* "Are these numbers right?"

Ezra leaned against the table and scanned them. "They appear to be."

"We should run it again to be sure," I said.

"I'll set it up again."

I moved off the chair and helped him into it. He wasn't as strong as he tried to portray.

"I'm going to take a look through Mother's journal."

"If you are looking for notes on the ice age, that's fine. But don't look for old magick or ways to fix me. I deserve this, Josephine. I deserve to pay for my sins."

"Everyone deserves an opportunity to redeem themselves." If it weren't the case, my family and friends would be doomed. We had all done things in the name of the empire that were regrettable. Not on the same scale as Ezra, but if he could earn forgiveness, then we could too.

I sat at the desk and flipped through the pages of Mother's journal from the beginning. There must have been others because this one was just the year of her ending. Where were the others? Most of this one focused on the ice age and the events, both human and vampire, around that time.

One repetitive entry got my attention. Every month, she had a reference point. She must have had a reason for documenting those points in time. I typed the dates into the computer.

"Quarter moons," I whispered. "The neap tides." I spun my chair around.

"Did you find something?" Ezra raised an eyebrow.

"Mother was a genius."

He nodded. "She was, but what are you referring to."

"We need to disperse it during quarter moons, where there is a neap tide. The difference between high and low tide is minimal then." I leaned back in the chair, astounded we hadn't thought of it. It was groundbreaking and the answer we needed. *Thank you, Mother.*

"That's brilliant," he said. "Your mother wrote that in her journal?"

"She had notes on it every month."

"Hmm..." He seemed impressed as he turned back to the computer.

I went back to reading the journal. If she had that, she might have something to help Father.

"How's it going?" Vin leaned against the open lab door.

"Lots of progress." I smiled at him. "How are our people?"

"Rumors and chatter of our guest are all over the gossip circuit," he said.

"It was a bit of a spectacle last night." I regretted many things since taking this position, but the decision to bring my father here wouldn't be one of them. Without him, I wouldn't have found this lab or the journal that might have given us our biggest breakthrough. "What are they saying?"

"It's mixed. They acknowledge Ezra's contribution last night, but they are concerned he is here, how long he's been here, and why they didn't know."

"Fair questions. I'll have the council address it. The people probably don't want to hear from his daughter right now."

"I think you should address it, Josie. You are who they want to hear from right now. Their Empress. The one who banded them all together."

"The council needs to take a bigger role in the future," I said.

"I agree with Vin," Ezra said. "They fought for you and stood by you, Josephine. Not the council. It's your voice they want to hear."

Vin cut his eyes at Ezra. He didn't seem pleased my father agreed with him. Vin tolerated him at best.

"If you both believe that, then I'll address them later today then. After I've had a chance to clean up," I said, aware my frustration was on display. The lab was where my focus should be.

"I can stay here with Ezra so you can take care of yourself and stop by to see your son."

It irked me and felt like a dig. "I'm fully aware of my responsibilities, Vin."

"I never said you weren't."

"Send word if the model completes before I get back. It shouldn't take very long this time."

"I will make sure you are notified," Vin said.

I took Mother's journal with me, feeling protective of it and the new knowledge found in its pages.

CHAPTER 14

JOSIE

Adam ran toward me. "Mommy!"

"Hi, my little man," I said. "Are you having a good day?" I had many moments like this with my mother but not with Ezra. My heart was grateful Adam had a father like Vin. Someone with a good and pure heart. Family was more important to him than anything else.

"Where?" He held up his hands and looked around.

"Who? Daddy?" I asked.

"No," he shook his head from side to side.

"Play trucks," he said. "Where play trucks?"

"Oh, do you mean your grandfather? Ezra?" I hadn't imagined the bond I saw form. It was almost instant. Adam found a part of Ezra I didn't as a child.

"Gr," he looked at me.

"Grandfather Ezra," I said.

"Grezra," he said.

I giggled. "Ok then. Grezra."

"Where?"

"He's working," I said.

"I work?"

"No, not yet. You have a few years." I ruffled his hair.

"I work Grezra." He whimpers.

"Maybe later. Maybe he can play trucks again if he feels like it."

Adam clapped his hands together.

"That makes you happy?"

He wrapped his arms around my neck and squeezed. "Wuv you."

"I love you too."

"Down," he said.

I stood him up on the ground. He looked so much bigger today.

"Where's Emilia?" I asked the nanny.

"Natasha said she wasn't feeling good today." A pit formed in my stomach. Vampire children didn't get sick. They healed too quickly unless they ingested something they shouldn't I hoped she hadn't gotten into my garden.

"I'll be back later today," I said. "Adam, be good for the nanny."

He nodded furiously.

I KNOCKED on Natasha's door. It flew open.

"I said..." she paused. "Oh, Josie. I didn't expect to see you." Her hair was a bit messy. Natasha was frazzled, and that wasn't her normal disposition.

"I heard Em wasn't feeling well and wanted to check on you both."

"Come in." She closed the door behind me.

Emilia was on the couch. She was pale even for a vampire. Em didn't look good. Pale vampire skin was an obvious sign of poisoning, but I didn't know how serious it was without more information.

"It started last night," Natasha said.

"What are her symptoms?"

"She felt nauseous at first. She vomited some blood, but that was hours ago."

"And has she improved or has she been this lethargic?" I asked.

"She's improved. She got up and moved around, but she got tired easily. Is this some kind of weird vampire illness I've never heard of?" Natasha sat next to Emelia and brushed her hair away from her face.

"None that I'm aware of. It makes me think she's been poisoned, especially if she is improving." I pressed my hand against Em's face and squeezed her hand. She squeezed back, but her skin was clammy.

"Who would poison a child?"

"Surely she wasn't the target. We'll need to test her blood to confirm it is poison. Could she have consumed some tainted blood?"

"I'll rip them apart with my bare hands if it is poison. She has started drinking from our cups, so I wouldn't say it's impossible. Would we see others who are sick?"

"It would depend on where the poison was added," I said. "Are you good with me examining her and drawing some blood?"

"Of course," Natasha said. "I wouldn't let anyone else near her."

"Have them empty the blood from your room and replace it and the carafes."

Natasha nodded, and I left to gather equipment.

I RETURNED from the lab with a kit of test equipment. Emilia was sitting up on the couch. I lined up the test tubes with reactive agents in them and drew her blood. She flinched when I stuck her with the needle.

"Just a few more seconds, Emelia," I said, keeping my voice soft for her. "Her blood is the right consistency and color, so that's a good sign."

Her blood wasn't coagulating. If it was poison, and I believed it was, it was mild and running its course through her body. I positioned the syringe over the first tube and dropped some in each vial. None showed an instant reaction.

"What's next?"

"We'll wait a few minutes to see if any reactions occur. Given her improvement, even since I've been here, there might not be much left in her blood. It may take a little longer."

It didn't take long to see the one turn bright purple. My middle section hardened with anger. This poison was lethal in certain doses. The administer was skilled at dosage.

"That's a reaction," I said.

Natasha kicked a chair into splinters.

"Mom," Emilia said, sounding more mature than a vampire should be at that age.

"Why would someone do this?" Natasha reigned in her voice but the anger still bubbled under the surface.

"I don't know," I said. "Emilia, has a stranger given you any blood or food lately?"

"No." She shook her head.

"What about last night while your mom and dad were away?"

"No." She shook her head again.

"Do you know what kind of poison it is?" Natasha asked.

"Jimson weed," I said. "It grows in the garden, but the doors are locked with guards posted."

"So, we need to review the activities of all the guards then," Natasha said. "Then I'll rip them apart."

"Mom," Emilia said again. "No."

I bit back a laugh. She sounded so much like Natasha, and I'd heard her tell Emilia no with the same inflections many times over the months.

"We'll get the guards on it right away, and if you want to oversee it, I'll sanction it," I said. "In the meantime, Emilia needs to consume some extra blood. I'd suggest staying away from human food until the poison is out of her system. We can test again tomorrow to see if the reaction is gone."

"I'll give her my rations," Natasha said. "I'm going to end their existence, Josie."

"I'll help you. Anyone that would harm a child is the lowest of our kind." I rubbed her arm. "But you can't starve yourself. That's already a mix of human and animal blood, so it's not as fulfilling.

"There will be issues if a friend of the Empress takes more than her fair share."

She was right. It might draw unwanted attention. "Then go to my room. The council insists I have my own supply. Take what you need."

"The council will not like that," she said.

"The council doesn't need to know about help between friends," I said. "I'll let Adam's nanny know to expect you."

"Anything else?"

"Don't end anyone while I'm gone."

Natasha smiled. It was tight, but it was a smile. "I'm not," she said. "Yet."

"In the meantime, keep an eye on her and come get me if anything changes. I have to get ready to address the people over the unplanned events last night."

"Thank you, Josie." She hugged me. "You are a true friend."

"We're family now, Natasha. I consider our kids to be cousins."

"Family," she repeated and pulled back to look at her daughter. Tears filled her eyes.

"Hey," I said. "Emilia will be fine." She improved with every minute that passed with the resilience of a vampire and a child.

I DETOURED to the garden and stopped to examine the crop of Jimson Weed. I looked for signs of tampering or harvesting. The entire plant offered poison, even the nectar and the beautiful flower. Toxins tainted it all. It was the reason I chose it for the poisonous gas we used on the Rogues at the Southern Compound. There were definite signs someone had been there.

Laughter rolled out of the lab toward me. I cocked my head to listen. It came again. Vin and my father were laughing together. Apparently, the Earth and Hell had both frozen over.

I inched forward to observe unnoticed. Vin leaned casually against one of the stations, and Ezra was kicked back in the chair with his hands behind his head. Smiles crossed both their faces, and laughter erupted again. I leaned against the door frame and waited for them to notice me.

"Hey." Vin crossed the room and kissed my cheek. "How's our son?"

"He's perfect as usual," I said. "Emilia though."

"What's wrong with Emilia?"

"She'll be fine. Natasha is watching over her closely. Someone tried to poison her with Jimson Weed." I glanced at Ezra.

His forehead wrinkled in concern. "The plant you used in the poison gas?"

"Yes, that's it."

"Where would they get it?" Vin asked.

"From my garden apparently," I said.

"But no one has access. There are guards posted twenty-four-seven.," Vin said.

"Let me show the damage they did to the plant."

I showed them the plant at the back. "Look at the hack marks. They didn't use the proper tools. It's possible whoever did this got a dose of poison too." If a vampire or human is sick, it would lead us right to them.

"That should be pretty easy to find," Vin said. "But why Emilia?"

"I don't know. Natasha is enraged though. She kicked a chair into oblivion."

"Maybe that's exactly why," Ezra said.

"What would they gain by causing Natasha to go crazy?"

Ezra grimaced. "Causing turmoil in your inner circle."

"He makes a good point," Vin said.

"I can't believe you two are agreeing on another topic," I said. "More importantly, we need to figure out who is trying to create chaos."

"I'd start with your council members," Ezra said. "Has anyone spoken outright against your choices?"

"Most of them at one time or another," I said. "I don't think any of them would do this, but if it is one or any of them, that will seriously undermine the integrity of the government we established."

"We vetted them, but vampires are convincing," Vin said. "As we all know." He cut a look towards Ezra. The lightness from earlier evaporated. I didn't expect them to be best friends, but I hoped they would be civil.

I considered the council members. "Julius and Darius are both very outspoken, but that's what I appreciate about them."

"Start with them. Darius never liked the number of created," Ezra said.

"But Emilia isn't created," I said. "But making her sick distracts you."

"I'll get Killian, and we can start the investigation," Vin said.

"Just keep it to the two of you for now. Let's see if we can figure it out without putting anyone on high alert. I'd rather they not know we are coming for them."

"They'll have to know you've seen Emilia by now."

"Maybe not," I said. "The wing is off limits to the general population."

"That just makes me think it is someone close to us," Vin said.

"Me too." I rolled my neck against the knots forming. It

added up. A vampire in our inner circle was the party responsible. We had to put a name and a face to the culprit.

"The model finished," Ezra said. "Results confirmed."

"Let's run it one more time." The results had to be repeatable for them to be valid and confirmed as a viable option for the reversal. I glanced over at him. "You're looking much better."

"Your mother would have done the same. Have you calculated the best quarter moon to start dispersing?"

"My initial thought is that we could disperse it at different quarter moons in different areas. That way it wouldn't be all at once and give the planet more time to acclimate to the change versus a sudden."

"It's a smart approach. We can incorporate that into the model this time if you have the schedule."

"I do," I crossed the room and handed him the chart I came up with. "My calculations might need tweaking, but let's see how it runs."

He inputted the numbers. His motion and balance seemed better, but his movements were slower. He didn't work like a vampire anymore. His breathing was humanlike.

"Ezra?"

"Yes."

"I think you might have transformed completely into a human." I watched his chest expand with each breath.

"Yes," he said. "It does appear that has happened."

"You don't smell human though."

"I can't tell anymore," he said. "Everyone smells the same now."

"What does it feel like?"

"Very mortal."

I laughed. "I suppose it would. You seem better though."

"I feel better than the last few months, but I do not feel normal."

"But you do not seem to be dying any longer." While not dying was a good thing, it made him vulnerable to be human. He'd be an easy target for our enemies, especially whoever was out to disrupt our plans.

"No, it must have been the transformation. I'm sure the council would gladly remedy the situation."

I wouldn't let them kill him. Not after the contributions he had made here. "You've been instrumental in solving the equation. They will listen to reason on this."

"The council and your people will want some kind of justice," he said, his tone candid.

"I'll negotiate for some form of exile," I said. "We'll figure out what that looks like when we get to that crossroads."

"Do you want to review this before I start the modeling program?"

"No, I trust you," I said, and I meant it. The old Ezra was horrible. This new Ezra was something different. He was honest and transparent.

CHAPTER 15

JOSIE

E zra's computer made a buzzing sound. "It didn't work with that cycle."

I ran my hand through my hair reminding myself not to pull it out. "Where was the breakdown?"

He pointed to the breakage point.

"Oh, that's early in it," I said. "So, maybe we spread them across a year."

"Do you think that will be close enough to maintain the progression?"

"Let's run it and see."

He nodded and inputted the change.

"How's it going?" Vin asked. He and Killian joined me behind Ezra.

"Would you mind moving? My new human nerves can't take people looking over my shoulder."

"Oh," I said. "Sure." I motioned for Vin and Killian to join me outside the lab. "We added in the quarter moon cycle to focus dispersement at the lowest tide point, but the first cadence failed. Ezra is entering an extended period now, and we'll run it again."

"Sounds promising," Vin said.

"How's Emilia?" I asked Killian.

"She's better."

"Did Natasha have any issues getting blood from my stores?"

"No, but she said she felt guilty for taking it."

"She shouldn't. What did you find out about who poisoned Emilia?"

"Nothing convincing," Vin said.

"How so?"

"The trail seems to lead to Darius." Killian stiffened. Darius' son and Killian had been friends when we were younger. He was a loyal supporter of Ezra's before the battle.

"Darius is vocal about his views," I said.

"Right," Vin said. "It seems a little too obvious."

As much as he rallied for my father and his ways, I couldn't see him hurting a child. "Darius is about his own needs, but I can't see him poisoning anyone."

"Me either." Vin glanced at the computer and my father.

"As much as I want to end the person who hurt my daughter, I don't think it is Darius either," Killian said.

I leaned against the table. "So Julius? Anything on him?"

Killian rub his chin as he considered the option. "He'd certainly gain from Darius being removed."

"But is he smart enough to pull something like this off though?" I asked.

Killian shook his head. "No, not on his own, but if he had help probably."

"What if Emilia wasn't the target?" Vin asked.

I wondered the same thing, and it seemed more plausible as we uncovered details of what could be a false trail.

"You think they were after me or Natasha?" Killian asked.

"I think Natasha might have been the target," Vin said. "She's Josie's biggest supporter, and she is vocal on the council."

My heart constricted. The idea that Em was hurt because Natasha and I are close was almost unbearable. "That would make more sense at least. Not that it makes me any happier."

"Julius and Natasha get along," Killian said. "He's visited with her numerous time."

"Maybe he's not as much of a friend as Natasha thinks," Vin said.

The bastard. I'd make him see justice. "If he's been to your apartment, then he's had the opportunity."

"Mother fucker," Killian roared.

"Reign it in, Killian," Vin said.

"The former vampire could hear that," Ezra called from the lab.

"Former?" Vin raised his eyebrows.

"He's transformed from vampire to human. Kind of the reverse process of when a vampire creates another vampire from a human," I said, my voice low enough that Ezra wouldn't hear.

"Interesting," Vin said.

"Back to Julius," Killian said, his voice strained.

"He had the motive and the opportunity. Let's get Natasha down here and get a plan to prove it was him." I wanted a swift resolution for Em from all this.

"She will not leave Emilia," Killian said. "Not even with the nanny."

"Fair," I said. "Let's make our plan then."

"What are you thinking?"

"I could set up a reason to test everyone's blood," I said.

"Too obvious," Killian said. "The council will see right through it."

"Blame me for the poisoning and incarcerate me again." Ezra joined us. "It will give the perpetrator confidence and embolden him." He didn't have vampire strength or healing anymore. It would put him at risk, but we could protect him.

"It's a good idea," Killian said.

Vin nodded his agreement.

"Okay," I said. "But I want one of us in the garden at all times."

"We'll need to make it look like we all leave," Ezra said. "Then, one of you can double back through the secret passage here."

"Secret passage?" He hadn't mentioned it when he showed me the lab.

Ezra looked at me. "Don't you remember playing in them when you were small?"

"No," I said. "I don't remember that at all."

"The passage runs from our old rooms to here." He walked over to the same wall the access panel for the lab was on. Two panels down, he pushed against the painted flower, and the panel slid to the side exposing a passage. Chilled air stirred around us from the pathway. "It feels like the climate control isn't working any longer." He shivered and closed the door.

"How long is the scheduled run time for the de-icer model?" I asked Ezra.

"Two to three hours max since we only adjusted the cadence," he said.

"The sun should have set by then. I'll come to the lab alone and see if anyone follows. Vin and Killian, you can hide inside the hidden passage. No one will know it's there but us, and it will be too good for them to pass up with me out in the open."

"Agreed," Killian said.

"Let's do it," Vin said.

"I'm ready to go back to my prison," he said, his tone resolved. "Let's make it public but not obvious."

"Where is the entrance to the passageway in our apartment though?"

"Is the portrait of your mother still up in the office?" Ezra asked. "Assuming you are using my old office."

"It is," I said.

"The panel next to it is the one you'll want to push." He gestured to the position he wanted me to locate.

"Let's all three escort him and retire to the private wing. Then you two can take the passage back to here as planned, and I'll have the guards walk me back." I didn't love it, but it wasn't the worst plan I'd been a part of in my existence.

We entered the hallway and before long, we crossed the main area. Humans and vampires stared. Darius appeared in front of us.

I stiffened at his appearance. He was focused on my father.

"Ezra," he said, his voice barely a whisper. He embraced my father and motioned for us to step into the drawing room.

"Darius, it's good to see you, even under these circumstances." Ezra clapped his hand over Darius's shoulder like an old friend.

"Empress, you shouldn't be parading your father around among the masses. The created have been talking assassination attempts."

Those threats went with the job. Father had them in his time as emperor, and I was no doubt they were discussed for me as well. "On me or my father or both?"

"Your father," he said. "The rumblings have been strong in opposition of his arrival since the Rogues arrived the other night."

I cut my eyes to Killian and Vin. They both gave a single nod that confirmed my suspicion. I wasn't naïve to think there wouldn't be when I set out to change the government in a radical departure from my father's rule.

"Are they just wanting him to pay or is there more to it?"

"They are questioning why you haven't dealt with him already."

"He's been helping me comb through my mother's research. Not that I expect anyone to understand the reasoning."

"I can help spread the word, but I'm not sure it will help those whose mind is already made up," Darius said.

"Thank you, Darius," I said.

He bowed first to me, and then to my father, and left us. We continued down the hall.

"Do you think he's trying to throw us off the scent or do you think he is genuinely sharing information?" I asked.

"No missing the bow to you and Ezra," Vin said. "His loyalty is still to the born vampires first."

"I think he's deft but genuine," Killian said.

"He's never been one to hide his motives," Ezra said. "He thinks it and speaks it."

"So, we still think Julius is the one," I said.

"The most likely suspect," Vin said.

❄

"I'm leaving the door unlocked in case something happens and you need to escape," I said. "If an incident occurs and you need help, hit the red button on the wall. It--"

"Sounds an alarm." Ezra smiled. "I had them installed when we built the labs."

"Of course, you did."

"Thank you for giving me a chance to do some good, Josephine."

"Hopefully, this time tomorrow we'll have the right formula and delivery plan, and we will have caught the one responsible for poisoning a child. If we do, you played a role in it."

Ezra placed his hands on either of my arms and squeezed. With pride, he said, "This was all you, my daughter, and your mother would have been very proud of you."

Tears welled up in my eyes.

"Don't," he said. "You don't want them to think you are crying over me.

"I'll see you later," I said.

He hugged me. It caught me by surprise. I hugged him back. He squeezed hard for a new human.

We left him in the exam room and made sure to stop and speak to a few people on the way to the apartments. We found Natasha in their room and filled her in on the plan.

"Did Julius come to visit you the night of the Rogue issue?"

She considered the question. "Not that I remember," she said. "He's come by a few times, but I don't think he did that night."

"Maybe it's not him then." I swiped my hands over my face thinking of who else it might be.

"You think Julius wanted to hurt Emilia?" Natasha said. "That doesn't make any sense. He's always bringing her toys and things."

"We think he might have been after you, my dear," Killian said. He crossed his arms tightly across his chest.

She reached up and put a hand on his arm. "Calm down. I'm fine. Emilia's fine... thanks to Josie."

"I just identified the poison. She was already getting better," I said, keeping my voice even.

"Let's get this bastard," Natasha said. "What's the plan?"

"I know what I'd like to do," Killian said.

"Yeah, me too," Natasha said. "It's not in the best interest for us to follow that gut feeling though." She understood how delicate our new government was.

"I'm not sure if you're talking about ending Julius or something else," I said. "But the plan is to catch the perpetrator returning to the garden."

"That's it?" She asked. "You're going to sit in the garden and wait like some backward ass stakeout the humans use to do? Seriously?"

"Well, when you say it that way, it sounds a little ... slow," Vin said.

"Damn straight it does," she said.

"Do you have a better idea?" I asked.

"Of course I do," she said.

"You had to ask," Killian said.

She leveled her gaze on him, and he flinched. Giant Killian flinched.

I covered my mouth and pressed my lips together to cover my giggle.

"As I'm sure you remember, I'm not a fan of wait-and-see tactics," she said.

"Well, let's hear it," Vin said.

She leveled the same gaze on him, and he took a step back.

I bit down on my lip to cover my smile. "Natasha, tell us what you think we should do."

"Simple. If it's me the assassin was after. Then let's make me more accessible," she said like we should have all thought of using her as bait.

Killian growled. "Not a chance, Natasha."

She set her gaze on him again.

He didn't flinch this time. "Unless you plan to use your power of persuasion on all of us, I will not agree to this."

"You know I keep them to myself these days," she said. "I promised you."

What? Killian made her promise to keep her special gift to herself. The gift was a part of her. That was like asking me to not have dark hair.

"Then, we stick to the original plan," Killian said.

"Her plan might have merit," I said. "If she was his target, he might not be more tempted if she's in the open versus me. He knows I have guards with me."

A smug smile crossed Natasha's face. "See."

CHAPTER 16

JOSIE

Natasha made herself known among the people in her not-so-subtle Natasha way. She strode through the main entryway and into the ballroom we converted to a gathering hall. Either people loved her or hated her. Nothing existed in between.

We watched from a side room that had once been a passthrough for servants. Natasha sat next to Julius.

I shook my head, but that was her. She hit everything straight on.

"She is direct if nothing else," Vin said, his voice a bit amused.

"It is her way," Killian said. "She drives me insane with it, but I love it too."

"And that is love, my friend," Vin said.

"So it is," Killian said.

It only took a few minutes for Natasha and Julius to be on the move.

"Let's go," Killian said.

"No," I said. "We have to wait for them to pass first. Spray Natasha's perfume to cover our scents."

"I don't think that will work," Vin said.

"You have smelled Natasha's perfume, right?" I whispered.

"It's hard for me to focus on scents here, so I tend to shut it off unless I need to track," Vin said.

"You're in for a treat then. Only Natasha would worry about perfume in an apocalypse." I peeked out the door. "Spray it now, Killian," I whispered and made sure to shut off my smell.

Killian pumped the bottle a dozen times.

Vin's eyes bugged out. *He must have taken a whiff.*

It was a spicy and strong floral scent mix comprised of ginger, tuberose, sandalwood, and a healthy dose of vanilla. I shook my head and listened for Natasha and Julius's steps to pass off in the distance. "She's taking him to the garden."

"Or he's taking her," Killian said. "Let's go."

"We should take the secret passage," Vin said.

I hurried to the entrance.

"It must be this panel," I said, looking at mother's portrait. I pressed my hand against the panel, and it slid aside easily. *How had I missed it before?*

I found the lever to close it once we were inside.

We dashed down the passageway and found our way to the panel near the lab. Natasha's voice carried through the panel, but Julius's was harder to hear.

The draft grew stronger compared to the slightness from earlier.

"The wind must be whipping up outside," Vin whispered.

"We haven't had a storm in months," I whispered back. The

temperature dropped in the passage, but it didn't impact us. It was good Ezra wasn't with us.

"Then we are due," he said.

"Would you both stop talking about the weather?" Killian whisper shouted at us.

Another voice came through. It wasn't Julius's, and it wasn't Natasha's.

I looked from Killian to Vin.

"That sounds like Mara," he whispered.

"I think it is," I whispered back. Was she working with Julius? I'd put more faith in her than the others. Dread hardened in my stomach.

Footsteps came closer to the panel, and I froze like a statue.

I made a motion to spray the perfume.

Killian shook his head almost imperceptibly.

The footsteps stopped in front of the panel.

I inhaled the scent. *Mara for sure. What was she doing here?*

A tap wrapped on the panel. "You can come out, Josephine. And I can smell Vin and Killian are with you. They can come too."

The blood in my veins ran colder than even a vampires should. I wanted to tear her head from her shoulders for the breach of trust and betrayal.

Killian moved to open the door.

I threw my hand in front of him. "Do we need a weapon?" I mouthed to him.

"No time," he mouthed back.

I looked at Vin.

He shrugged.

Damn.

"Come on out. We'd hate for Natasha to come into contact with one of your dreaded lovelies here. Or should I say your mother's dreaded lovelies since she cultivated them?"

Venom filled my mouth as I pushed forward. Vin held my arm and shook his head.

Killian released the lever, and the door opened. The draft gusted around us.

"Ahh. There you are." Mara turned to face us. Her face twisted in a smirk. I imagined what it would feel like to sever her head.

Killian snarled next to me.

Natasha sat on the edge of the flower bed, her hands behind her back.

Laughter from the far corner by the back wall of glass drew my attention. Emilia and Adam sat playing with his toy cars. A feral growl reverberated around me, and I wasn't sure if it was mine, Vin's, or Killian's. Maybe it was all three of us in unison.

"Why are our children here and what is going on?" I asked, choking back my desire to tell her how she will die.

"The children are fine as long as you cooperate," Mara said.

"As long as I cooperate with what?"

"For starters, you and your friends will leave this compound. Go somewhere north," she said. "The most impor-tant thing is that you announce me as your successor before you leave."

"Why would I do that?"

"Because you want your children to live," she said, in a matter-of-fact tone.

I dug my nails into the palms of my hands. Natasha jerked. Killian and Vin remained still. Too still.

I followed Vin's gaze to a half dozen vampires blocking the exit from the garden. They carried various weapons from the armory, particularly those we would use against Rogues. This group of traitors was prepared to kill us if need be.

"Why do you want to replace me, Mara? We are just getting started on our work here." I tried to stall to buy us some time to assess the situation.

Mara walked around me like she was sizing me up. "Josephine, you said yourself that you didn't intend to stay in the position. The council was never going to succeed without a leader. I'm just securing the future by doing so."

I turned as she spoke, keeping eye contact with her. "We could have had the conversation without the dramatics. If you had just come to speak with me, I would have been open to listening."

She stopped short of moving between me and Vin. "Ezra's daughter is a good listener," she said. "That sounds like a contradiction. You've been wrapped up in your troubles. And now you've brought your father here?"

I hadn't heard the alarm from the other lab, so I assumed he was still safe. "Mara, I've been working on the major issues we are facing. Ezra has helped with one of those. He's been key in identifying a potential solution."

"And what have you shared with the council on these major issues? Are the things you considered the major issues what we would choose to focus on?"

She was short sited and not seeing the big picture we were. "It's survival, Mara. A chance to rebuild society."

"In what way? The way you and your father determine." She shook her head.

"This isn't my father's vision. He's only helping me."

She paced back the other way. "Still you defend him after sharing his sins with all of us and evicting him from the throne?"

"We have no throne, and he is not the same person he was then." I thought I protected the people by keeping him hidden, but I should have made Ezra's contributions since his return more prominent. I should have updated the council more and our people.

"Not the same vampire he was for hundreds of years?" She asked. "You're naive if you believe he has changed."

"He's changed in many ways that might surprise you," I said.

"Why don't you ask me yourself?" Ezra called from the secret passage. He emerged and looked every inch human. His skin was a peachy color with rosy cheeks from the draft in the passage.

I was relieved to see him, but I wished he'd stayed back.

Mara's nose jutted up in the air as she whiffed his scent. "What trickery is this?"

"No trickery here," he said. "Josephine and I completed the Vampire Rite. The vampire version of me died and transformed. The transformation made me human, and it only completed after I came here."

"How is this possible? Vampires cannot become human," she said in disbelief.

"Old magick can do many things, and in this case, it turned a born vampire into a human," Ezra said.

"No one has yielded old magick in centuries," Mara said. "That bloodline died off."

"All except for one," Ezra said. "I didn't even know it was anything more than a casual interest until Josephine evoked the Vampire Rite ceremony. Her mother was the last of the old magick vampires until Josephine was born. We didn't think she carried it in her, but she does."

Was it true? Did mother belong to a special line of vampires? And now I'm the last of them? Would Adam be one?

"I'll do whatever you want, Mara," I said. "Just let Natasha and Killian take the children and go."

She held a hand up toward me. "How do you know this is true?"

"How else would I be standing here before you as a human?"

She walked toward him and sniffed the air around him. "Hold out your hand."

Ezra complied.

Mara drug a long fingernail across his palm until bright red blood beaded along the line. She licked the red drop from his hand, an easy way to taste without worrying about venom mixing. Her face contorted. She spat the blood out on the floor.

"Human, but it tastes different, bitter, and unappetizing." She smelled him again. "Same with your scent. Human but unappetizing." She looked at me. "How did you do this, Josephine?"

"I don't know. It seems to be a reaction from the ceremony we took part in."

"Could it be done on other vampires?"

"The Vampire Rite is a fight to the death, either physical or metaphysically," I said. "I don't know many vampires willing to take part in that kind of ceremony."

Mara's gaze became distant. "There has to be a way to do it without invoking such an archaic ceremony."

"Maybe with time and trials we could figure it out, but I'm not sure how it would be useful."

"It would make a great punishment for those who break or abuse our laws," she said. "Like your father."

Control. She wanted to use it as a way to exert power. She concealed this side of herself well. "Mara, the balance between humans and vampires is dangerously close to the point of no return. We need to return a climate balance to the world, so the human population can recover if we want vampires to survive as well."

"How by turning them into humans like your father?"

"No," I said. "By reversing the ice age. We are very close to figuring out the formula."

"Haven't you been close for some time?" She asked. "Why should we continue to wait?"

Killian motioned two fingers to Natasha and toward the kids. I met his eyes. They had the father look I grew up seeing, and I knew it all too well. We would fight our way out of this. We had been outnumbered before, but it was against my father, not with him on my side and not with him as a human. I'd do my best to protect my father, but there would be no choice if Adam was in danger.

I looked at Natasha. She gave one swift nod in understanding of the plan. I entwined my pointer finger with Vin's. He returned it with a single-finger squeeze.

"Mara, this will not bring your only child back," I said.

"No, it won't," she said. "And I can thank your father for that."

The faint sound of the computer behind the lab door rang through. It wasn't the buzzer of a failed model. It was the bells of success. I closed my eyes to hold back the tears. We had done it. We had the formula and now we had to continue to exist to protect it.

Ezra stepped into the middle. "Take me then," he said. "I am the one to blame. You do not need the rest of them. The statement you want to make can be made by using me."

"No," I whispered. *Had he missed our plan or was he that willing to sacrifice himself?*

"This is not your decision, Josephine," he said. "I'm offering this deal to Mara."

He looked at her. "While this offer would have been tempting years ago, I need the Empress to renounce her position."

"The people love her, Mara," he said. He was stalling, keeping her talking. I recognized the tactic. He hadn't missed our subtle gestures. "They will not accept she has stepped down. Nor do they know you well enough to accept you."

"You took your position when your father-in-law died."

I never knew that.

"It wasn't by force. My beloved wife put her support behind me and those who loved her followed. It had little to do with me and everything to do with her. You need that same kind of support. If you send Josephine away, who will throw their support behind you?"

She considered what he said as if she was filing through her memories to confirm.

I had to give him credit. He kept her thinking and talking. Vin, Killian, and I were able to change our stances in subtle motions to prepare to fight without her noticing.

I didn't know Mara well enough to know most of her story or age, but I do remember her devastation when her only child turned Rogue. A beautiful vampire who had only lived a couple of dozen years before the ice age hit, close in age to me. She begged Ezra to research a way to turn the Rogues back into vampires and had a hard time understanding when Ezra explained it was impossible to do so.

Now, Ezra stood before her as a born vampire transformed into a human, and it seemed like there was hope again. I could read it on her face. The way her eyes had widened as they talked. She bought into the gift he offered.

"Escort them all to the Empress's apartments," she said. "For now, while I consider this information."

Killian gave a single shake of his head from side to side. Our plan was put on hold.

CHAPTER 17

JOSIE

The kids played in our bedroom while we sat around the table in the waiting area of my suites.

"You need to deal with her swiftly, Josephine, before she reconciles there is no bringing a vampire back from Rogue," Ezra said.

"Our community is wise. They will figure out something is amiss quickly," Killian said.

"So we just end her? Someone driven by grief?" I asked. "And a council member I chose." It didn't set well with me. There would be discontent among the people for actions like that.

"She's past the point of reason," Vin said. "I'm not sure ending her is the answer, but banishment, as she was ready to give us, sounds fair."

It was a better option than ending her.

"Have you all forgotten we're the ones imprisoned?" Natasha asked, her eyes wide like we were all idiots.

"Not really," I said. "We still have the secret passageways."

There were several branches, and my childhood memory of them was sketchy but coming back.

"But she knows about those," Natasha said.

"Does she know where they all are?" I asked. "Would she have put us here if she did?"

Ezra smiled. "My daughter is smart."

"I can thank my parents if I am. Did you hear the bells from the modeling software when we were in the garden?" My desperation to get back to the lab was second only to making sure the people in this room, my family, were safe.

"No," he said. "It completed?"

"It did," I said. "It was successful. We have the formula and the delivery cadence."

His eyes filled with tears, and he opened his arms.

I hugged him. "Thank you."

"This changes everything," he said.

It meant success. It meant survival for us all, and it meant redemption for him.

"We must end her before she garners more support," Killian said.

"I don't want to be the Empress that snuffs out every point of opposition. We need it to challenge us." The image of her dying at my hands after threatening my child thrilled me, but I would hold any of our people accountable for that type of action. As much as I wanted Mara ended, I wanted the people to see a new way. I imagined what it would be like to yank her head off and set her on fire, and it was satisfying... at least in my head.

"Opposition is different from sedition," Vin said.

"I can't argue with that," I said. "But we need to handle this right. We've all learned from the wrong path, so let's not repeat those mistakes." The people needed an example, and that had to be me in this situation. Not that I liked. If we were going to rebuild a society, we had to move from vigilante justice to real justice.

"I agree with, Josie," Natasha said. "We have to be judicious about this or the groundwork we have set will be for nothing. We need to live with the same rules we expect the rest of the people to live by."

"You can't ignore the insurrection," Killian.

"It's hardly an insurrection." Natasha rolled her eyes. "There hasn't been any violence."

"Yet," Vin said.

"Let's see if we can do this without death or bloodshed," I said. "I have an idea." I looked at the plant in the corner. Another gift from Mother.

"Not more poisonous gas," Natasha groaned.

"No not poisonous," I smiled. "The scent of a Gardenia is known to make humans sleep. Ingesting it has the same effect on vampires."

"Won't they notice the taste?" Vin asked.

A smile formed on my lips as it came together. "It has a sweet flavor, so it's easily mixed into drink or food."

Natasha studied the plant. "How much would a vampire need to consume though? There are only a half dozen or so blooms on the plant."

"The equivalent of one bloom per vampire should be enough," I said.

"My daughter, you are truly a genius in your own right," Ezra said. "I am in awe." He bowed before me. "My Empress."

His reverence was meant to be a show of support, but this wasn't the path forward. No one should bow before the other.

"Mara has a penchant for human food, so she should be easy," Killian said. "The rest of the group only drinks blood."

"Let's plan a council meeting. Two carafes of blood. One for Mara and her crew. One for us," Natasha said.

"We can toast to the future," I said. "The sweetness though."

"The human cook has been making these delightful little cakes. They smell very sweet," Ezra said.

"The petit fours?" I asked.

"Yes, those."

"We'll have a couple of plates of those brought into the room and sat on the table next to the carafes."

"What if her soldiers do not drink?" Killian asked.

"Then, we might have to do a little quick thinking and maybe a little fighting. Just be cautious not to kill anyone unless it is life or death."

I took the scissors from my desk drawer and cut the beautiful white blooms from the plant. "Sorry."

"Did you just apologize to a plant, Josie?" Natasha asked.

"Yes. Wouldn't you for butchering it like this?"

"Um no," she said. "It's just a plant."

"It's not just a plant," I said to myself and stroked the leaves. No one else would understand the connection he held for me to my mother. I looked back at the group. "Now, we just need to get it ground up and into the carafe."

"Leave it to me." Natasha smiled. "I was born for this."

Killian growled. "Natasha."

"It's a good cause." She patted his arm. "I'm not doing it for personal gain. It's to help Josie and the greater good."

He grabbed her hand in a swift motion and kissed it.

She smiled. "See, not so bad."

I retrieved a hand towel from the ensuite bathroom and wrapped the flowers gently in it.

"You can take the passageway to the kitchen," Ezra said. "There is a cutoff just before you hit the halfway point. Take a left there."

I handed the towel to Natasha.

Ezra pushed the panel. "Good luck."

"I've totally got this," she said.

My turn. I stepped into the hall. My heart quickened like a nervous human instead of a steadfast vampire.

A guard approached me.

"Let Mara know I wish to convene the council immediately to discuss the transition."

He nodded and waited for me to return to the room.

I walked around the room. Natasha should be back any second. She had to be.

"Stop pacing," Vin said like he could read my mind. "She'll make it back."

Killian stared out the window. "Natasha doesn't understand failure. She'll be here."

I worried Natasha would get caught, and I worried she wouldn't make it back in time and our plan would be exposed. If this option failed, we would be forced to fight. There would be ultimate death, and I would have another coup to work through.

The door opened and one of the guards requested Nanny Ann's presence in the hall.

"I'll get her," I said.

The kids giggled in the bedroom. I opened the door to find them playing an old board game. I smiled at their innocence, completely unaware of the danger around them. They deserved a life without constant struggle for survival. Our very existence was on the line, and we had to succeed.

"What are you playing?" I asked.

"This game with slides and ladders," Emilia said.

"I remember that one."

"Do you want to play? Nanny Ann has been teaching us."

"No, not tonight, but I will next time. Have fun." I looked at Ann. "The guard asked for you to meet him in the hall."

She gave me a weak smile as she walked past me. I closed the bedroom doors behind us. If luck went our way, we would have more chutes than ladders over the next few hours. The suite door slammed shut behind her.

I resumed my path around the room. Ann came back before I made my way around once.

"I'm to watch the kids when you meet with the council." Her hands nervously smoothed her shirt.

"You know where to find them," I said. Part of me wanted her behind a door before she noticed Natasha was missing. The other part was happy the kids would have her nearby. "Ann?"

"Yes." She tucked her hands behind her.

"If anything should go," I paused afraid the tears in my eyes would spill over. I cleared my throat. "If we should not return from the council meeting, will you make sure the children get out of the mansion safely?"

"Of course," she said, her voice soft enough that it wouldn't carry to the hallway. "The support is with you, Empress."

"Thank you," I said. She knew the importance of children, but I didn't know her well. The situation required me to have blind faith that she wouldn't let them perish. I swiped at my eyes. "The care of the children is a debt I could never repay."

"The debt is ours," she said. "For saving us many times over." Her eyes darted to Ezra like she expected a reaction from him. He gave none. "I'll check on the children now."

I nodded and waited for the bedroom door to close behind her. Bloodshed and endings weren't the goals today, but I would do it for my children if it came to it.

I worked the same path across the room I had been since Natasha left. She should be here back by now. "Where is she?"

As if on cue, the panel opened and Natasha emerged. Relief waved over me. I wanted to hug her, but we had to act as if she'd never been gone.

"Done," she said. "No one doubted me, did they?"

I pressed one finger to my lips. "Ann is here to watch the children when we leave."

Natasha motioned for us to huddle together. I did as instructed. We looked like an old football team deciding their next play.

"Our end of the table should have the decanter with the pointed topper. Mara's end will have the flatter one. Just in case the idiots get the placement wrong. By the way, this stance is completely unnecessary, but I thought it was fun."

I laughed and stepped back. "You're awful.

The suite door opened, and a guard entered. "We'll escort you to the meeting room, Empress."

I walked toward him. Natasha had calmed my nerves, which I suspect was her goal, and I had confidence in our plan. "We're ready."

I followed the guard out the door with Vin, Natasha, Kilian, and my father behind me.

"Not you." Another guard threw an arm out in front of Ezra.

"He comes with us," I said. "I'm still the Empress."

The guard held steady and met my gaze like he wanted to challenge me, but he withdrew his arm.

Ezra walked next to me. "It was not necessary for you to intervene." He didn't want the altercation, and I understood that. He didn't have vampire strength or healing anymore, and I didn't trust what they would do if he wasn't protected.

"We go in as a team," I said. "You are part of our team now." He belonged with us on this journey.

He looped an arm through mine. "You are a far better leader than I could have ever dreamed of for you. You deserve a long reign."

I patted the hand that rested on my forearm. *No one should reign for a long time.* I kept the comment to myself, but saying it out loud might have felt better.

The double door to the council room opened, and no one was there. Relief washed over me when I saw the petit fours on the table as well as the carafes of blood. The sweet smell of the petit fours mixed perfectly with the gardenias. The sharper point one was on my regular end of the table.

Vin, Natasha, and I took our seats at the table. Killian and Ezra stood behind me. Our fate, the fate of the nation and our people, rested on a flower and some little cakes. No one would believe this if we survived. Our plan was almost laughable, but we worked with what we had.

Mother, I hope this is what you envisioned when you planted that Gardenia. Thank you to whoever tended it after her death. And thank you that I didn't kill it when I transplanted it to the planter in the apartment.

Mara entered the room followed by Julius and the half dozen guards. She carried herself with unfounded confidence.

We could end it now, but it would require us to end them. Not that we hadn't ended plenty of vampires to get here, but this was different. We were trying to build something better, and I wanted to get there in a more peaceful way. The guards stood around her, protecting her, and Julius sat on her right. He had a smug smile on his face.

A low growl came from Natasha's direction. I touched her arm to remind her why we were there.

"Where is everyone else?" I asked, hoping my gut was right.

"It will be only us for this meeting," she said.

I mentally sighed, but my body tensed. I suspected the other council members weren't part of this treason, and I was glad she confirmed it.

"I have thought about your offer," she said. "You will remain here and offer your support of the transition. We will make arrangements to dismantle the council, and once that is done, you will leave this city and nation."

"How long do you foresee this transition?" I asked. *Eat the cakes. Take a drink of the blood.* I tried to will them to reach for the snacks.

"Two to three months at most. Hopefully, sooner."

I nodded, not believing a word from her mouth. She use me as a puppet to build her platform. "And you will guarantee our safety during those months and as we leave?"

"I will," she said, her eyes narrowed on me.

Nothing about her tone or demeanor fostered trust, but I faked it.

"Agreed," I said. *Eat the cakes, Mara.* The meeting can't end this quickly.

"Shall we toast then?" She motioned for one of the guards to pour the blood into glasses.

Finally. "Yes," I said. "Natasha?"

"Of course," Natasha responded. "Let me help serve." She quickly filled our glasses from the carafe on our end of the table. Then passed out the cakes on our side.

Ezra took one and bit into it. "Mmmm. Humans have the most exquisite taste in pastries."

"Julius." Mara motioned to the plate on her end.

Even as a human Ezra could toy with vampires and manipulate them. I wanted to laugh at how well his skills worked on her, but it would give us away for sure.

Julius held out the plate, and she took one. Then she motioned for him to give one to the guards.

I glanced at Natasha, and she winked. *What had she done now?*

Everyone in the room had a cake and a glass.

"To alliances," I said and held up my glass. *Drink it down, Mara.* I bit down on my lip to keep from smiling. The advantage was shifting to us, and Mara's tactics would be stopped.

"To alliances," Mara said and drank deeply from the glass.

I trailed my eyes around the room and watched everyone sip the blood, except our one human participant.

"And betrayals," Natasha whispered.

I choked on my blood and coughed through it.

"What was that Natasha dear?" Mara asked.

"Just wondering how they make these little cakes. They are so good." Natasha flashed a big fake smile.

Mara was the first to slip into sleep. Before Julius could tend to her, he fell into a slumber as well. The guards stumbled against the wall and slid down.

It worked. "Let's get them to the prison right away. I'm not sure how long that will last."

"I'll take Mara, and I'm not going to be gentle." Natasha swung Mara's limp body over her shoulder.

"Julius is mine," Killian said with a growl. "And I'll release your personal guard to come get the rest."

"Put Mara and Julius in separate cells, please." It was more of a statement than a necessity to separate them.

"Wouldn't have it any other way," Natasha said. "We will check on the kids on our way back."

They dashed out at top speed. Ezra stood by the door to monitor for any unwanted activity on the outside. Vin and I stood over Mara's guards while we waited for the others to return.

Moments passed and my personal guard appeared at the door. They entered the room and stepped over the down guards Mara had. Each one took a knee in front of me. They were somber.

"Empress, we serve you," the lead guard said. "We will not accept a usurper and apologize for our failure."

"Please rise," I said. "We don't bow to anyone in our nation. Those times have passed."

"Yes, Empress." The lead guard stood and the others followed. "What shall we do with these traitors?"

"Put them in the cells for now," I said. "Be sure someone we trust is watching them at all times."

"Yes, Empress," he turned and went to work.

CHAPTER 18

JOSIE

Natasha dropped into her seat. "The kids are with Ann and are fine. There were no other guards nearby."

Killian entered the room. "All the traitors are secure in the cells awaiting your decision."

"Convene the council," I said, proud that we contained them without bloodshed. "They need to know what happened and have a say in how to handle the small group."

"Father, although I wouldn't mind you staying, I don't think the council will look highly on it. Adam would be happy to see you though."

"I understand," he said. "Time with Adam sounds more inviting."

"Please feel free to retire to my apartments until we return," I said. "If you are in agreement, Vin?" I looked for his approval.

"Yes, agreed," he said, no animosity in his tone.

"Very well," Ezra said, pleased with the agreement from Vin. "I shall see you after the meeting."

"You're calling him father now?" Natasha asked.

"Yes," I said. "I think he's proved he is not the same person he was."

"But father?" Natasha grimaced.

"Let it go, Natasha," Killian said, from the doorway. "The council approaches."

She sat up straight in her seat. Vin took his, but I remained standing. I prepared myself for disbelief and a debate on the facts with them. Nothing was easy about the decisions ahead.

Darius entered first. His face was marked with concern. "Empress, we heard of a scuffle earlier. Is everything resolved?"

The news had made it to them, and they did nothing. That stung. The council should be leaders, not followers.

"What did you hear, Darius?" I asked.

"We heard Mara called a meeting with you excluding the other council members," he said.

"You knew and yet you allowed it?" I crossed my hands over my waist.

"It is not for me to say who the Empress takes an audience with or doesn't." Darius maintained his confusion and took his regular seat.

The others filed in and took their places. I wondered if any other traitors were yet to be exposed.

Darius looked at Julius's empty seat. "Where is--"

"Julius? He and Mara worked together to dismantle the government we have been working to build." The room fell silent. The remaining council members stared at me. "My question to you all is who is with Mara and Julius and who supports what we are trying to do?"

I tasted fear in the air. I couldn't tell if it was fear of what they thought I might do or fear of getting caught.

"I'm not punishing anyone, but this is your opportunity to hear your voice in its own right. We can determine how to move forward at that point. What I will not tolerate are threats against my family or my inner circle." I wouldn't punish any dissenters, but I would remove them from the council if they supported Mara and Julius.

"I've always supported you, Empress," Darius said, his tone sincere.

"Thank you, Darius," I said.

The others voiced agreement.

I'd suggested change in a slow methodical fashion, but the recent events seemed like the changes needed to be quicker.

I gripped the chair in front of me. "One change is needed if I'm to remain the leader. I'd prefer to no longer be known as the Empress. How does the council feel about the head of state being known as the President? Similar to what humans had before the ice age. A leader who is elected on a regular cadence."

The council buzzed, but the smiles on their faces showed agreement.

I met each council member's gaze. "Can I count on your support in this change? Do I hear a motion?"

Darius stood, "I make a motion to vote the head of state shall be known as President and the title of Emperor or Empress will be here forth retired."

"I second the motion." Natasha stood and took my hand. "It's time to end all division including a gender specific title."

I smiled at her. She'd always believed in me. If the council's faith had wavered in me as a leader, it seemed strong now. I turned back toward them. "Shall we vote?"

"Aye." Natasha started.

"Aye." Vin stood and smiled at me.

"Aye," Darius said.

And each council member stood for the vote.

"The vote carries unanimously. I am proud to be your first President," I said. "Your next tasks are to determine how long my term will be, when we will vote, and what are the qualifications to run. Be considerate in your discussions, and I'd like to review what you have next week. Sooner if you are ready, but I'll not rush you."

"Will you have a Vice-President like the humans did before?" a councilwoman asked.

These were the discussions that needed to be had, and I knew who I would choose as my vice-president if they created the office. *Natasha.* "That will be up to your plan. I'll let you present what you think the structure should be."

She nodded. "We will make you proud, Madame President."

"If everyone will be seated, we do have another matter to discuss. Mara, Julius, and their half dozen guards are imprisoned in the cells for the acts committed against me and my family." My chest tightened. This wouldn't be easy for them. I glanced around to see if anyone seemed uncomfortable, and they all did.

"What will you do?" Darius asked, his voice soft.

"I want us to decide together. I don't want our people to be afraid to speak, so I'm not willing to put them to death. I'll listen to other options you have to present though."

"Let them rot in jail," Darius said.

While I didn't disagree with Darius' assessment, we should discuss any other options the council members had. "Does anyone else have another idea?"

Saoirse, a born vampire from the old Irish vampires, cleared her throat. "May I?"

"Please do," I said.

"Mara has violated the sanctity of her position on the council. The breach of trust must be punished, but since the indiscretion was not public, perhaps the punishment can be more of a private nature as well," Saoirse said.

I was impressed. "What did you have in mind?"

"Perhaps she is sent to one of the smaller settlements," she said.

I considered it. It could work if it was enforceable. "What guarantee do we have she will not try to raise another force? Maybe a bigger one that causes an insurrection?"

Saoirse continued. "We don't, but if we send her to one of the more isolated locations, then it would be less likely."

"It's an interesting idea," I said. "How does the rest of the council feel about this option?"

"I don't think they should be let go so easily," Darius said. "But a remote area could offer its own kind of punishment."

I nodded. A remote area and small settlement would be a daily struggle to exist. That would occupy their time.

"What say the rest of you?" I asked.

Natasha and Vin sat silent, letting the rest of the council members discuss, and offered their support as the conversation came to a close.

The council voted and came to an agreement on the punishment.

I agreed with their choice, and I would send them to one that we could monitor. "We'll let them sleep off the gardenia treats today. In the meantime, we can assign a group to escort them to the settlement."

"Which one will you send them to?" Saoirse asked.

"The one in Missouri," I said, keeping my voice even. "It's a very isolated one."

"Isn't Mara originally from that area?"

"Yes, Saoirse. She was from there."

"That is a punishment in and of itself," she said. "All her demons are there."

I cleared my throat. "I didn't think it was a punishment to return here, and this is my home. I was grateful."

She looked down at her clasped hands in front of her like she had something else to say but hesitated.

"Saoirse, if I'm missing the point, please help me understand." I waited for her to respond.

"I just wonder if it is far enough away," she said, not looking up.

"It's far enough and remote enough to prevent easy access, but it's not so far we cannot check in. Did you have another one in mind then?"

She raised her eyes to meet mine. "New York, perhaps? I hear they are thriving again but their numbers are quite small. They could use extra hands."

My stomach sank. *Livia. Luna.*

"Have you heard news from New York?" Natasha asked a hint of desperation in her voice.

"I had word from my cousin there. He said a few vampires have found their way there. They are living on animal blood in the absence of human donors."

Had Livia and Luna made it?

"Any other news?" Natasha pressed.

"No, that was about it. The satellite phones had a poor connection."

"I'd be interested in hearing more information," I said. "Can you try to contact your cousin today to see how many vampires are there? If it seems sustainable, we will consider sending them there."

I wanted information about Livia and Luna, but if they needed hands, I'd consider sending our prisoners there or maybe splitting them up. It would be easier to monitor them if they were in one place though.

"Yes, if I can be excused, I'll do it now."

"We'll leave the group incarcerated until we hear from you. The council will reconvene then, but I think we can close the meeting until then if there are no objections."

No one objected.

When the council cleared the room, the tension I carried melted some. "I don't know about the rest of you, but I'd like to spend some time with the kids."

"That sounds like an excellent idea," Natasha said. "Let's go see what our little destructos are up to."

CHAPTER 19

JOSIE

O ur two little minions plotted a demolition derby on the bed where we found them sound asleep.

"Did the playing wear them out?" I asked Ann. She sat in a chair next to the bed, reading a book.

Ann walked with us out to the living room where Ezra was sitting.

"Yes," she smiled. "They found a box full of cars, and played furiously with them the entire time you were gone."

"Why don't you go eat?" Natasha said. "We've got our kiddos."

Ann nodded. "I can come back later if you need me.

"My new human stomach is telling me it's time to eat. I'll head to the kitchen and meet you back here afterward," Ezra said. "If that is ok?"

"You are free to do as you please," I said. "Just be careful. You are fragile now."

"Not so fragile. Just human," he said.

"We can go to the lab and start prepping our plan based on the model results later," I said.

"I look forward to it." He bowed in front of me. "Empress."

"No more Empress and no more bowing," I said. "I'm the President now."

He smiled. "Madam President then," he said with a prideful smile. "I haven't used that term in more than a hundred years."

"It sounds right though," I said.

"It does." He touched my arm and followed Ann out.

Natasha and I leaned on the door watching our children in such a peaceful state.

"Look how much bigger Emilia is than Adam," she said. "He's growing fast, but she is still outpacing him."

"She has slowed down though, Natasha." I looped my arm through hers.

She rested her head on my shoulder. "I hope it's enough."

"Once we reconcile the plan to reverse the ice age, I'll tackle the growth rate again," I said. "I promise."

"I know." She squeezed my arm. "You don't have to do it all alone. You've got us. All of us, Madame President."

"My impulsiveness got away from me on that one," I said. "But it felt right."

"It was," she said. "It was the right time."

"Will you take the position if they add a VP?" I wanted her to be the one to take the position, but only if she wanted it to.

"I don't think I'm exactly VP material, Josie." She watched the kids.

"You are exactly vice-president material," I said. "You're real, and you're vocal."

"She certainly is." Killian slipped his arms around her waist. "Mind if I steal my family away for some downtime?"

"You don't have to ask that." I waved them on. "Have fun!"

Killian scooped Emilia off the bed, and he and Natasha left in a blur.

When the door closed, Vin and I watched Adam for a moment. The day had been challenging, but our son didn't have to know that. Adam could sleep through anything. Vin took my hand and led me to the couch.

"You are one amazing woman, Josie," he said.

"I don't feel very amazing to have not seen what Mara and Julius were doing," I said.

"You'll never see everything coming, but how you react when it does is very telling," he said. "Who else would have thought to use Gardenias?"

I laughed. "It sounds so impossible." The humor left me. Saoirse's mention of New York had my thoughts on former residents there. "Do you think Livia and Luna made it to New York?"

"We might know when we hear from Saoirse," he said.

"Trust is hard for me right now," I said. "And something is nagging me about New York coming up twice now. Do you think Saoirse knows about Livia and her daughter?" I didn't disclose it, and Livia went largely unnoticed here due to her depression.

"There's no way to know," he said. "Trust is faith in someone, and I think you should trust them until they give you a reason not to."

"Even when there is a pit in my stomach saying to pursue it." My trust had been misplaced in Mara and Julius, and I wouldn't make that mistake again.

"You are someone who should never ignore your gut," he said. "You are the President. How does it feel hearing your change in action?"

"We'll see when the council decides our structure, and we announce it. I suppose that means a trip to the Southern compound too," I said. "I want to make sure we get the ice age reversal process going before I embark on any tours though."

"Makes sense," he said. "I'm so proud of you."

"Thank you." I leaned in to kiss him.

Our lips met in an explosion of emotion. Tears ran down my face for the threats we faced, the triumph, and the future.

"Little man is on our bed," Vin said, disappointed.

"He is," I said, my voice thick with desire. "But the shower is free."

"Shall we Madame President?"

"I declare it a law," I said.

"Mmm," he nuzzled my neck and pulled back to look at me. "I like when you bring down the law on me."

"I'm going to do more than that." I wagged my eyebrows at him.

He lifted me off the couch and walked towards the bathroom. "You better."

I STRETCHED as we watched Adam sleep. "He's so peaceful when he's not destroying everything in sight," I whispered.

Vin chuckled. "He doesn't always destroy things."

I covered my mouth to stifle my laugh. "No, he doesn't, but when he does, he leaves a trail to follow."

Adam's eyes blinked open. A smile spread across his face. He was so happy when he woke up.

Vin and I moved toys over on the bed to sit with him.

"Did we wake you?"

"No, Mommy," he said. "My eyes wake."

"They did." I kissed the top of his head.

"Are you hungry little man?" Vin asked.

"I not little, Daddy," Adam said.

"You're littler than me, right?"

"Mea..." he thought. "Measure, Mommy." He scooted across the bed and tugged on Vin's hand to stand up with him.

Vin obliged. "Measure, Mommy." He smiled and shrugged.

"Ok. Stand side-by-side."

Vin helped Adam move to the side. "Stand here so Mommy can measure."

"It looks like you've grown, Adam."

He clapped his hands.

I took my hand and swiped from the top of Adam's head to the spot on Vin's leg it matched up to. "Look how much you have grown!"

His face lit up. "See Daddy. I not little."

"No you're not," Vin said. "You've grown several inches since we measured a few days ago." Vin looked at me.

Vampire children didn't stay children for long. He was not catching up with Emilia, but he was growing fast.

"Do you want to eat in our room or do you want to go down with the other people?" I asked. "In the big room?"

"Emilia!" He yelled. "Eat with my Emilia."

"Your Emilia?" I asked. "Does she like you calling her your Emilia?"

"My friend," he said.

"That she is." Vin picked him up. "Let's go knock on their door and see if she wants to go to the dining hall with us. Mommy, are you coming?"

"Mommy!" Adam dove toward me.

I laughed. "Yes, it looks like I am." I took him from Vin. "I guess you do like me."

"Wuv you." Adam hugged me.

"I love you too."

"Daddy!" Adam practically leapt from my arms.

"Wuv you."

Vin laughed. "Love you too."

We stopped at Vin and Natasha's door. Adam knocked with both hands on the door.

Killian opened the door, amused by the random knocking.

"Where my Emilia?"

Killian raised a single brow.

"He means his friend Emilia." I laughed.

"I see," Killian said.

"We're heading down to the dining hall, and Adam wondered if Emilia and her family could join us."

"I'll need to ask her mother, but I think that will be ok," Killian said.

"Emilia?" Adam called. "Where?"

"I'm here, Adam." She peaked around Vin. She'd grown even in just the couple of hours we parted. Her hand reached out for Adam, and it was much large than his. I hid my worry, but that had to be the first thing we worked on after we fixed the ice age.

He smiled and squeezed it. "Wuv you, Emilia."

"Love you," she said.

"Uh oh," Vin said.

"We're in trouble already," I said.

"Go ask your mother if she feels like going to the dining hall," Killian told Emilia.

"She's still in the bathroom."

"Still?" Killian said. "Come in and sit down. I'll check on Natasha."

He held the door open.

We didn't get but a few steps inside when his panicked voice reached me. "Josie? Can you come help?"

I walked into the bathroom to see Natasha's head buried in the toilet. *Poison? How?*

"What's going on? Did she come in contact with some of the poison?"

"Not that I know of." Killian shook his head.

"Oh my god," she said. "Are you two blind?"

Killian and I exchanged looks. He looked as confused as I felt.

"I'm pregnant," she said, her voice rough.

Killian grabbed the counter.

"What?" I mumbled. "How?"

"How do you think?" Natasha held her head.

"Never mind. Don't answer."

"Killian, say something so I know this news didn't end you," she said.

"I didn't think it could happen," he said. A smile broke out across his face. He knelt near her. "I love you, Natasha."

She held up her hand. "Do not try to kiss me. I need some privacy and a toothbrush."

"Of course," I said.

"No, you stay," she pointed to me. "You go," she said to Killian. "For now."

I closed the door.

Natasha pulled her toothbrush out of the drawer. "Do you think this is a natural pregnancy or do you..." She slammed the drawer shut.

"I don't know," I said. "We could probably do some tests for the marker. How far along do you think you are?"

"It feels like six weeks or so, but I could be wrong if the baby is like Emilia." Her voice shook with worry.

"The most important thing is that we keep you healthy and strong, and thereby keep the baby healthy."

"Woohoo!" We heard Killian shout from the living room.

Natasha and I both laughed.

"I think he's happy about it," I said through laughter.

"I never doubted he would be." She stuck the toothbrush in her mouth. "How do you think the childless people are going to react to my belly growing again?"

"They should be happy for you," I said. "But I think you can expect some serious jealousy."

"Mmm hmmm."

She spat the toothpaste in the sink and rinsed her mouth. "I don't want to be a science experiment."

I rubbed her arm. "I know. We won't let that happen."

"I just want this baby to be healthy." Her eyes filled with tears.

"The baby will be fine, Natasha." There was no reason to think the baby wouldn't be fine.

"If something happens," she said.

"It's not," I said. "Have faith."

She wiped under her eyes. "I hear we are eating in the dining hall tonight."

"Are you up to it?"

"Yes, I'm starving. Even human food sounds good," she said. Hunger was a good sign.

"Let's get the kids and the men and go." I smiled.

We found Ezra sitting with Darius, and he welcomed us to

the table. It felt good to sit like a family. Lots of eyes stared at us, but I ignored them. The kids didn't seem to notice.

"I'm heading down to the garden," Ezra whispered in my ear.

"I'll meet you down there after we put Adam to bed." I turned to watch him walk out of the room with his head high, seemingly with no regard for the stares. A lesson I could learn.

CHAPTER 20

JOSIE

V in and I walked down the hall. My guards had cleared the path well ahead of us. Vin's hand found mine and squeezed. I stole a glance at him. He'd been so patient with me. Our life together had been put on hold while we built the new government, and he didn't pressure me. He was patient.

"Do you think it will happen for us?" I asked Vin.

"What?" He looked at me.

"Another baby."

He stopped in the hallway. His face dropped, and I saw shock there. "Are you ready for another baby already?"

"Whenever it happens, I am. What about you?"

"I want as many as you are willing to have but..." His voice trailed.

"But what?"

"It was horrible seeing your body ripped apart." He bowed his head and pinched the bridge of his nose. When he looked back up, pink tears trickled from the corners of his eyes. "I thought I lost you. I don't know if I can handle it again."

The worst of it he witnessed wasn't part of my memories, but he remembered every bit of it.

I wiped his tears away. "Not every birth is like that. Don't you want more?"

"Not if it means losing you."

"I'm still here, aren't I?" I took his face in my hands. "I have no intention of leaving any time soon."

He kissed me. "You better get down to the lab. Ezra will be wondering where you are."

"I guess I should. He is on human time instead of vampire time now." I kissed him hard. "Walk me down to the lab?"

"It would be my pleasure." We resumed our path behind the guards.

"Do you think I'm doing the right thing with my father? Having him here? We wouldn't have any of the major break-throughs without him,

"Don't second guess yourself, Josie. There is a lot of hate for him here, but there is equally as much love for you. The people will trust your decisions, and once the ice age is reversed, they will understand your why."

"I hope you're right because I really could not have gotten this far with the formula without him. If hadn't known about Mother's private lab, we'd never had her journal."

"He will never be able to make amends for what he has done in the eyes of the people, but they might not send him to his death."

I worried about what would happen when we did reverse the ice age. *Would the people support me if I don't condemn him to a human death?* "I won't be able to give them his life if they demand it. There was a time I wanted him dead as the people do, but he's not the same person. He'll never be that person again."

"None of us are the same person." He paused. "You need to be true to yourself. That is why your people respect you. Just don't keep them in the dark. The transparency builds trust."

"It does, and I've done the exact opposite since my father has been here. I need to do better." I stopped in front of the lab entrance.

"And you will because it is who you are in here." He pressed his hand over my unneeded heart.

"Some think we don't have hearts." I gave him a sad smile.

He leaned down to my ear. "And they would be wrong." He kissed my cheek.

I put my hand on the keypad and opened the door.

"Be safe, Madame President," he said.

"I'll do my best, and I like Madame President so much better than Empress."

"It suits you."

"Wuv you," I said, imitating our son.

Vin laughed. "Wuv you too."

I stepped through the doorway. "Hey," I said, feeling the need to alert my newly human father to my vampire presence.

"Josephine." He smiled. "I was starting to wonder about you."

"I needed to talk to Vin for a minute," I said.

"All good?" His brow creased.

"I think so. How about with our model?"

"It looks positive for deployment once a year at the neap tides. Everything checks out."

Pride in our accomplishment together settled in my chest. "That's wonderful," I said. "Can I take a look?"

"It's your work." He gestured to the computer. "I just facilitated."

"These numbers are great," I said. "We can present to the council tomorrow in the regular meeting." The council would be excited to hear this news.

"You can present them. I don't think I should."

He needed to be part of the discussion so his vital contribution was understood. "Of course, you should. You helped achieve this milestone, and you deserve to have some good in your legacy."

"I do have good in my legacy, and that is you."

My heart softened. "What we are doing here is more important than me, and we have done this together. That should be known."

"You are probably the only one who believes that, Josephine."

"Even if I am, it will be entered into the official record of my presidency. You earned that legacy." I'd make sure he wasn't remembered only for his bad deeds. His ability to recognize his wrongs and make them right would be recorded too.

"I'm not sure I have, but I believe you want that for me."

Was that it? Was I trying to remake his image into something I wanted to believe?

"I want you to present with me. Can that be enough for now?"

"It can," he said. "There's something I want to show you. I found this looking for some decent paper for the printer." He handed me a leather-bound journal like the one we found in the lab.

I opened it to see familiar writing. It was another one of mother's journals. "You found a different one?"

"Yes, and this one was from when things were good," he said. "I thought it might be good to remember me by."

"Remember you by?" He can't leave. Not yet.

"I can't stay here forever, Josephine. Your people are not going to tolerate it, and I am human now. I will die at some point."

"You seem so healthy right now," I said. "Surely that will be a long time from now."

"How do we know with my human body?"

"We don't, but that is the beautiful thing about being human. The fragility of it makes it incredibly special." The human lifespan was such a small fraction of a vampire's that every moment meant something.

"And incredibly short," he said, resigned to his new fate. "But I did live a very long vampire life, so I will not complain."

"I need to ask you about something." Natasha wondered and so did I if he'd had anything to do with her recent conception.

"Anything. I'm an open book for you."

"Natasha is pregnant again," I said. "I have to ask if this has to do with your and Calidora's experiments?" I wanted him to say no that it wasn't him.

"She is pregnant?" He sounded excited. "No, I haven't had access to any of the experimental components, so it's not from me."

Relief replaced my worry. "We haven't seen Calidora in months," I said. "Is it possible from earlier contact?"

"No, I don't see how," he said. "It worked similar to the fertility treatments humans used. There was a specific time the treatment had to be administered. It sounds like her pregnancy is natural like yours with Adam was. This is a good thing for the vampire world."

I smiled. Natasha could celebrate her pregnancy with excitement instead of worry. At least for this child, Em's growth rate was still a concern.

"Emilia is still growing extremely fast," I said. "I have to tackle that research next."

"You need a team, Josephine."

"There's just not enough of us to do it all. I worry about it day and night." His lack of judgment when it came to me made it easier to share.

"Have you told Vin this?"

I shook my head. "Not the details."

"Killian? Natasha?"

"No, but they see it too. They've told me I can't spread myself around so much."

"They're right, Josephine. You are a vampire, but you have limits too. Albeit not the same limits I have, but still limits."

I nodded. "Will you stay and help me? We can make it work."

A guard emerged at the door before Ezra could answer. "The council has requested your presence."

"Thank you," I said. "I'll be there shortly." If they convened, then they must have some questions on our new government status or they reached the contacts in the Northeast. Probably the latter.

"You should go," Ezra said. "We can talk about this later."

"Saoirse must have made contact with New York," I said. "I'll come back after. I hope there is news of Livia and Luna."

"Me too," he said, his tone sincere.

The guard escorted me to the chamber. News of Livia and Luna would be ideal, but an update that the settlement thrived would be good too.

Everyone stood up as I walked into the room. "Please be seated," I said, taking my seat. I met Saoirse's gaze, and she looked pleased. It would be good news today. Natasha and Killian were absent, but Vin was in his normal spot. Natasha and Killian hadn't missed many meetings. Perhaps they would be here soon. I was thankful Vin was here.

"Saoirse, have you made contact with the New York encampment?"

"Yes," she said.

I struggled to find the words and sounded formal when I finally did speak." And how do we find them?"

Saoirse cocked her head to the side like I confused her. "They are doing well. Their numbers are about one hundred now, and the animal blood is sustaining them."

"Any humans?"

"None. There aren't enough human food sources to sustain the residents."

I wouldn't be able to banish Mara and Julius there. *Had Luna and Livia made it there?* "And where are the vampires from that have joined them?"

"Mostly from that area, but there are a few from outlying areas, so that is good news."

It was but not specific enough for me. "Any children?"

"None reported." Saoirse shifted in her seat. It registered on her face what I was after. She'd put it together.

The news crushed me, but I couldn't show it here. *Where were Livia and Luna?* "Anything else to report?"

"No, Madame President."

"Thank you. Then, if there are no objections, we shall send a team to escort Mara, Julius, and the rest of their group to Missouri instead of New York given the food concerns. Any objections?"

The room was silent. No one voiced any concerns.

I was thankful there were no questions. "Anything else for now?"

"Not that I'm aware of," Darius said.

"Good. Tomorrow, we can review the results of the environment reclamation testing and plan." The excitement I had for the results was dampened with Livia and Luna's whereabouts unknown.

"You have findings to present?" Darius asked, curiosity in his tone.

"Yes, we were very close when the incident happened, but we are now in a position to share a plan for the council's approval."

"That is fantastic news, Empress," Darius said.

"President, please," I said. "And I believe the council will be pleased."

"We are looking forward to it." He smiled.

I forced a smile to match his enthusiasm. "I'd like to craft an announcement for the title change and our new process. When does the council believe they will be ready?"

"We should be ready by the end of the week, Emp... Madame President," Saoirse said.

"Wonderful. I look forward to your plan as I'm sure you do mine."

I stood and headed for the door with Vin at my side. The pieces were fitting together as I hoped, and that gave me confidence in our success.

CHAPTER 21

JOSIE

K illian skidded to a halt in front of us. He was frantic. "Natasha."

I stopped in the middle of the hall. "Is she sick again? I can mix up an anti-nausea--"

"No, she's missing." He motioned for us to follow him.

My stomach tightened. "What do you mean missing?"

"We were taking a nap. Natasha, Em, and I. Emilia woke me up saying mommy was gone." Killian's eyes widened. "I've been all over the grounds, and she is not on the premises."

"Vin, we need your nose," I said. "Let's start at their rooms to see if you can pick up the scent."

I darted to their door with them. *She's fine. She woke up and decided to walk around.*

Vin entered the room and took a large whiff. "It's been a while since she's been here."

"How long did you nap?"

"We laid down shortly after we parted with you and just woke up maybe a half hour ago."

"That's a long nap for a vampire family," I said. "Vin, do you smell gardenia?"

He inhaled again. "Yes, it's very faint."

This was deliberate and a slap in the face using the gardenia. Whoever did it wanted us to know they knew what I did, and it scared the vampire out of me. "Someone used my tactic against you. We need to get on Natasha's trail right away. Vin, is there enough of her scent to follow it?"

"I think so. It might get challenging mixed with others."

Killian growled.

"We'll find her. Maybe you should stay with Emilia," I said. He wasn't in his normal military composure, and his emotions could lead to a mistake.

"Not a chance," he said. "The nanny is with her now."

"Very well," I said. "We'll take my guards and track her."

He nodded once.

One of my guards met us halfway down the hall in a brisk jog. "Madame President, I was on my to you. Julius has escaped. It appears someone set him free."

Just Julius? Of course, he would take Natasha. "Mara and the rest?"

"They were still in their cells. Whoever did it specifically released him," the main guard said.

He had help, and it wasn't Mara. "Thank you. Natasha is missing, so it is likely Julius is the one who kidnapped her," I said. "Did they say anything?"

"Mara refused to give any information, and she was not very alert."

The gardenia from the meeting should have mostly worn off. "She may have been given the same sleeping potion Natasha and Killian were," I said. "Julius is smarter than we give him credit for. We need to find them and find who is helping him."

"Yes, President," the main guard said. "The rest of the guard is awaiting your orders at the end of the hall."

I refused to let myself think about the possibility Natasha could be harmed. She would be fine when we find her. "We're going after them. Tell the guards to prepare for a quick hunt."

"Very well, ma'am." The guard pivoted and headed quickly down the hall.

"I need to go check on Ezra before we leave," I said. I wanted to make sure he wasn't one of Julius's targets as well.

"I'll go with you," Vin said.

"I will meet you both with the guards at the gate," Killian said.

I nodded and sped towards the lab.

"He's not here." Confused, I spun around like that would magically make him appear.

Vin sniffed the air. "There is gardenia scented on the air, but it could be coming from the garden itself."

"And Ezra?"

He took another whiff towards the door. "His scent is stronger than Natasha, but it is fading. They might not be that far if his scent is any indication."

It gave me hope we could stop them before they were able to get any distance away from here.

"Let's get to Killian and the others."

Vin and I rushed to meet them at the gate. *How did Julius get out of the cell? Who helped him?* Natasha and my father were tough. They would be fine. We would end those involved to save them if needed.

"They took Ezra too," I said. "Do you think they know about Natasha's condition?"

"How could they?" Vin said.

"No one knew," Killian said.

"I told Ezra earlier in the lab and asked him if his experiments had to do with it," I said. "He didn't know she was pregnant, but the door was open. If someone slipped through and was hiding, they could have heard." Guilt shook me. I should have shut the door.

"They must have been," Vin said, his tone resigned. "We should have been more diligent."

"I'll end Julius for touching Natasha. How dare he." Killian said, incensed.

"Remember what Ezra said before we knew for sure who it was? He said they wanted to cause disruption." The disruption I thought we stopped was just a distraction.

"They have certainly done that," Vin said.

"Let's show them what happens when we get angry," Killian said. He let out a roar that reverberated off the gates.

I agreed with him. The dissenters had taken the hint when we tried to be diplomatic. Our justice would be immediate this time.

"I'm usually the one asking for a non-violent solution, but I'll make an exception today," Vin said.

"We attempted to handle it kindly. The time for kindness is gone," I said. Anger built in my chest and filled my words with venom. "Vin lead us to them."

Our small group headed out in the direction of Ezra and Natasha's scents. Vin followed it like a bloodhound. My guards flanked us.

"Julius is definitely with them." He snarled.

"Can you tell how many others?" Killian asked.

"Maybe five," he said.

Fresh snow fell over us, and I wondered if Ezra was warm enough. The numbers were on our side. "How far ahead are they?"

"Not far," he said. "About two miles or so."

Visibility wavered as the wind blew the snow into our faces. It blotted out the sun enough that the Rogues would be able to venture out. The Rogues moved freely, and that amped up the danger for Natasha and Ezra, especially if they were incapacitated.

"What are we going to do when we get there?" I asked.

"Rip them apart," Killian said. "We should send some of the guards ahead to block them in case they try to run."

"Good idea." I motioned for the head guard. "Take your men and head up front. Block any escape route. Take a wide berth so as not to give your location away."

Vin clasped the guard's shoulder. "And keep an eye out. Rogues are in the area. I've been whiffing their scent randomly in the air. They could be close."

The guard nodded and took the men ahead at a brisk pace.

I lurked at a slow pace, giving the guards time to get in place. It was silent around us like when we were at the cabin.

"The Rogue scent is getting stronger. It's overpowering the others," Vin said.

Killian scanned the trees around us. "Get ready in case they attack."

"Isn't there a small clearing ahead?" I asked. We were being herded. I knew because it was what I would do.

"There is," Killian said. "We appear to be walking right into their plan."

Vin alternated between looking at the ground and sniffing the air. "They are very close," he whispered.

"Which ones?" Killian asked, his voice low with no emotion.

"All of them," Vin whispered.

The hair on my arms stood up. Chills ran up my neck. "I don't have a good feeling."

"You shouldn't," Vin said.

I got a first glimpse of the clearing. It reminded me of the fight we faced not so long ago against the Rogues as we claimed power, and I hoped we didn't see as much bloodshed as we did that day.

Natasha and Ezra were both laying on the ground in the middle of a circle of vampires. Neither was moving, but I could see Ezra's chest rise and fall. He was beating. Julius lay in that circle too with two vampires on either side. It took a second to realize the circle was made of Rogues.

"I don't understand," I whispered. "What are we looking at there?"

"Have the Rogues bitten them?" Killian asked.

"It doesn't look like it," Vin said. "I can smell their scents. They are pure and untainted."

Their actions were bizarre like they were being controlled, but Ezra was out, and it wasn't Vin. "It's like they are guarding them," I said. "But why?"

I got my answer. Calidora strolled out of the woods, alone but confident in her stride. She wasn't wearing the Grecian-style gown this time. She was dressed like a human in boots and a heavy coat. Pure hatred bubbled inside me. My mother's killer was in my presence.

"You have done well," she said.

The Rogues took a knee in her direction.

"I should go alone," Vin said. "She's my mother."

"It's my father on the ground," I said.

"And the mother of my child. We go together," Killian said.

"Agree," I said.

Vin started to protest. "Jos-"

"No, we all have someone to lose here and someone to fight for. We do this together," I said with every ounce of conviction I could muster.

We emerged into the clearing side-by-side. Calidora greeted us with an evil smile. Bile and blood rose up in my throat. I wouldn't forgive her for what she did to me or the prison she held Natasha in or for subjecting her own son, Vin, to experiments.

"There you are," she said. "I was wondering when you would stop hiding in the woods."

"Why are you here, Calidora?" I asked.

The Rogues snarled at me.

I glared at them. *If I am ended today, I'll take as many of them with me as I can.*

"I'm here to claim what is mine, of course."

"There is nothing here that is yours," I said.

"My son stands next to you. My future daughter-in-law is here. My future husband." She looked at my father.

I fought back vomit.

Killian growled next to me.

"And my youngest son is here."

I followed her gaze to Julius. *Not possible. Could it be?* Confused, I turned to Vin.

He shrugged and mouthed *I don't know.*

"Your level of insanity has reached a new peak, Calidora," I said.

"You will let them go," Killian said.

"I will not," she said. "And my pets will make sure I leave with my prizes."

"Vin, I know she's your mother, but I'm going to kill her." I clenched my fists. My nails dug deep, ready to break the skin and drive the Rogues insane.

"Not if I do first," Killian said. He shifted his weight to the other foot and took his pre-fight stance.

"She's my problem. I'll deal with her," Vin raised his voice. He set his shoulders.

"Deal with me?" She echoed him. "You're coming with us too."

Not today, Calidora.

"I'm not leaving here with you," he said.

"If you want the children to live, you will do as I say." She smiled towards the woods behind her.

I smelled Adam before I turned around to see him in Ann's arms. Emilia held her hand. Venom flooded my mouth with the rage in me. The kids were not pawns, but now for the second time, they were being used against us.

"Ann?" She had been loyal and swore to protect the kids. *Why?* "Bring Adam and Em to me."

"I'm sorry, Empress." She wouldn't meet my gaze.

My chest ached with a heaviness. The children were safe for now. I had to keep them that way. No matter what I had to do.

"She owed me a favor," Calidora said. "Don't be too hard on her. Bring the children here, Ann."

Ann lowered her head and took Adam and Emilia to her.

Calidora took my son in her arms.

Her hands on my child amplified my fury. I wanted her head, and I wanted it in my hand. I stepped forward. Vin grabbed one of my wrists, and Killian took the other. "Let me go," I said, my voice not my own.

"Josie, she is taunting you, and we can't risk the kids," Vin said, his voice strained.

I struggled, but Vin's words sank in for me. I stopped fighting them.

Calidora pushed Ann toward the Rogues. "Dinner my pets." The Rogues descended on Ann.

My heart pounded. *What is she doing?* I looked at Adam and Emilia. Terror rippled over their faces. The Rogues ripped Ann apart. Their gnashing drowned out Ann's screams. Adam's scream hit my ears. Vin and Killian's grips tightened on my wrist. I yanked my hands. Adam covered his ears. Emilia buried her face in Calidora's waist. I wrenched my wrist free from Vin and went to work on Killian's grasp. Vin wrapped his arms around me, pinning my arms to my side.

"Take her, Killian." He spun me around into Killian's arms.

Killian held me tight.

I head-butted Killian, but he took it without any reprieve in his firm hold.

"I have to go, or we will all die today," Vin said in a resolved tone.

Tears of anger spilled from my eyes, blurring my vision.

"She will not leave with my son," I said. "Vin..."

"We can't risk her hurting the kids, Josie," Vin said. "And we know she values little in this world over her ambitions."

I swallowed hard, fighting back the tears. I tried to regain self-control. "Don't ask me to stand by and watch her walk away with my son or our goddaughter."

"Trust me," Vin said. "Trust that I will always do the right thing."

"I trust no one more," I said. I shut my emotions off. It was like I died inside if that was possible for a vampire.

Vin kissed my cheek. "It will all be ok." He turned and walked toward his mother.

"You can let me go, Killian," I said.

"Are you sure?" He asked.

"Yes," I said. "Release me."

He loosened his grip, and I moved to his side. No emotions didn't mean I couldn't comprehend the situation, nor did it remove the goal of ending Calidora.

Vin stood in front of his mother, blocking the children's view of the Rogues as they worked what was left of Ann. Movement from Natasha caught my eye. She stirred to wake and would be ready to fight as soon as she saw Em.

I waved a hand at her to not move. Ezra hadn't woken yet. His human state could take longer to recover.

She froze at the sight of our children and the epitome of evil holding them.

Julius woke and stood up. "Was that necessary, Mother?" He wobbled on his feet before getting his bearings. He strode over to Calidora side. "Eww," he said, at the sight of the Rogues finishing Ann's remains. "Disgusting."

"How did we not know he was Calidora's son?" I whispered to Killian.

"Mara vouched for his creation," Killian said.

"So, he's a born vampire?"

"I can hear you, Josie," Julius said. "No, Mother created me to have the perfect son." He looked Vin up and down. "Since her other one is flawed."

"My boys will not fight," Calidora said. "You are both my favorites for different reasons."

"Why do you need me," Vin said. "Us?"

"Oh, I don't need all of you." Her tone dismissive, she looked at Killian and me. "Just my family."

"You don't have a family," Vin said. "Unless you count your puppets."

Julius drew back his fist, but Vin didn't flinch. Calidora placed her hand on Julius's fist and pushed it down.

"We will not fight," she said. "Among ourselves."

The muscle in Vin's back twitched.

I cut my eyes over to Natasha and blinked once. She blinked once back.

I lowered my voice to below a whisper. "When Vin moves we move. Whistle for the guards at that time."

"Are you sure?" Killian asked.

"Positive."

We waited.

Vin's movements were frozen.

Calidora smiled. "Ahh, it seems my pets found the rest of your crew."

I focused on the direction we sent them. The sounds drifted to me. I grabbed my stomach.

"Fuck," Killian said, under his breath.

My emotions returned in a pang of regret. "I sent them to their end."

"You are not to blame," Killian said. "Only one vampire here is."

"Well, maybe two." I stared at Julius. He stared at Natasha. I lowered my voice for only Killian to hear. "If Vin still makes his move, we go with him. She's not leaving here with our kids."

Vin didn't move though. "We'll go with you," he said, his tone defeated.

"What?" I asked.

"If you leave the children with Josie and Killian. All of them," Vin said.

Natasha stood then. She positioned herself in a stance that would maximize her trajectory. She was going to jump.

Calidora stared at him like he had suggested the most absurd thing she'd ever heard. "No, I want my entire family."

"You will not leave here with all of us, so which do you choose?"

"I do not wish to shed family blood here, but I do not trust you not to attack if I release the children. The children stay."

"He's trying to be tricky anyway, Mother," Julius said. "Natasha is pregnant again." He cast a disgusted glance at Killian. "By him."

"How is this possible?" Calidora asked in disbelief.

She didn't know. That was the reason she was here.

"Natasha, come here," Calidora commanded.

Natasha rolled her head in my direction and rolled her eyes. Never one to like commands, she faced forward to Calidora. "I'm good."

"Julius, bring her here," Calidora said.

"Oh, please do." Natasha laughed. "I would love to see how that ends."

Julius took a couple of steps forward and turned back to Calidora.

"Go ahead," she said.

"Yes, Julius. Please come get me." Natasha taunted him. "I have so much to show you that I learned from your mother."

Natasha wanted blood and payment for what had been done to her. If Julius advanced on her, he would pay that price. The moment we entered the clearing, I knew we wouldn't leave without spilling blood.

She crooked a finger toward him. "Here little Julius. I have something for you." The old Natasha was coming out. Not that I didn't understand, because I did.

I let my emotions flow back in and rolled my head around as they flooded back in. *Fear. Fury. Fight.*

The Rogues' feeding frenzy had ended on Ann, but the sounds in the woods could still be heard. Sadness came swiftly for the vampires lost. I tucked it away, but my rage powered me for the battle ahead.

"We don't know how many are out there," I said for only Killian to hear. "Is there a chance to outrun them?"

"If we move fast, I think so," Killian said.

I looked at Ezra, still out cold. "I'll carry Ezra. He's my burden to bear anyway. You get the kids."

Killian glanced at me. His voice skeptical, he said, "You're assuming Vin will end Calidora."

"Yes," I reached for the sunshine stick at my waist.

"We'll go with that then." Killian put his hand on his belt.

"Go on, Julius," Calidora said. "Get her and bring her here."

"Mom?" Emilia peered around Vin. Calidora gripped her shoulder to stop her from going further.

"Close your eyes and cover your ears, Emilia. Mommy has to do some bad work," Natasha said. It wouldn't block sensitive vampire hearing, and I doubted Emilia's control was developed enough to focus elsewhere. It was a nice thought though.

Julius approached Natasha slowly. He looked like a wolf stalking a deer.

A smile crossed her face. She wanted to make him suffer.

"Natasha, we're friends," he said, his tone cheerful. He moved within her reach.

Bad move, Julius.

"I believed we were until you poisoned my daughter and kidnapped me." She landed a kick into his chest.

He stepped back and spit blood onto the white snow.

"This will be too easy," she said. "You should go back to your mother."

"I have to take you with us," he said, his voice full of regret. "She commands it."

"Then she commands you to your end."

"She will end me if I don't," he said. "So either by your hand or hers. It is the same."

Natasha's face softened. Something in her broke, and she stepped back, remaining in the fighting stance.

It made me pity Julius, but it did not diminish what he had done.

"Then I will show you mercy, but only because my daughter is here," Natasha said. "You can die at your mother's touch. I'm not going anywhere with you."

"Aagh." Blood gurgled at Julius's lips. It wasn't Natasha's kick that pained him. His mother was trying to assert her control over him.

I glanced at Calidora. Her intent was focused on him. This was our window.

"Fight it," Natasha whispered to Julius. She spent years in

Calidora's house before her escape with us. She understood what it was like to be under Calidora's control better than any of us.

Vin moved swiftly. He leaped into the air and planted both feet into Calidora's chest. She stumbled backward and Adam flew in the air.

I dashed to catch him and found Emilia planted firmly in the snow, almost as if she had sat down. My son was safe in my arms, and I took Emilia's hand in mine.

Killian jumped in the middle of the Rogues, but they weren't fighting us. They stood still as if... waiting for a command.

A crack echoed in my ears, and I turned to see Vin's foot connect to Calidora's chin.

"Natasha, come get the kids. I'll take Ezra," I said.

"I'll get him," she called over her shoulder.

I maneuvered our children away from the fight.

Julius dropped to his knees. Blood pooled on the snow in front of him. He gasped like a human in need of air.

Natasha glanced up and down at Julius and bent to pick Ezra up. She froze. I looked over my shoulder to see a number of Rogues so large I could not quickly count. I backed toward her, putting the children between Natasha and me. Killian was first in front of us.

Vin stood behind us. "Stop. They are all around us. We are surrounded."

Ezra finally stirred awake.

Thank the Gods.

"Who's ready for a fight?" Natasha asked.

"I'm always ready for a fight, but we are grossly outnumbered here," Killian said.

Natasha patted his shoulder. "We sacrifice it all to protect the kids. Everyone agree?"

"Agree," we all said in unison.

"How in the human Hell did we get in this situation?" Ezra asked. His confused gaze went to the circle of Rogues.

They shrunk the space around us. Our kids were positioned in the center with five of us around them.

An opening parted in front of us. Calidora stepped through, looking unscathed from Vin's attack. Her poise intensified my hatred for her.

"Now, I get it," Ezra said, glancing down at Julius. "What does the little created vampire have to do with it?"

"She created him, so you know, the whole control thing," I said.

"Ahh. Yes."

"Calidora, what is the meaning of all this disruption?" Ezra gestured around at the Rogues. "You have no claim here."

"But I do dear Ezra," she said. "My family is here. Just as yours is."

"I think the time for that sentiment passed when Josie took over the kingdom. This is her nation now," he said. His strong voice boomed out like a vampire.

CHAPTER 22

JOSIE

Calidora approached Ezra. "I've missed you," she said, her voice soft. "Our children are so rebellious, aren't they?" She held out her arm for him to take.

He looked at me, but he took her offered arm. They strode around the circle perimeter.

"Remember our plans?" She asked. "What the world was supposed to look like by now?"

"Our plans died a long time ago. We are far past the days where that dream could be realized."

"We are so close," she pouted.

"No, we are not, Calidora," Ezra said. "We have gone too far. Each day pushes us too close to the tipping point."

"You're siding with your daughter."

"I'm not. Our actions now will determine if our days on Earth will end or continue."

"We need your mind on it. That's all."

"Calidora, I'm human now. I can't move like a vampire, including to do the research needed."

"I heard about the disservice done to you. So you want to

give up?" She asked. "So easily? We could find a way to turn you back."

"It's been a century. It's time to admit our ideas failed. We need to try another way."

"But reproduction has restarted," she said. "Your daughter had a natural pregnancy. Natasha is pregnant a second time. There will be others."

"And what blood will sustain these new vampires? We are running out of sources. Humans are closer to an extinction rate than we are, and the animals are in the same race. We'll all end up Rogue."

"I don't want to be one of my pets," she said. "You don't think that would happen do you?"

"Yes, I do if we keep on this path," he said, his tone conciliatory.

My blood boiled in anger the longer they circled. Calidora acted like she was oblivious to the fate we were all destined to if we didn't reverse the ice age, and Father was pacifying her.

"Josephine has done an excellent job on the research to move us in the correct direction. It will not be easy, but it can be done."

"I will not go back into hiding," Calidora said.

"The times of hiding in the shadows have long since passed. You can't put the vampire back in the coffin," my father agreed.

Calidora laughed, presumedly at his corny joke. "We'll retreat for now," she said. "I haven't made up my mind yet. Come, Julius."

He joined her, and they walked through the ring where Rogues had parted the way. The Rogues filed in behind them and marched in military fashion. Calidora's control of them was impressive. No doubt she'd long known control of them was possible.

They exited as quickly as Calidora had emerged.

I picked Adam up and held him tightly to me. Vin wrapped his arms like a cocoon around us. My little family was safe for the moment.

Emilia yelled, "Mom!"

"Let's get back to the compound before she changes her mind," Ezra said.

"On my back, Ezra," Killian said. "We're going back at a vampire's pace."

"I will not," Ezra said, insulted.

"Do it for me," I said. "Please, Father." The word sounded foreign like I tested it out. *Could I call Ezra by Father all the time again?*

He let out a big sigh and climbed on Killian's back.

"Look at the mighty Ezra." Natasha laughed.

"Stop, Natasha." I shot her a look to back off.

We were inside the walls of the compound in minutes at most. The snow had slowed and visibility had returned.

"My body aches like I didn't even realize a vampire could experience this kind of exhaustion," Natasha said. "I'm going to take Em up for a nap."

Killian set Ezra down. "I'll sit and watch over you. I don't think I'll sleep for a while."

I nodded to them. Adam was asleep in my arms. His ability to sleep anywhere amazed me. Even though he had witnessed horrible things today, he was home safe. "I promise we will make the world better for you," I whispered to him.

"Want me to take little man?" Vin asked.

I was reluctant, but I passed our son to him. "Yes, I should go to the lab for a while."

"Would you like me to join you?" Ezra asked.

"No, I'm really looking for a little alone time," I said. I dashed off before he could respond. It wasn't anything against him. I needed to decompress.

I put my hand on the panel in front of the lab.

A haze of smoke filled the room. Shock froze me for a split second. *Fire.*

I reached around the corner for the emergency fire retardant button. My fingers found it, and I slammed them into the button. The doors started to shut, and I jumped out of the way. The hum of the fire-retardant system was audible. I turned around, pressing my back to the wall. I slid down to the floor. Everything we needed was in that lab and coated with a sticky residue.

Damn. I rested my head on my knees. *How can I explain this to the people? It is within our reach, and if that computer is destroyed...* I refused to let myself think about those consequences. The computer would survive, and we would be able to push forward. *What could have caused a fire in there? No one had access but Ezra and me. Did I leave the door open? I don't think I did.*

If it wasn't salvageable and if all our research was lost, I'd find a way to recreate it. I had to.

I'd find Ezra to help restore what we had lost. If it could be done he was the right person to help me do it.

The system required a couple of hours to remove the toxins from the air in the lab. Ezra wouldn't be able to enter until that was done. I looked at the position of the sky. Everyone would wake soon, except for the guard who was posted late for us. And the kids. They will need therapy after what Calidora did in front of them today. Anger festered in my heart and expanded out through my body. I wanted her to pay. She would pay.

I wonder if Julius wasn't controlled if our options would look differently. Would he have still followed her if he hadn't been controlled?

"Guess we will never know," I said to myself.

The doors of the lab would remain locked until the system released. I paced through the garden checking the roses and smelling them. I turned around taking in each aspect of the garden and considered how much care Mother had put into it before she died. Those loyal to her and her plight had maintained it for almost a century. It's almost like they had known it would all lead to this point. The point where we would have to make a decision that would lead us to existence or extinction. Everything in the garden looked in the appropriate place other than the Jimson weed Julius had taken. I stopped at my mother's favorite and mine. The petals of the flesh-colored rose I picked were like velvet in my hands. The softness and fragility reminded me of humans.

"Hey," Vin said over my shoulder. "The guard told me there was a fire alarm in the lab, but he said the suppression system engaged. I came right away to make sure you were ok."

"Mmm hmmm," I said, letting the petals fall through my fingers to the floor. "I am. I'm not so sure our research survived though."

"You haven't checked yet?"

"No, the doors will not unlock until the chemicals are cleared from the air," I said. "It'd be bad for the plants to force it open anyway. How are the kids?"

"Adam is still sleeping. He's exhausted, but he'll be fine," he said, his tone worried.

"That was a pretty horrific scene for him to see," I said, the bitterness in my voice like poison.

"Our little man is resilient," he said in a sincere tone.

"He is, but still," I said. "How about Emilia?"

"Killian said Natasha is firmly wrapped around her and may never let her out of her sight."

I chuckled. "Sounds like Natasha. She's not afraid of anything except losing the family she gained."

Vin pulled me into his arms and held me tight. "Sounds familiar."

I rested the side of my head against his chest. "Me?"

"And me," he said.

I looked up and studied his face. He was there for me like he had been with all the love he had to give. "Are you worried about losing our family?"

"I'd worry less if you'd finally marry me," he said.

I sighed.

"But I am worried this is all going crumble in front of us if we don't get the ice age reversed. I know it's bad, Josie."

"It is," I said. "We can't afford any delays. A month. A week. It all matters at this point."

"We'll make it happen."

"The only way the model shows success is a years-long rollout at the lowest tides," I said. "The neap tides. Mother had the answer in her journals. She never got the chance to execute it. We need to start with the next low tide, which is only a week away, and we have to do them in a specific order." If it was still possible, and I wasn't sure it was until I could see what was left in the lab.

"Them?"

"The deployment to the atmosphere. We have to go past the troposphere but not beyond the stratosphere to get the right dispersion."

"And you have the delivery system?"

"Yes, it's the same way the ice age was created. There are still some here, but we'll have to travel back to Chicago to have enough of them."

"Where do you start?"

"We'll start here in North America. It's easiest here, and if something goes wrong, the rest of the remaining populations can learn from it. We can move most of our people to the Southern Compound just in case. Before launch, Ezra and I will transmit everything to the other locations for awareness."

"Josie, if something were to happen," he said, his voice troubled.

"We should have enough time to evacuate. It's only a safeguard to move everyone else."

"I'll stay with you," he said. He had so much conviction in his tone.

"You need to go with Adam, especially now that Ann is..." I shook my head against the horrible memory. "Gone."

"I can't leave you," he said.

"We can't leave Adam alone." Tears pricked my eyes.

"Then marry me before you do this," he said.

There was too much to do in preparation for the deployment. I didn't have time to plan a wedding. "You already have my love, Vin. There is not anything else I could give you. Other than a world without ice."

"Say yes. Grant my deepest wish to be your husband."

"It's such a human thing." I ran my hand over his chest. "Surely, there is something else you want."

He tipped his head back. "I thought we were past all this human thing versus vampire thing. Besides your dad is human now, or at least something close to it."

A nervous giggle escaped my lips as my thoughts scrambled. "Something close to it sums it up."

He put his lips close to my ear. "There is nothing else I want more than to be bound to you for the rest of our eternal lives."

His breath tickled my ears, and I closed my eyes. In my unneeded heart and in my head, we were already bound for eternity and longer. He needed something more tangible than my word, and this I could give to him. I pressed my lips against his.

He leaned back and looked me in the eyes. "So, what say you, Madame President? Will you profess before our friends and family that I am the best thing to ever happen to you?"

I laughed and slapped his chest. "Madame President doesn't marry."

His face dropped.

"But Josephine, the vampire who loves you eternally, will marry you."

He pressed his lips to mine. It was a soft kiss that coaxed my lips apart. I welcomed him in and enjoyed the slow entanglement. The sensual caress reminded me of how gentle he could be. He could read me and my needs, and I'd been blind about how perfect we are for each other.

I pulled back. "Vin, I know you wanted a marriage. I'm sorry I drug my feet on planning a good ceremony and saying we should wait until everything around us settles."

"All I want is to be able to call you Mrs. Cavanaugh," he said.

"I've never had a last name before," I said with happiness. "That feels very human."

"Join us, commoners," he said.

"Gladly," I said. "Josie Cavanaugh sounds really good."

"It sounds perfect." He lifted me and spun us around in a circle. This was happiness. This was love, and Vin deserved everything I could give to him.

CHAPTER 23

JOSIE

I steadied myself for Natasha's response when I told her the news.

"We deploy the first one next week," I said. "Vin and I have decided to have a wedding ceremony before then, and I was wondering if you would be the best woman or whatever they call it."

A smile spread across her face. Her eyes widened.

I leaned back and braced for her reaction.

"So, wait," Natasha bounced up and down on the sofa. "You want me to stand up with you?"

"Yes," I said. "I consider you my sister now, and there isn't anyone else I would think of asking."

"I'd be honored to be your maid of honor." She frowned. "Are you going to ask Ezra to walk you down the aisle?"

"I was planning to," I said. "He has changed, Natasha, and I don't just mean from vampire to human."

"In my experience, people don't change so easily," she said in a frustrated tone.

"From our conversations, I don't think it was that easy for

him." I understood her mistrust, but he not only helped me breakthrough on the formula, but he also convinced Calidora to leave. He didn't try to sway the situation for himself as he would have in the past.

"Don't you think the people will have an issue with it? Do you think they even know he's not a vampire anymore?"

"They have to," I said. "Wouldn't they?" I considered it. He moved slowly and only ate human food now. "How would they not?"

"Maybe they aren't talking about it." Natasha shrugged. "Or maybe they are scared to say anything because he is ... well, Ezra."

"True." I sighed. "It's going to take him a long time to earn back their trust. Maybe his whole human lifetime."

She leaned her head back on the couch and stared at the ceiling. "Would you turn human if you could?"

"I haven't even thought about it, but I don't think so. There will never be enough years with Vin and Adam for me to want to be mortal. Would you?"

"Before Emilia and before whoever is in here." She rubbed her belly. "And before the ice age, I might have. I have too much tied up in the vampire world to do it now."

I understood what she meant. Family changed my perspective of how I look at the world too. "I can't imagine leaving Vin and Adam voluntarily."

"That has to fuck with your head though," she said.

"What does?"

"Ezra, I mean." She turned her face toward me. "Going from an immortal to mortal. How do you reconcile that?"

"He seems at peace with it, so I guess that resolution came

easier than some. I think he believes it is penance for his crimes." We all had our crimes and most of them were from our time under Ezra and Calidora's rule. The notion of my own penance weighed on me. To pay the price Ezra had would shatter me like an icicle on a hard surface. I hoped our redemption came as the goodness and unification we created spread.

"Ok. So have you thought about what you want for the ceremony?" Natasha's face lit up like she'd been waiting for this her whole life.

"We only have a few days. I'm not sure how much we can do." Humans took months before the ice age to plan these things.

Natasha rolled her eyes. "We're vampires, Josie. We can do a lot in a few days. So, what do you have in mind?"

"For flowers, I'll carry some of Mother's flesh-colored roses from the garden." From the moment I agreed to marry Vin, I wanted to make sure Mother was represented in the ceremony.

"Good choice. What about a dress?"

"I've got some dresses in the trunk from the Southern Compound. I don't even know where to find a wedding dress." *How can I think about wedding dresses when there is still so much to do to save all of us? Save the world? It can't become too much of a distraction from the work. I can do this, with Natasha's help, because Vin needs it. It will provide hope for our people. And I want to declare myself to Vin for the world to see.*

"I'll check out the mall we uncovered and see if anything suitable survived. Maybe we can find something to alter."

"Ok. If not, I'm sure there is something around here that will work. One of those dresses I brought will be just fine."

Natasha stared at me for a moment and narrowed her eyes at me. "Music?"

Why are human ceremonies so complicated? "Do we need music?"

Natasha nodded. "There is that piano someone was tuning. I'll see if they know any wedding music from the human ceremonies."

"Oh, that march they use. That would be good."

"The Wedding March?" Natasha laughed.

I giggled. "Yes, that's it."

"What about rings?"

Another question. Couldn't we just meet at the altar and do it like that?

"I have the ring Vin gave me." I held out my hand and wiggled my fingers.

"But rings for you two to exchange. That jewelry store we uncovered still has tons of stuff in it. I bet we can find matching bands there."

"Natasha, I have a lot of prep to do before we launch the device. I'm not sure I have time for all these other activities. Maybe this was a bad idea." So many decisions. It overwhelmed me to think this all had to be done while we were trying to get the first device active. Provided the fire suppression system hadn't destroyed everything. I needed to get back to the lab.

"Leave it to me. I'll coordinate the food and everything. The thing I can't do is write your vows for you. You'll have to do that yourself."

"I have to write my own vows?" I leaned back and covered my eyes with my arm.

"You don't, but I'd bet my mortality Vin will be."

I peeked out from under my arm. "He will. That's him. You're right. Why did I agree to this?"

"Because you love him. You can do it. I bet once you start it will be easy," she said, her voice full of encouragement.

I sat up. It will all get done for the wedding and what doesn't will be fine, because I'll be married Vin. Warmth settled in my chest. "Maybe so. Speaking of my other duties. I need to get Ezra and head to the lab to make sure neither the fire nor the fire suppression goo damaged our research."

"Fingers crossed," Natasha said. "You work on saving the world, and I'll work on saving your wedding."

"Thanks, Natasha."

We got up off the couch, and I hugged her. "And I mean it. Thank you."

I took my time walking to Ezra's room, not sure if I was ready to see what was left of the lab. At least the trip with him was a human pace, but it gave me time to run through too many scenarios. *What if the fire destroyed the computer... or Mother's journals... or both.*

"Let's see what we are dealing with." I pressed the panel for the doors to open. They made a grinding noise but gave way. I closed my eyes not sure if I was ready to see it.

No smoke and no chemical smell. I squinted through my lids before opening them wide. The system did its job well. My knees buckled with relief, but I right myself in vampire speed.

"It's clear, Ez... Father," I said. If I wanted everyone else to see the difference in him, I had to start acting like there was too.

"Father?" I turned to look at him.

He regarded me. "It sounds so strange coming from your

mouth," he paused. "I thought I would be Ezra to you from now on."

"You are more of a father since your transformation."

"Thank you, Josephine, but I'm not sure I'm worthy of such praise."

"You are if you keep growing in your humanity," I said. "I wanted to ask you something."

"Ask me anything. I will keep no secrets from you."

"Vin and I have decided to get married."

"Congratulations." He hugged me. "You and Vin deserve a commitment ceremony."

I returned his embrace, but it was an awkward hold on my side.

"We're doing more of a human-style wedding ceremony." I chewed on my lip. *Why is this so hard to ask him?*

"Ahh. Their traditions are a little different than ours," he said. "Well, yours. Not mine anymore."

"Yes, and I'd like to ask you," I paused. "Would you walk me down the aisle?"

Tears welled up in his eyes. "I'd be the proudest father, human or vampire, to do so."

I hugged him in a more graceful way this time. "Thank you," I said. "It means a lot to me. I just wish Mother could be here for it too."

"I do too, Josephine," he said. "I do, too. Not sure I will ever forgive myself for her death."

Even knowing Calidora was the one responsible for having Mother ended, I wasn't sure I could forgive him for his culpability in it, but I reminded myself to try.

"What does a human father do for his vampire daughter when she gets married?"

"I think you are supposed to throw a rehearsal dinner." I shrugged.

"Ok. When will the event be?"

"Like two and a half days. Vin wanted to do it before we evacuate everyone to the Southern Compound."

"He wants witnesses." Father leaned against the table and crossed his arms.

"I think it's more he wants the world to know about our love."

"There is no doubt he loves you, Josephine, and he is a great father to your son. Much better than I ever was to you."

His admission quelled the anger I carried under the surface.

"He is the most amazing father," I said. "My life and how I look at it would have been different if Vin and I had never met. We might not be saving the world if he hadn't always challenged me on my moral code."

"Vin is good for you, Josephine. I saw it from the beginning. You stopped going through the motions of the day when you met him. The light came back in your eyes."

"Is that why you never objected to him?"

"When you first rescued him at the gate, I thought he would be a pet for you, and you needed something with meaning. Vin gave you that while you grieved your mother," he said. "I didn't learn his identity until much later after you had broken up."

"He did help me through my grief. I'd contemplated many ways to end my existence before him." I'd never told anyone that, and it sounded odd to say it out loud almost a century later. Father had Agata brought in around that time, and she watched my every move... until Vin.

"He gave you love when I was incapable of providing that for you. I was driven before but I shut everything off when your mother was murdered. I didn't realize how much until I became human, and it pains me to know you wanted to end yourself." He wiped at his eyes.

I studied him. This honest and vulnerable side of my father was new. In all my existence, I'd never seen him talk about his emotions with such candor.

"I do love you, my infinitely wise daughter," he said.

My own tears pooled then. "We've got to stop crying like this." I laughed. "I love you too, Father."

"Maybe one day I will be worthy of your love," he said. "Enough tears. Let's see how our work faired against this system."

"Why don't you check the computer, and I'll look for the source of the smoke."

"Whatever you say, Madame President."

He grabbed some supplies from the cabinet and sat at the computer area to clean it.

I milled around the lab investigating the general direction I thought the smoke had come from, but I'd only had moments, seconds at best, so it could have been anywhere.

A small round device caught my eye. I'd seen one of these before. The release mechanism was open. It had been discharged. I picked it up and sniffed. The strength of the smokey smell gagged me.

"Are you okay, Josephine?"

"Yes, I found the source of the smoke," I called over my shoulder.

"Deliberate?"

"Absolutely." I walked over and sat it on the table next to Ezra.

"I haven't seen one of those in decades. That's the smoke device we used to smoke humans out of hiding when they were still abundant."

"Someone gambled and won on the reaction I'd have finding the lab filled with smoke," I said.

"What would they gain from this? We all benefit from ending the ice age."

"We know one person who doesn't think so," I said. *Calidora.*

"She left," Father said, a perplexed expression on his face. How would she have gotten in here and opened the lab door?"

"Great question, and I think the answer is that she still has someone inside."

"How would they gain access here though? Through the guards and then to the lab itself." He looked confused.

"They did see us come through the secret passage, and those passages aren't guarded." That would have to change. I leaned down to whisper in his ear. If we still had Calidora supporters in our midst they could cause major disruption in our plans... beyond a fire in the lab. "And I suspected the lab was being monitored after Julius knew Natasha was pregnant. No one else knew but Natasha, Killian, Vin, and me until I told you in here."

Ezra casually glanced around and grabbed a piece of paper. He scribbled on the paper. *Cameras?*

I shrugged.

He scribbled some more. *Give me a task, and we'll look around for it.*

"Let's get the rest of this cleaned up." I gestured to the film covering almost everything in the lab.

I walked to the desk I had been using and pretended to clean off the suppression material while looking for listening devices and cameras.

Ezra did the same.

I worked my way down the side of the room I was on, and Ezra worked down his, albeit at a human pace.

He opened the cabinet at the back of the room and pulled out one of the electronic charge items. They were used during our training early in the ice age and packed quite a punch, but they could be used to do target disablement on other devices. He tilted his head toward a corner. The area had a good view of the entire lab.

I met him over there.

He stood to the side and pointed at a small device. Anger permeated me to the core, but shame twisted with it for missing something like this. Smaller than any of the others we had used. This was not something from our nation as far as I was aware. *How had he recognized it?*

"I can clean this area, Josephine. Why don't you go see if the computer will fire up?"

He didn't want them to know we had found it. I went over to his area and pretended to work on the keyboard.

Zzzp. The noise from the electronic discharge wouldn't be heard by human ears, but I picked up on it. "Everything good over there?"

"It is. We should destroy it just to be safe."

I returned to where he was standing. "Have you seen this before? Should we dissect it?"

"Yes, it was a prototype we had collaborated on with Calidora's team. They don't store any data and only transmit sound, but they can transmit long distances. We never finished them at the Southern Compound."

"It looks like she did. We know what we are looking for now. Are we sure that is the only one?"

"I didn't see anything else on this side. I can run over your side to be sure."

"I'd feel better if you double-checked. I can destroy this one." I crushed it in my hand and dropped the dust into the trash bin beside the table. "You would think vampires would build stronger equipment."

Ezra laughed. "I don't think you realize how strong you have actually become, Josephine. Inside and out."

I smiled. Compliments, especially genuine, were never his strong suit. He'd told me as a child that compliments were a way weak people hid the truth. He changed every day he became more human, and I liked this version of him. I tried to not get caught up in flattery, but it was harder when it came from him.

"All clear as far as I can tell," he said. "But you should have the guard sweep the room regularly. Get the cameras online. Your mother had them disabled for her privacy. And have the guard monitor for any stupid enough to come to see why their listening device stopped working."

"Yes, sir," I said. His direction dropped me back to the Southern Compound and setting up the lab there. I'd wanted his approval and executed his orders without fail in hopes he would assign me to missions instead of research.

"I'm sorry," he said, in an apologetic tone. "Sometimes the Emperor still comes out."

"It was your job for a long time. I'm sure that is not an easy transition."

"Easy? No. Worth it? Yes." He smiled. "I have my daughter back, so there is no price too great, at least not to the human me. The vampire me can burn in the hottest fire." He looked at me. His lips turned up on the corner. "Don't raise an eyebrow at me. You know he was an ass, as Natasha likes to remind me."

"I'm glad you found a better version of yourself."

"Me too. Let's see how our computer fared through it all." He swapped out the keyboard and mouse with one from the cabinet. "Ready?"

"Ready," I said.

Please work.

He turned it on, and the computer booted up. His hands moved over the keyboard. "The system itself looks fine, and the backups are in place."

"Yes," I said. "Thank goodness."

"Our notes are there from the last simulation, but the simulation itself is missing. We can run that again. The results shouldn't change, but you'll want that to present to the council. Shall I run it?" It was frustrating, but so much better than what I expected to find when we reentered the lab.

"Yes, Father." I rested my hand on his shoulder. "Please run it again."

CHAPTER 24

JOSIE

I opened the door to my room and was tackled by a cute little boy. "Adam, I missed you."

"I miss yoooooo," he said. "Wuv you."

"Love you too."

"Down."

"Ok." I sat him down on the floor.

"Daddy!" He ran across the room to Vin.

Vin scooped him up. "We're going to leave and give you ladies some time to bond."

"Ladies?"

He cut his eyes over to the study. Natasha had all kinds of wedding stuff spread across the room, and there in the middle of it was Agata, my former maid from the Southern Compound. She had her hair in a bun and wore street clothes.

I rushed over and hugged her.

"Madame President," she said. "I'm in awe of the changes you have made already."

"We will have none of that. You'll call me Josie like all my friends. What are you doing here?"

"Natasha called the Southern Compound and of course, I had to come."

"I can be pretty persuasive." Natasha flipped her hair and smiled.

"We are aware," I said, throwing some tulle at her.

"We'll be back later." Vin kissed my cheek. "Have fun."

"Thanks," I said. "See you later." I wagged my eyebrows at him.

He chuckled and walked out the door with our son hanging upside down from his arms.

"Weeeeeeeeee," Adam waved. "Bye-bye."

"Bye-bye." I waved back.

Natasha turned me around to the room of bridal things. "Ok. Focus. Vin only gave me two hours, because he thinks you need to rest even though we're vampires."

"Where do we even start?" Bags covered every piece of furniture in the study. I warmed inside but a little fear nagged at the corners of my excitement.

"Let's start with the dresses," Natasha said. "We'll build everything else around the dress."

"Dresses?" *Please don't let Natasha have brought the entire store here.*

"Yes, Agata and I raided an old bridal store in the mall. Most of the stuff was ruined, but we found a few gems preserved in perfect condition. Fingers crossed you like at least one of them."

Natasha pulled the first one out of a bag. It was a satin gown with a deep plunging neckline and a long train.

"That's you. Not me," I said.

She looked it over. "You're right. We'll save that one for later." She tossed it across a chair and opened the second bag.

It was a wrap-style dress with shoulder pads and a shawl collar.

"That looks a little matronly to me," I said.

"Hmmm. Yes, that's not going to make Vin want to rip it off of you," she said and tossed it on top of the first one.

"Agata, you want to do the honors on the next one since you found it."

"I'd love to," she said.

Agata unzipped the bag and gently removed the wedding gown. "It's handmade lace," she said.

It was a sheath-style wedding dress with long sleeves. The back and sleeves were made of nude mesh, so the lace made a tattoo-like effect. Small beads accented the lace. It was styled to skim the body but gave way to a beautiful chapel train in the softest tulle. The back was brought together by at least thirty buttons.

"It's beautiful," I whispered.

"Try it on. Let's see what kind of alterations it needs," Natasha said.

Agata grabbed some pins.

Natasha rolled her eyes. "We can turn around if you want."

"Modesty isn't a vampire virtue, but I'm feeling a little..."

"Vulnerable," Natasha said. "I get it." She and Agata both turned their backs to me.

I slipped on the dress. "I'll need help with the buttons."

"Can we turn around yet, Madame President?" Natasha exaggerated my title.

"Yes, but only if you help with the buttons."

"On it," Natasha said. Her fingers worked the buttons swiftly, and she turned me around to the free-standing oval mirror. Tears filled her eyes.

My eyes welled. "It's like it was made for me."

Agata took my hand. "Perfect."

Natasha nodded. "Perfect. No alterations needed."

She messed with my hair. "Do you think up or down, Agata?"

"For Josie and this gown, I think down but with one side pinned up with one of the rhinestone hair accessories we found."

"I like the idea," Natasha rummaged through the dozens of accessories.

"No crowns or tiaras. That's not a statement I want to make," I said.

"I figured as much," Natasha called over her shoulder. "Found it." She swept the left side of my hair back in a beautiful silver comb that combined vintage and modern.

The comb complimented the dress well with the clear and blue crystal wildflower and overgrown foliage design.

"I love it."

"Oh shoes," Natasha said. "I guessed you'd be a size seven."

"I am," I said. "Good guess."

She offered a shoulder for balance that I gladly took while Agata helped me into the white satin-covered shoes. They had rhinestone adornments on the toe of each one.

"Now, you are perfect," she said.

"Thank you both for doing this," I said. "The only thing missing." I swallowed and looked down at the floor.

"Is your mother," Agata said. "That's why you have this. I found it in Ezra's things at the other compound." She held out Mother's blue sapphire ring. I could have sworn my heart gave a beat at the sight of it. The ring had been in her family for generations from what she said. I thought it was lost in the chaos of the move. The Art Deco style matched perfectly with the old-world charm of the dress and hair comb. I closed my eyes and remembered when she put it on my finger for the first time and told me one day it would be mine. She told me it was always passed from mother to daughter.

It was like having a piece of her here with me. My heart swelled in my chest.

I slipped it on my right hand. It fit better than it did when I was a kid. Mother would be with me in many ways on my wedding day. I brushed a fresh set of tears away. "I feel ready now."

"I'm going to take all this back to my room, so Vin doesn't see," she said. "I told the cook red velvet for the wedding cake. Are you good with that?"

"Yes, that's fine. The vampires will not eat much of it, obviously, but we need to make sure there is enough for the humans. Do we have enough champagne for the reception?"

"We raided a liquor store and brought back twenty cases in the snow rover. Plus a couple of cases of whiskey and scotch for those with different tastes."

I laughed. "I'm glad you remembered the booze."

"The human teaching piano lessons does know the Wedding March and has agreed to play it. Tomorrow, Agata and I will be decorating. Is there anything else you need?"

"No, not that I know of," I said. "You would have to tell me if I did."

"Pretty sure we've got it covered," she said. "Agata, anything you can think of?"

"Humans have the tradition of something old, something new, something borrowed, and something blue."

"The dresses are new, as in unused. That counts right? And the hair comb has blue stones in it," Natasha said.

"Plus my mom's ring is old and is a sapphire," I said.

"Something borrowed." Natasha tapped her finger on her lips and stared at the ceiling like something borrowed would materialize from there. "I could give you my bra, but it probably wouldn't fit."

"Natasha." I slapped her arm.

"It sounded funnier in my head," she said.

"Do you actually think about things before they come out of your mouth? I thought you had no filter."

She laughed. "I really don't. Not much of one anyway. Back to the something borrowed."

"It's not a concern. We're not held to human superstitions."

"I have the perfect thing," she said. "I forgot Killian had given them to me. I have a pair of sapphire earrings he found on one of their outings."

"You mean patrols?"

"Yes, on one of the patrols. They will go great with the ring and the hair comb."

"Thank you," I said, grateful for their help. "Thank you both."

"You're welcome." Natasha rubbed my arm. "Get changed, and we'll get all of this out of the room. Be prepared for an excellent rehearsal tomorrow. And tell Vin I was under the two-hour mark."

"I will," I said.

"Good night, Josie. I'm so happy for you." Agata hugged me.

I dropped down on the couch after seeing them out and closed my eyes.

A THUMP against my chest woke me.

"Mommy!" Adam yelled in my face.

"Hey, my little man." I pulled him tightly to me. "You marry daddy?"

Vin leaned against a door frame and smiled. His hair was messed up, probably courtesy of our son, but he was sexier that way. It made him look relaxed and maybe he was or maybe that was love on his face.

"Yes, in just a couple of days. Do you know what that is?"

"No." He held up a truck for me to examine.

"It's a celebration when two people love each other."

"You wuv Daddy?"

"Yes, I do."

"I wuv Daddy."

"I know you do, and he loves you," I said. "And I love you."

"I go play?"

"Yes, play in your room."

"K, Mommy. Wuv you." He took off at a dead run to go play.

Vin slid into the open spot next to me on the couch. "The whole compound is abuzz with news of our nuptials."

"I hope we can live up to their expectations."

He wrapped his arm around my shoulders and tucked me closer. "They need something good to celebrate."

"I hope we can give it to them. I'm worried about the amount of food, both human and vampire we are using, but Natasha and Agata picked out some wonderful things for me to wear." I couldn't wait for him to see me in the wedding dress and accessories we picked out today. *Will he be surprised? Will he like the choices?*

"You are going to reverse the ice age and soon human food will no longer be a worry."

"I hope I garner the support of the council when we present the plan tomorrow. We can proceed without them, but I'd rather they share our decision," I said. If the council comes together and supports this action, it would be a sign of our ability to achieve a healthy society.

"It will be a success. Just as our wedding will be."

"If I can stop Natasha from trying to turn it into the wedding of the century," I said.

"You are the sitting President of the nation, Josie. It is the wedding of the century," he said.

"Ugh," I grumbled. "By the way, Natasha said to make sure you knew she finished under the two-hour allotment."

Vin laughed. "I guess I owe her then."

"Did you two have a bet?"

"I told her I would trade patrols with Killian next rotation if she let you get some rest."

A crashing noise came from Adam's room. I sat up and moved in his direction.

"Adam?" Vin called out.

"I'm K."

"We need to find another nanny, but I thought I would ask Agata if she minded accompanying Adam. I know Natasha will be there, but with her pregnancy and Emilia."

"Are you sure you want to send Adam away?" Vin asked.

"No, not at all, but I don't want to risk him being here if something goes wrong either," I said. My heart constricted thinking about being apart from them.

"Agata loves you, Josie. She wouldn't say no if that's what you're worried about."

"I don't think she would ever tell me no, but her family is so large."

"When I met her and Natasha in the suite, she said more of them are working since you made it possible. That's something to be proud of, my love."

I smiled. "I'm glad it is helping them."

"Did you know that the technical services program at the Southern Compound has graduated more than fifty, including Agata, since you became Empress and started it back up?"

"Let's hope we double that number with the government changes. I'd like to see vampires from other compounds come and train. We shouldn't be the keepers of knowledge, and maybe we can send some of ours to train in their specialties."

"That's a wonderful idea. You are changing the world, Josie. How will anyone follow in your footsteps to live up to that?" Vin smiled.

My gut twisted. It was meant as a compliment, but it reminded me of my childhood. Always expected to be kind and smart like my mother or cunning and a leader like my father. I didn't want that for Adam.

"Adam needs to know he is free to do whatever he wants. He doesn't have to choose politics or technology. If he wants to be a farmer or a seamstress or a chef, he can be any or all of those things."

"Hey, what brought that on? Our son's current passion is hanging upside down, and he certainly doesn't feel the need to ask permission to do it."

"There was so much pressure on me to be..." I said. "Perfect.

I felt like a failure in my father's eyes every day. I don't want Adam to grow up feeling that way."

Vin cradled my face in his hands. "You are not your father. You never were like him. You never will be like him, and our son will be loved for who he is."

I nodded. "Can we just move to a deserted island to raise him?"

Vin hugged me to his chest and chuckled. "Josie, I think all parents must want to build a protective wall around their kids, but they learn by their mistakes and our mistakes. We don't have to be perfect parents, and he doesn't have to be a perfect son."

"Thank you," I said.

"For what?"

"Being the voice of reason and reminding me we don't have to be perfect."

"Josie, perfection is an idea, an unattainable idea, that doesn't exist." He kissed the top of my head.

He pulled back and reached into his pocket. "Natasha found these in a jewelry store, but I had them engraved." He opened the box to two plain platinum bands. "Look at yours."

Both had engraving on the outside and inside. I picked mine up. "Josephine, my Josephine." I giggled at the outer inscription, and on the inside, it read one word. "Finally."

"Mine next."

"Eternally yours," on the outside, and "Forever" on the inside of the ring. "Vin these are beautiful." I pressed my lips to his,. He slid me into his lap, and folded his arms around me.

CHAPTER 25

JOSIE

E zra sat on the couch in my apartments. He smiled and patted the seat next to him. Vin and Killian left early to patrol for Rogues and signs of Calidora. Natasha and Agata took the kids down to eat. I sat on the edge of the cushion. My nerves wound up from the earlier incident, and what we still had to do today.

"Presentation day," Ezra said. "Ready?"

"Not really," I said. "I might vomit." The council's support was important to me for this effort, and it would be important if the effort had to be carried on without us.

"A little apprehension is normal when something is important," he smiled.

"Then why don't you seem nervous?"

"I'm not the one who has to present." He stretched his arm across the back of the couch and rested his hand on my shoulder. "You are going to do great. I'm proud of you."

"You're still coming, right?" I said. I felt stupid asking.

"Of course," he said. "I've loaded everything on this laptop, and I asked Vin to hook up a projector in the council room." He passed the device over to me.

"Oh good. You found one. I was worried everyone would have to gather around the laptop." I opened and closed the lid.

"Stop stressing. You did this when you were younger too," he said. "Before one of the sparring matches when you were training, you would second guess everything and try to think of every possible scenario."

I flashed back to those days of overthinking how to drop Killian to the mat. It seemed like a much simpler time. A time before the fate of the entire world rested on my shoulders. My stomach gurgled and bile rose up in my throat.

"Let go of that negative energy. Tap into the feelings in the energy of the room and respond in a way to shift it in the direction you want to go."

"Is that how you did it?"

"Every time," he said. "I opened myself to the room and ebbed with each wave."

"Isn't that exhausting?" I asked.

"It can be," he said. "If you are not careful. Never take their emotions into yourself. You want to taste it and understand to respond. Then, let it go."

"You make it sound so simple. It's not that easy."

"Easier than you think," he said. "Let's try something. Stand up and close your eyes."

He got up from the couch, and I followed.

"Now, touch the energy in the room. Feel what I am feeling, but don't go so deep you get lost. If you start feeling lost, let go."

I inhaled and smelled his human, but not, scent and thought of how he is feeling.

"Pride," I said. "You feel pride." Warmth enveloped me.

"Yes, and what else."

"Love and happiness." Tears filled my eyes.

He took my hands in his. "Now pull back and open your eyes."

I did, and his were filled with tears as well. He rolled Mother's ring around on my finger. "Where did you find this?"

"Agata brought it with her. She found it in your things at the Southern Compound."

"I thought it was lost in the skirmishes there. This ring was a symbol of your Mother's family. A ring each mother passed down to their daughter. I'd planned to give it to you one day, but each day it seemed less and less important. Seeing it on your finger, though." He wiped at his eyes. "The importance is restored."

"Josephine, sit down. I want to tell you about your mother."

I sat down, ready to receive what he wanted to share with me about Mother. "She had told me the ring was passed down through generations."

"Yes, each generation would add something or modify it in some way." His finger touched a tiny diamond on the side. "Your mother added this when you were born."

"I never knew that," I said.

"No, I don't suppose you would. Your mother was very old, Josephine. She was a direct descendent of the original line. You are the last surviving direct female descendent."

"I don't understand," I said. "Original line of what."

"The original vampire line. The first. It is why I was so hard on you. The expectations are different for your mother's line."

My mind raced through what he told me. "Does it even matter anymore?"

"It does," he said, his voice solemn. "It's no accident the rite worked for you when you challenged me."

"And you accepted it knowing what would happen?"

"I didn't know for sure. Your mother has been gone almost a century, and I had no idea if you would have the old magic connection."

"But you suspected," I said.

"Yes," he said. "Even though the rite was old, it didn't seem possible that a ceremony like that would awaken the magic in you."

"But I'm a vampire," I said.

"With very old blood running through you and old magic too."

"Why tell me now?"

"Because it might be the only way you can defeat Calidora when she returns and she will return," he said. "With more Rogues, she can control, and you need to be prepared.

"I don't know how to access it or use it. How can it help me?"

"In the library is a special section that was all your mother's personal books. On the top row, there are books within books, hidden in plain sight. Those books contain everything she had on old magic."

"Why not tell me this when we were working on the research to reverse the ice age?" I asked, wondering why he'd held onto the information.

"It wouldn't have helped there," he said. "I'm sorry your mother isn't here to pass down her knowledge to you, but the answers are in your blood. When you read the books you will feel it as she did."

"Was she practicing this craft while you were together?"

"She did," he said. "In secret."

"I'm done with secrets," I said. "Never again."

"You might want to rethink that," he said. "As everything transitions back to what it was before and centuries pass, vampires will fade back into the shadows of myth and lore. You, especially."

"I don't believe that," I said. "I can't."

"Your mother and I were together for over three centuries before you were born. We watched it happen once. I'm thankful for my newfound human frailty so that I will not see it again. The only thing I'm sorry for is that I will not be here to guide you through it," he said. "You are strong, Josephine. So strong, and you will find your way and make sure our heritage is preserved."

"When we were told our history as kids, I never..."

"Imagined they spoke about your family?"

"Not at all."

"Read the books. They will explain it so much better than I can. It's not my story, but it was your mother's."

Old magick not only exist but was in my family tree. It still didn't seem real.

I glanced at the clock. "We better get to the chamber and make sure everything is ready to go."

My father patted my knee. "You're going to do great."

Except I'll be distracted and thinking about old magic the whole time.

CHAPTER 26

JOSIE

The proposal went well, and the council gave their unanimous support to our efforts. They even thanked my father, which surprised me. I should have focused on building the future and eliminating the ice age, but I couldn't wait for the meeting to be over to head to the library.

I had a good idea of what section Father meant was mother's special collection. The top shelf of books was wrapped in more modern covers just as he said. I locked the door and sat in a chair with the first one.

Incantations and ceremonies were detailed on the pages. I flipped through them, but it didn't feel like a connection. The next book sat differently in my hands, the weight a little heavier and a mild vibration radiated off of it. I opened it and turned the pages until handwriting caught my attention. *Mother's.*

Her notes about what she remembered. Updates to magic rites and daily rituals she must have performed. I stopped in the middle. A folded piece of dark parchment marked the halfway point. I unfolded it gently. It was connected to the book binding. Names were written back through time. I ran my hand across it tracing with my finger until I found Mother's name. The names glowed like antique gold when I came in contact with them. And there, under her name, was mine and the year I was born. Father hadn't exaggerated that Mother was old. If this was right, she'd been over fifteen hundred years when I was born. I traced back up toward the top. The tree went back thousands of years. I added them up in my head. *Almost six thousand years. The beginning of civilization time?*

"Where are they all now?" I asked out loud even though there wasn't anyone here to answer. Some of them lived almost a thousand years but not many were as old as my mother. Some outlived their children. Interesting that only women were represented. All one-to-one. One mother to one female child. My family dated back to the birth of society. I couldn't wrap my head around how that was even possible.

The doorknob jiggled, and I jumped up.

"Josie?" Vin's voice came from the other side.

I crossed the room and unlocked the door.

"Are you hiding in here to avoid the wedding?" He winked at me.

I smiled. "No. Never." I moved aside for him to enter. "Come on in. There's something I need to show you." I took his hand and led him to the spot where I'd left the book. "Pull up a chair."

He lifted one and sat it beside me.

I picked up the book and dropped into the chair.

"What have you been reading? Old vampire matrimonial tips?"

I laughed. "Something like that." I unfolded the parchment

and turned it toward him. "This is my family tree on my mother's side," I paused. "This is me at the end."

His mouth opened slightly as he traced it back. "How is this possible?"

"Father told me Mother was old the other day, and today he pointed me to her section of the library. She had old magic books concealed on the top shelf, including this gem."

He studied the brown parchment. "But that would make you--"

"Part of the original unbroken line. The only one left intact."

"There aren't any others?"

"Not direct descendants," I said. "Other borns are from the broken lines but I haven't found the details yet. Created vampires could reproduce then, but the ability disappeared as they evolved in the first thousand years. Maybe that had something to do with it. See here." I flipped to an entry in the book.

His eyes darted back and forth across the page. "This is incredible history, Josie. And proves how wrong it is to treat created vampires as subservient. What are you going to do with this information?"

"I want to keep it between you and me," I said. "At least until I understand it more." I stared at the shelf of hidden books. "I want to know more about it before I decide to share."

"What else did Ezra tell you?" Vin's voice dropped to a low menacing octave. His anger at Ezra was always below the surface ready to bubble up.

"The reason the old magic in the Vampire Rite worked the

way it did when I challenged him is because I am an original bloodline descendant."

"So you can use the old magic?" Vin leaned back in the chair, putting distance between us.

It hurt, but I understood, even if I didn't have the choice. "I'm not sure. The rite would suggest I can, but I didn't feel connected to any of the incantations. This book with my lineage drew me to it."

"Have you used magic on me?"

He couldn't think I would do that. Not really. I avoided him for almost an entire century. It'd be laughable if he wasn't staring at me with a stern expectant expression.

"No, Vin," I said, my tone even. "I can't believe you would even ask that. I don't even know how to use it."

"So, you could have used it on me without either of us knowing?"

"That's what you are worried about at this moment?" I took the book from him. Everything I knew about my family changed today, and he was worried if I had put a spell on him with some old magic I don't even know how to use. I needed time to think, and his negativity made it hard to concentrate. "Maybe you should go."

"Josie." He stood for a moment in front of me. His face softened and tempted me to give in. He was a talker. I was a scientist and needed to understand what this meant before I could talk to him about it.

"Just go." I picked up the book and immersed myself in it.

The door clicked behind Vin. I considered locking it again, but no one had entered or tried to except Vin. I'm not even sure how many people came to the library besides me.

As I read through the book, one thing, in particular, leapt out at me. There was nothing about my original ancestors' birth. *Was it a mutation and the science didn't exist to explain it then? Did the old magic create my ancestor as a conduit? How did it happen?*

I supposed that information had been lost over thousands of years. Hard to believe with the other meticulous record keeping, but still possible.

I set the book aside and chose another one. My mother's handwriting left notes in the margin on many of the pages. The book focused on meditation and centering the mind. *I could use some of that centering now.*

Most of the meditation required incense and different materials no longer available, but I found one that only required focus. I laid the open book on top of the one with my lineage and closed my eyes.

I set my intention. *Focus and clarity on what the new knowledge means.*

The phrases repeated in my mind from the page.

Knowledge comes from both light and dark.

True sight doth require both.

Fear not the truth for it brings hope.

My mind stilled. Memories that were not mine came to me. I was in awe. A movie of past events played through in my head. I let myself go with the flow and floated through the scenes. *History. This was our history. My history.*

The scenes stopped, and I opened my eyes to a room filled with pale blue lines crisscrossing like lasers. *What is this?* I reached out to touch one. There was no weight to it, but it had a silky texture against my fingertips. My mother and I dancing in the ballroom when I was nine moved up and down the line. My mother's voice came through. "You are special,

Josephine. You don't know just how special, but one day I will show you." The memory had long been forgotten, but it stood out vividly now. She had intended to show me these ways. "I love you, my very special daughter." *Her voice. Those words.*

All the grief of her sudden death crashed on top of me as it had a hundred years ago. I dropped to my knees. Tears fell through my fingertips to the ground. My concentration was lost. The connection broke. I looked up to see the blue lines fading away. "No." I grabbed for them, but they were no longer tangible. I curled into a ball on the floor.

The door creaked open with a quick couple of taps. "Josie?" Natasha called. "Vin said you were in the library."

"I'm here," I said, my voice rough with hunger. My throat was sore, and my belly ached. This wasn't hunger. It was near starvation, but I'd eaten not long ago.

She knelt beside me and touched my shoulder. "Josie, are you okay?"

"It's a very long story, and not really," I said.

"Give me the TL;DR version," Natasha said.

"Parent drama," I said.

"I will kill Ezra and pulverize his frail human body for this," Natasha said, her voice full of vitriol.

"It wasn't him," I said. "Well, not exactly."

"This doesn't have anything to do with the wedding, does it?" Natasha said.

"Other than my husband-to-be doesn't trust me?" I asked.

"Josie, Vin loves and trusts you. I don't know why that would even enter your mind."

"Long story again," I said. "I'm really hungry."

"I think you're hangry," she said.

I giggled. "That too. Is there any blood in here?"

She helped me sit up. The magic weakened me, and I wondered if it had been that way for Mother and those before me too. Or was it because these tools needed to be exercised? Natasha buzzed around the room.

"Here." She thrust a glass in my face. "It smells old, but it'll do."

"Thanks." I guzzled it down.

"I've never seen you drink so fast."

"Is there more?" I asked. It was bitter and my hunger was not satisfied.

"Yes, let me grab it for you."

She returned with another one, and I was able to sip on it, my strength returning.

"Do you want to talk about it?" Natasha sat on the floor next to me.

"Not yet," I said. "I need to figure some things out." It wasn't that I wanted to keep my best friend in the dark, but I didn't even know where to start.

"It usually helps to have someone to work through it with you." Natasha had a gift for reading people. It was useful at times, but I hated it at the moment.

"It does, but I'm not ready," I said.

"Fair enough," she said. "I came by to tell you everything is ready for the rehearsal and your big day tomorrow. You still want to get married right?"

"I do. I don't know about Vin. We had a disagreement," I paused, biting down on my lip. "I think we are still fine. I guess we'll know before the rehearsal. Was there something you needed from me?" I needed to talk to him. I regretted telling him to leave earlier, but I still needed to understand what happened.

"No, but are you sure you are alright?"

"I will be. How much time do I have?"

"You need to be in my room in two hours. I found the perfect dress for you to wear to the rehearsal."

"Ugh," I said. "Natasha, please tell me it's not cut down to the navel."

"It's not." She smiled. "I promise." She stood and held her hand out to help me up.

"I'll see you then." I hugged her.

She pulled back and looked at me. "You're staying here?"

"Yes, I want to think for a bit," I said.

"You don't think," Natasha said in a concerned tone. "You overthink."

"Sometimes," I said. "I'll see you in a couple of hours."

She squeezed my hand and left me alone.

Vin needed an apology and answers, but I had to find the answers first. I closed my eyes and repeated my intention from earlier. *Focus and clarity on what the new knowledge means.*

Then the phrases from the page in mother's book.

Knowledge comes from both light and dark.

True sight doth require both.

Fear not the truth for it brings hope.

The movie began to play again.

CHAPTER 27

VIN

I pounded on the door, but it opened, left unlocked. "Josie? Are you in here?"

She didn't answer, but her scent told me she was here. I moved through the room and found her crumpled on the floor, book in hand, and blood running from her nose and ears.

I knelt down beside her and brushed the hair out of her face. My heart raced.

"She's in here," I yelled over my shoulder.

I took the book and tossed it away.

Her skin was pale, almost translucent. A scary sight even to a vampire. I imagined it must have been the same feeling she had when I almost died refusing my mother's call.

I slid my hands under her gently and pulled her into my lap.

"Josie? Can you hear me?"

She didn't move. I refused to believe magic would take her from me.

I whispered into her ear. "Fight it, Josie. Whatever is happening in there, fight it. Fight like you told me to."

What had she been doing? I looked around at the stack of books and saw the one she had shown me earlier. It laid closed. The one I chunked laid on the floor face down. I picked it up and read the old language. It sounded like a simple meditation spell, but my limited understanding of old magic told me nothing about it was ever simple.

Natasha burst through the door. "What happened?"

"I think she was doing this spell," I said, passing the book to her. "Ezra told her earlier her mother was part of a very old line with old magic. I think she was trying to do a meditation spell."

"Old magic is bad news," Natasha said. "That must have been what was going on when I found her earlier."

"What happened then?"

"She was crumpled on the floor and hungry. I gave her blood, and she seemed to be fine."

"Well, she doesn't seem fine now," I growled back. "Josie, open your eyes." My body shook, and I tried to still it and control my fear.

"I'll get some blood."

"And how will she drink it, Natasha? She's unconscious."

Ezra and Killian breached the door.

"Get him out of here." My voice roared at our former Emperor. The entire compound might have heard, but I didn't care.

Killian looked at me and his eyes darted from Josie in my lap to Natasha and finally to Ezra.

"Did you do this?" Killian asked. His hand seized Ezra's arm.

"No," Ezra said, his tone dejected.

Forcing my voice back to normal. "He sent her here under the guise of finding remnants of her mother's memory."

"Is this true?" Killian asked.

"No," Ezra said. "Vin, this is who she is. She had a right to know."

I rubbed Josie's cheek. She stirred slightly giving me hope.

"And you thought turning her loose by herself with old magic was a good idea?"

"Ezra, you wait here," Killian said and walked over to us.

"She dabbled in old magic?" Killian whispered to me. "I thought it was dead with the ancient ones."

"It was," I said. "It should have been."

"She just said family drama earlier," Natasha said, her voice stressed. "I didn't know."

"She wanted to keep it a secret until she understood it," I said.

Josie's body jerked, but her eyes remained closed.

"Come on. Open your eyes," I said.

"How did I?" Killian asked.

"May I?" Ezra asked from the doorway.

"If you touch her, I will kill you a third time," I said.

Ezra held his hands up and walked closer to us. "Josephine is descended from the original line of vampires. A line that has remained intact for thousands of years. The line from which old magic was born, and the only line that can wield it. A line passed from mother to daughter."

"You fucking idiot," Natasha said. "You know how desperately she misses her mother. Why in fuck's sake would you send her alone to do spells?"

"I did not send her to do spells. I gave her this information to find something strong enough to stop Calidora and her Rogue army," Ezra said, his tone even.

Calidora. My mother's army. What?

Josie's eyes fluttered open for a brief moment and closed again.

"Open them, Josie. Just open them. We are all here." I held her close. Panic rose in me the longer she stayed out.

"What?" Natasha stood and faced him.

"We have a large enough force to take on her and her army," Killian said. "Besides she agreed to the truce."

"She has a way of twisting words into a careful web to get what she wants without breaking her word," Ezra said. "Her army is much larger than you realize. She controls many Rogues. The Chicago research center we visited? That was her home base before she moved underground."

A memory cut from my mind returned. She had been there when the experiments were done on me. I fought the urge to vomit and turned back to Josie instead.

"Open those blue eyes, Josie." I looked up. "Someone do something."

"She has overextended herself. It will get easier with time, and she will get stronger. Her strength will return with rest and blood. This happened with her mother early in our years together."

His lack of concern pissed me off. "She is your daughter. Do you not care for her well-being at all?"

Ezra's demeanor remained calm. "It is for her wellbeing, and that of my grandchild, I told her of this."

"We're not going to solve this here," Natasha said. "Let's take Josie to your room and let her rest. Agata has Adam and Emilia giving them an etiquette lesson."

I looked at her.

"Don't raise an eyebrow at me, mister. Agata is her own woman."

"Ezra, I'd appreciate it if you gave us some space. Maybe go visit your grandson if you can keep from telling him ghost stories."

He gave one nod.

I scooped Josie up and carried her to our room, placing her gently on the bed. I stretched my body out beside hers.

"I'm sorry I made you think I didn't trust you earlier. I do, and I know you wouldn't use magic on me. I was in shock, and I'm sorry."

"Is that all you've got?" Her voice was raspy and gravelly, but it was hers.

I chuckled in relief. *Thank the Gods.* "You were expecting more?"

"Maybe an 'I love you' would be nice." Her eyes opened. Blood pooled in them, but the whites were visible. The red dissipated to pink, so her eyes were clearing. She was healing.

"I love you," I said.

"That's better." She tried to push up and dropped back to the bed. "My head is killing me."

"Looks like you overdid it," I said. "Imagine that."

She flung her hand against my arm in a weak hit.

"Do you want some food?"

"A large glass of blood would be great."

"On it," I said.

Natasha paced in the living room.

"She's awake and hungry," I told Natasha.

Natasha reached the carafe before I could and poured the glass.

"I'll take it to her."

She hesitated but handed me the glass.

I rushed back to the room.

Josie tried to sit up again, but it was a struggle. I propped up some pillows behind her.

"Here," I handed her the glass. "Drink up, and we'll get you some more. Natasha is in the living room whenever you feel like company."

Josie drank the glass in a couple of gulps and sat it on the table. "She probably thinks I'm crazy."

"Mmm... maybe," I said.

She laughed.

"Mainly, she is concerned for her friend."

"I feel fine now," Josie said. "Still hungry but fine." She moved to get off the bed.

"Let's go slow. Like human slow," I said. I helped her to her feet. "Steady?"

"Yes, I really do feel fine," she said. "Let me talk to Natasha, and then you and I can talk alone."

"You might want to wash the blood off your face and ears first."

She looked in the mirror. "That's attractive." She stepped into the bathroom and clutched the edge of the counter.

I soaked a washcloth and wiped the red off her face. "It's in your hair too."

"That can wait." She held her hand out to me.

I took it craving the touch.

"We've got this, right?" She asked.

"Of course we do," I said, hoping I sounded more convincing outwardly than I did inwardly.

We walked out hand in hand to meet Natasha.

CHAPTER 28

JOSIE

Vin held my hand as we walked into the living room, and I knew we would be ok. One moment of doubt wasn't enough to break our love.

"Josie." Natasha rushed over to me.

"I'm fine. Sorry to worry you." I sat on the couch, still a bit weak.

Natasha plopped down next to me. "Girl, I've seen you on the floor twice today. Let's not do any more of that until after the wedding."

"Did I ruin the rehearsal?" I asked.

"No, we still have plenty of time," she said. "Apparently, when you are the President, you are excused for tardiness."

"That's not the example I want to set though," I said. I flashed back to the lectures on responsibility Father use to give me.

"No one knows what the reason is except us. We can keep it among friends," Natasha said.

Gratefulness filled my heart, and I shared a small smile with her.

"Speaking of," I said. "Where are Killian and my father?"

"They are with Agata and the kids."

I nodded, thankful the kids were away from here. "Can you give Vin and me a few minutes? Then, I'll meet you in your room to get ready."

"Of course," she stood up. "I have everything ready for you," she called on her way out the door.

"Finally alone." Vin pulled me into a tight embrace. "I love you, Josie, and I never want you to doubt my trust for you."

"I love you too," I said. "And I'm sorry I didn't pull you into the conversation when Father told me."

"It doesn't change anything for me," he said. "You are still the vampire I fell in love with a century ago."

"Thank you," I said. "I'll tell you everything. I don't want to keep any secrets between us."

"It can wait until after the rehearsal," he said. "We're still getting married, right?"

"You're not getting off that easy, Mister Cavanaugh."

"Glad to hear it, the future Misses Cavanaugh." He whispered in my ear.

My heart skipped a beat. *We are getting married.*

"I better get to Natasha's room before she loses it," I said.

"See you downstairs." He kissed my cheek.

I didn't want to let go and had to force myself to. "See you there."

We parted ways at the door, and I made the short trek to Natasha and Killian's suite.

Natasha paced the floor when I entered the room. "I told them to give us 30 minutes."

"Is that enough time to make me presentable?" I ran my fingers through my hair and tried to smooth it down.

"We're vampires, Josie." She put her hands on her hips. "Of course, it is."

"Where's this wonderful rehearsal dress you mentioned?" I asked.

"Let's do your hair and makeup first," she said. "I want the dress to be a surprise."

She went to work on my hair and did a partial updo. "Thank goodness you didn't get blood in your hair."

I laughed because I had. She didn't notice. "Glad that was your worst concern."

Her hands paused. "It's not," she said. "I just know not to pressure you about it." She looked at me in the mirror and went back to styling the perfect coif.

"My hair has never looked better, Natasha."

"Oh, it will tomorrow." She smiled at me in the mirror.

"I don't see how." I turned my head from side to side admiring her careful attention to detail.

She placed a single fleshed-colored rose on the side.

Tears welled in my eyes. "It's the perfect nod to my mother. Thank you."

"You're welcome." She squeezed my shoulders. "Wait until you see the dress. Dry the tears. We need to do your makeup."

I grabbed a tissue and dabbed at the tears. "Done."

She did my makeup in no time, obviously more practiced at it than me. She used a lot of mascara and eyeliner, but I still looked like me. "This is more makeup than I usually wear."

"It's a special occasion. You need to be a little more glam," she said. "If it's too much, I can tone it down."

"No," I said. "It's nice."

"Great," Natasha said. "Let's get you into this dress."

She pulled the dress from her closet and unzipped the

garment bag. It was an elegant ivory color one-shoulder midi dress designed to be figure-hugging. The fabric gathered at the single shoulder to drape in a panel on either side.

"Wow, Natasha. This is very sophisticated. I love it."

"Do you really like it?"

"Yes, I do."

"I'm so glad. I told Agata it was the one for the rehearsal, and we didn't need a backup. She was a little nervous."

"No need to be. It's perfect."

"And we found some nude heels that will work with it," she said. "Same size as the ones you tried on with the wedding dress, so they should fit. I'll step out, so you can change. Call if you need any help."

I slipped into the dress. The zipper was on the side with the one-shoulder, and I could easily get it fastened on my own. I slid the shoes onto my feet and admired the outfit in the mirror.

Dresses had fallen out of favor in my wardrobe choices since we moved here, but it was nice to be in one again. I smoothed the dress out. My engagement ring and my family ring stood out against the fabric, shining like stars. I didn't need any other jewelry tonight.

I opened the door and Natasha stood up. She smiled and took my hands in hers.

"You look beautiful, Josie," she said. "Tell Vin to go easy tonight because tomorrow will be better."

I laughed. "Only you, Natasha."

"No, everyone is going to be saying it," she said. "Trust me."

"I'm ready if you are."

She walked around me. "I have some jewelry picked out, but I don't think you need it."

"I don't either. The flower and rings are enough for me."

"Agree. Let's head down to your wedding rehearsal then." She smiled.

I smiled back at how magical Natasha had made everything so far.

Vin, Killian, Ezra, Agata, and the kids waited for us outside the chapel. We exchanged quick hellos, but I didn't miss the up and down Vin gave me with a wink.

A blush crept across my cheeks.

"The ceremony rehearsal will be private, but then there will be a party for the rehearsal dinner in the dining hall," Ezra said. "The group tonight is smaller than the reception after the ceremony tomorrow where we will host the entire compound."

"You took your father of the bride duties seriously." I greeted him with a hug. Sweet scents wafted our way. "Petit fours?"

Ezra smiled. "Of course."

"You couldn't resist."

"I wouldn't have ruled this nation if I didn't understand the subtle art of a well-placed reminder."

I stifled a giggle. "Touché."

Agata opened the doors, and I entered the chapel.

With fresh flowers at a premium, they had found enough silk to make what looked like hundreds of flesh-colored roses. Tulle draped in careful cascades down the pews and over an arch at the end of the aisle. I caught my heel in a mound of tulle and pitched forward.

Ezra caught my elbow. "Let's get that out of your system tonight."

"Are you afraid you might have to catch me tomorrow?" I laughed.

"Not at all."

"If everyone can look this way," Natasha said. "Josie, you and Ezra stand here at the chapel doors. Vin, you and Killian take your positions up front. Tomorrow, you two will enter from that door over there." She pointed to a side door.

Killian and Vin got into place, and Ezra and I stood against the door.

"So, Vin and Killian will take their places first," Natasha said. "Then Agata will lead the kids down the aisle to take their places."

Agata took the children's hands and did as instructed.

"I'm next," she said and tossed her hair over her shoulder. "When I get to the last pew, the chapel doors will open."

As if on cue, they opened and a human joined us. I recognized him as the human's spiritual guide. He was tall like Vin, but his hair was curly and lighter and his shoulders were broad like Killian's. He wore a suit that looked new, and I wondered if he saved it for the few weddings the humans had.

"Thomas," Natasha said, warmly. "Thank you for coming. We just started the rehearsal."

"It's great to see you, Natasha. I'm assuming I'll be standing on the other side of that arch."

"Yes, please," she said gesturing towards it. He made her nervous, and I was curious why filing that back to ask later.

He walked into place and turned to face us. He smiled and appeared happy to be here, even if it was for two vampires.

"Tomorrow, Thomas will lead Vin and Killian out," she said. "As I was saying when I get to the final pew. The Wedding

March will start and you and Ezra will come down the aisle in time with the music." She pointed to the piano player, who hit a few notes and began the march. "Everyone will stand up," she said over the music. "And you will float down the aisle like the beautiful bride you are." She waved us forward.

Ezra held out his arm, and I took it. "Are you feeling ok?"

My head felt light, and my stomach quivered. *Nerves. Did human brides go through this?* I focused on the end of the aisle. "Yes, why."

"You feel cold. Do we need to turn up the heat? I'd hate to think we were freezing the humans."

Ezra chuckled. "I'd phrase that differently, but the temperature is perfectly fine."

"Good."

We reached the last pew. "So tomorrow, maybe a little less chatting on the aisle," Natasha said.

"Whose wedding is this?" I asked.

"Don't pull rank on me now," she said. "You turned the details over to me, so you have to follow instructions."

"Yes, ma'am," I said.

She laughed. "Once you get to this spot, Thomas will say." She held out an impatient hand to him.

"Who gives this woman in matrimony?"

"That sounds so archaic. Can we say it another way?" I asked. *I'm the leader of a nation, and I'm marrying the love of my life. Our voices are the ones that matter here.*

"We have used 'Escorted by her father, does the bride freely give herself in matrimony' in some of our recent ceremonies. Do you prefer that version?"

"Yes," I said.

Thomas took notes on a little card.

"And you have your own vows, correct?"

"Yes," Vin answered quickly.

I'd yet to write mine but answered the same. "Yes."

Panic hit me. I had to get them done tonight.

"And do you want a prayer or references to God as would be in a typical human ceremony?"

"I'm not sure your God would welcome us," I said. "But I'll leave that decision to Vin."

"No God references," he said, his even tone never wavered. "But a simple prayer for peace and strength as we restore Mother Earth would be welcomed."

"Nice choice." I smiled.

"Noted," he said. "And for the final introduction, how will I be introducing you?"

"Mr. and Mrs. Vincent Cavanaugh," I said. "It's the first time I've had a last name, and I want to use it."

The group, including Thomas, erupted in laughter.

"Very good," he said. "Then once I announce you, you will be free to head down the aisle and to the reception."

"Does everyone know their roles and responsibilities for tomorrow?" Natasha asked.

"Yes," we all said in unison.

"You missed your calling," Killian said. "You should have been a drill sergeant."

Natasha laughed. "Two things I don't mess around with," she said. "Fashion and parties, and we haven't had enough of either lately."

"True," I said. "Shall we retire to the rehearsal party?"

"It's all yours," she said.

We wound around the way over to the dining hall, and it was decorated in the same tulle and silk roses.

Vin leaned in close to my ear. "You look stunning, but that dress will look better on the floor."

Desire swirled in my belly. "That's a promise I hope you plan to keep."

"I keep all my promises," he said. "Especially to you." He kissed my temple.

The tables were set up in a rectangular shape with the middle open. The council was already in the room along with several non-council members I recognized, both human and vampire.

We received their congratulations before Ezra asked us all to be seated. Glasses were filled with an old wine I assumed was found when they uncovered the liquor store.

Ezra held up a glass. "Tonight we celebrate two unique and incredibly loving people. My daughter, Josephine, and her husband-to-be, Vin." He paused. "I've learned so much from the relationship they share, as I'm sure many of you have, but the biggest lesson they have taught me is forgiveness. I know there is no greater love on this planet than exists between the two of them, and that love has blossomed into the hearts of the people here. It's where they have found the strength to stand up for what is right, even under the most challenging circumstances." He cleared his throat. "And it is why they will continue to lead the people of this nation into a better world. Long live Josie and Vin."

"Here here," Darius said.

Cheers and applause erupted around us.

"Let us partake in this feast in their honor," Ezra said and sat down next to me.

"That's the best speech you've ever given, Ezra," Vin said.

"It was really good," I said. "Thank you for the kind words."
I touched his arm.

"All true, Josephine. Every word." He patted my hand. "I
know I wasn't great at saying it for decades, but I am proud of
you, and I do love you."

"I love you too, Father, and I'm proud of the man you have
become."

He smiled and turned his attention to the center of the
tables.

Adam and Emilia twirled in circles for our entertainment.
They earned applause from all of us before Agata and Natasha
ushered them out.

We ate human food. No blood was served.

Vin leaned in next to my ear and whispered. "Have we
been here an acceptable amount of time yet? I'm ready to see
what this dress looks like on the floor next to our bed." His
hand slid under the table and trailed along the slit.

My body woke up to his touch.

"Yes, I believe we have." I stood up, and he followed my
lead. "Thank you all for coming tonight, and please stay as
long as you like. Vin and I have had a long day and need to
prepare for tomorrow. We will see you all soon."

"We'll keep Adam tonight for you," Natasha said. "Practice
makes perfect." She winked.

Killian chuckled. "Natasha, where does practice get you?"

She playfully slapped his arm.

"See you tomorrow," I said. "Rest well, Father," I called to
Ezra.

He gave a wave.

CHAPTER 29

JOSIE

The sun was high in the sky and shone a path across the bedroom. The snow took a break, and I hoped that was a good omen for the environmental reclamation project.

I ran my fingers through Vin's hair and down his back. He nuzzled into my neck.

"It's our wedding day," Vin whispered in my ear.

"Technically, it already was our wedding day before we went to sleep." I stretched and wrapped my arms around his neck. I can't wait to be your wife."

"Good," he said. "Because I can't wait to be your husband."

"I just hope I make you happy, Vin."

"You do make me happy, Josie," he pressed his lips to my neck in a soft caress. "As long as you love me, that's all I need."

My cheeks burned and must have glowed. He'd loved me through the worst of it and for decades when I tried to turn it off. He'd loved me when everything had fallen apart and had to be put back together. My stomach fluttered. "I love you so much, Vincent Cavanaugh."

He pressed his lips to mine. "I hate it when you say Vincent," he said.

"Vin," I said, my voice soft and deliberate. "I love you."

He smiled and peppered my face with kisses.

Laughter rolled out of me. "Stop."

"We should probably get up."

"Probably. Do you think Adam let anyone sleep?"

Vin laughed. "He had an active day. I bet he slept a few hours at least."

"You know what Natasha said last night about practice," I said.

"Yes." He wagged his eyebrows at me. "I enjoy the practice."

"If we were to get pregnant again, and it's a girl..." My voice trailed off.

"If it happens and it's a girl, we will love her as much as Adam."

"It's just in the book, the one with my lineage. It only traces one mother and one daughter. No sons. No second daughters. What do you think that means?"

"I don't know, but think how old that recording system is. It might just be an old archaic inheritance chart."

"Maybe, but it definitely didn't feel like that when the book was in my hands." The power in that book hummed like a generator. I'd never experienced anything like it before.

"We'll go through the books together and see if we can decipher it after you save the world with the de-icing device you and Ezra have. That's still your top priority. Right?"

"Of course," I said. "None of the other matters if we can't make the de-icing happen at the right pace and at the right time."

"Then let's tuck away all the old magic stuff until after

today. Let's focus on you and me and Adam and celebrating with our family and friends."

"I can do that," I said. "But I do need to run to meet Ezra for a few minutes to make sure everything is on track with the devices we are launching from here." The calibration had to be finalized for the launch this week, and I wouldn't have time later.

"Then get it done, so we can get this wedding going."

His enthusiasm over this wedding stirred excitement in me. I wanted it too.

I rolled out of his arms to the edge of the bed. "I'm a little nervous about traveling back to the Chicago compound, especially now that we know it was Calidora's space and what was done to you there."

He scooted up beside me and kissed my shoulder. "It gives me an uneasy feeling too," he said. "When Ezra mentioned it, I had a piece of memory she erased come back. Not only did she know about the experiments on me, but she sanctioned them."

"Too bad we can't turn her human-like my father." I slipped into my robe.

"I'm not sure being human would give her a conscious," Vin said. "Ezra always wanted to do what he thought was right, even if it was misguided and jaded. Calidora wants more of everything, Blood. Power. Control. That's all that matters to her."

"No memories of goodness in her?" I caressed his cheek.

"None. I don't think goodness exists in her. Her mind feels corrupt. The air tastes bitter, like poison, when she is near."

"I can't imagine anyone would know better than you as to

whether she could be saved. You are the moral compass for the rest of us."

He stood beside me and rested his head against mine.

"Ezra thinks the only way to defeat her is for me to evoke old magic," I said. "But I haven't got a clue as to how to do that."

"Maybe it's one of those things we need to figure out together." Vin pulled back and studied me. He's brows pulled together in concern. "After the wedding."

"Deal." I forced a smile and pushed old magic out of my mind, at least for the day. "I'm going to run to the lab and check on Ezra. Do you want to get Adam from Killian and Natasha's and meet me there?"

"It's a plan." He kissed my cheek.

I showered and dressed quickly and took off to the lab. As I suspected, Ezra was at work.

He glanced toward the door when I entered. "I didn't expect to see you here today."

"It's only a few days until our first launch," I said. "I still have duties."

"There isn't much left to do. I'm monitoring the weather changes and making small calibrations for it, but we are ready to go with the next neap tide."

"There was something else I wanted to talk to you about, Father."

He turned to face me. "This sounds serious."

"Why are there only women in Mother's family tree and only one daughter to each mother listed?"

He sighed. "In the old ways, a mother declared a successor, which was usually the first female child, but it could have been a second or third child if the magic was stronger in them."

"But always a female?"

"Yes," he said. "The old magic is always stronger in a female, and the original line started with a female, at least that is what we were told."

"So, it must be genetic then, something on the X chromosome but not the Y."

"If it were something tangible, then that is a possibility, and that is likely a reason the succession and knowledge were kept such a secret. However, I'm not sure it is so easy to pinpoint."

"When I did an incantation from one of the books, a web of blue lines appeared in the room. I touched one and saw a memory of Mother telling me I was special and that one day she would tell me just how much. Do you think she was talking about old magic?"

"She would have thought you were special with or without magic," Ezra said, his tone sincere. "Many in her line were not kind, Josephine. She was pure and radiated kindness. It was her, but there were so many before her who abused their power. She wanted to make sure that never happened again," he said.

"And she married you," I said. I bit down on my lip ashamed I was spiteful. "I'm sorry. I didn't mean it like that."

"It's okay, Josephine. I wasn't always the tyrant you remember, and I hope to make up for at least a small piece of that time."

"I know," I said. "You have changed, and I want other people to see it. Just sometimes..."

"It's hard to forget the past and let go of those hurts," he said.

"Yes, exactly."

"But you need to, Josephine. Those are the things that make us bitter and resentful. Stay true to yourself and the path your mother set you on, which I believe is the same path Vin wants. That is the right direction."

Adam's laughter echoed through the garden. Ezra smiled, and I returned it.

"My son might not carry a magic gene, but he is certainly magical to me."

Ezra nodded. "He is incredibly smart for one so young."

"I know," I said. "He's too smart sometimes."

Ezra laughed. "Reminds me of another sassy child I knew."

We walked out to meet them just outside the lab entrance.

"Hello, my handsome men," I said.

"Mommy." Adam stretched out toward me with grabby hands.

"Hey, little man." I took him into my arms. "Did you behave for Natasha and Killian last night?"

"No." He shook his head.

"No?" I fought back a smile. "Why not?"

"He refused to go to sleep and kept getting up to play."

Adam leaned over to Ezra. My father took him in his arms.

"Hello, my grandson. I believe you have grown overnight."

A reminder that he grew at vampire speed, but Emilia was still growing faster. Another task we had to solve before it was too late... after we reverse the ice age.

"Play," Adam yelled and leaned over backward. He sat up in Ezra's arms and looked at me. "Down, Mommy."

I smoothed his messy hair. "No, we can't get down in here. There are too many 'no no' plants in here."

"Down." He started to fake cry.

"I see we have a recent addition to our drama skills." I took him from Ezra. "Let's go get you some food instead."

"Cake!" he shouted and smiled.

"We'll see," I said. "I'll put you down, but you have to hold my hand."

"K. Mommy. Wuv you." He squeezed my neck.

"I love you too."

"Pop Pop come?" he asked.

"Who is Pop Pop?"

"Pop Pop!" He pointed to Ezra.

"That would be me, I guess." Ezra raised an eyebrow and chuckled. "Pop Pop would be happy to come with you."

Vin wrapped his arm around me, and I hooked my hand around his waist. My hand held Adam's, and Ezra held his other hand. We walked through the garden and down the hall like a family. *Mother would have loved this.* A year ago, I wouldn't have believed I'd be walking down the hall with my future husband, my son, and my father. We had to save our future. This was too special to lose.

The dining hall was closed under Natasha's wedding directives, so everyone was crowded in a smaller ballroom. She was afraid the decorations might be damaged by curious people. It made them more interested in the event, and several gathered in the hall to sneak a look.

Ezra picked Adam up, and I could see a bond already formed.

"I'll be back," Vin said. "I have some official business with those guards." He touched my back and crossed the room.

As if someone knew Adam's cravings, there was a cake on the buffet. He made grabby hands at it, and I put it on a plate for him.

"Are you ready to eat?"

"Yes, Mommy," he said. "Pop Pop down."

Ezra put him on his feet. Adam took his hand and led him to a table.

"Sit, Pop Pop," Adam pointed to a chair. "Mommy, sit." He pointed at another one.

We both obliged, and he crawled up in Ezra's lap.

I stared out the window.

"Wedding nerves or thinking about the reversal plan?" Ezra asked.

"Both," I said. "I'm worried about disappointing Vin - either with the wedding or failing to reverse the ice age. And most importantly, I'm worried about if Adam will have a world to grow up in."

"You are your mother's daughter," he reached across the table and extended his hand.

I placed mine in his. "That's not the first time you've said that."

"And every time I have, it's been a compliment to you and a testament to her." He squeezed my hand.

Natasha slid in beside me. "You have three hours until you are due in my room for Agata and me to dress you. Vin, Killian, Adam." She leveled a gaze on my father. "And you, Ezra, will all get ready in Josie and Vin's room. The rest of them need to be down at the chapel in the side room at least thirty minutes before the ceremony. You will need to wait outside of my room to walk down with us."

"As you wish, Natasha," Ezra said.

Vin slid into a seat across from me.

"Don't fuck up the day for Josie and Vin. This is about them," Natasha said, her voice hard.

I touched her arm. "We've got it."

"Fuck," Adam said, under his breath but plainer than any other word that came out of his mouth.

Vin sat on the other side and covered his mouth. I could see hints of a smile under his hand.

"Thanks a lot, Natasha."

"Sorry," she said.

"Adam?"

He looked up from the cake to me.

"Little boys shouldn't say that word."

"What word, Mommy?" He sounded older today.

"Mmm. Hmmm." I turned back to Natasha.

She shrugged and picked up the glass of blood in front of her.

"Fuck," Adam said, his voice soft.

I rolled my head back to him and stared at him with the look my mother used to give me.

"Sorry, Mommy."

Vin laughed followed by Natasha and finally my father.

I stood up to go find my glass of blood and pointed between all of them. "You better figure out a way to fix this, and he better not yell it during the ceremony tonight."

As soon as my back was turned, my hand went to my face to cover my laugh. I'd embarrassed my mother plenty of times at Adam's age, and I'm sure Adam would do the same to me.

CHAPTER 30

JOSIE - VIN

Natasha and Agata guided my wedding gown down over my head, careful not to mess up the side-swept hairdo Natasha had created for the ceremony. The handmade lace dress rustled down over my body and pooled around my feet. I inhaled a familiar delicate rose scent.

"Why does the dress smell like rose water?" I asked. Vin told me this scent always made him think of me. I wore it when we met and after the move to the Southern compound. It'd been hard to find time to make it here with anyone else. They didn't know, but this was a gift for him as well.

"I pulled some from the garden and steamed it with the oils," Agata said. "You wore it for so many years, I thought it would be perfect for your wedding day. It smells nice, right?"

"It is wonderful," I said. "Thank you."

"Better than that preservation smell," Natasha said. She smoothed out the dress and adjusted the shoulders. Her fingers paused, and she looked up. "It was a brilliant idea, Agata." She smiled.

"Thank you," Agata said.

"You two make a great team, you know," I said. "Can I look yet?"

"No, we haven't even got you buttoned up yet," Natasha scolded me. "Agata, maybe put the earrings in while I finish the back."

"Of course," Agata said. She picked up a pair of oval sapphire earrings surrounded by tiny diamonds and put each one in my ears. "Perfect," she said.

"Buttons are done. Let's put your shoes on." Natasha picked up the shoes and held them out for me, and I slid them on. "Last but not least your rings."

Natasha handed me my engagement ring first, and I put it on my left ring finger. I gazed down at it and thought of the engraved bands Vin had made for us. I smiled.

"And this beauty," she handed me the sapphire and diamond ring. "I wanted your earrings to match it."

"My mother's family ring," I said. "The earrings were a good choice for it."

"It sure is heavy," she said.

"Is it?" I weighed it in my hand. It didn't seem unusual to me. I turned it over, but it just looked like a ring. "I remember it always being on my mother's hand. She never took it off." I slipped it on my right ring finger.

"Let me slip the comb in your hair. Then you can look." Natasha took the comb from the tray on the table. She slid it into place and adjusted it. "Beautiful."

"She looks like a cover girl from one of those old bridal magazines. Doesn't she, Agata?" Natasha smiled.

"I'm turning around," I said.

Natasha grabbed the train and held it up while I faced the

mirror. She let it down and Agata helped stretch it out behind me.

Tears filled my eyes, and I fought them back. Today wasn't a day for tears.

Natasha leaned to the side and met my gaze in the mirror. "Do not destroy your makeup," she said, her voice stern.

I snickered. "Yes, ma'am."

Agata hand me a tissue. "You look like your mother today."

I dabbed the corners of my eyes.

"Enough sappy stuff," Natasha said. "Except for a group hug."

Natasha and Agata encircled me with a gentle embrace. "You are part of my family. Whatever that word means in this ice age and into the future, you are a member of it for me. Always."

"Ride or die, bitch," Natasha said.

I laughed. "Ride or die."

A soft knock on the door broke the moment. Agata walked to answer it. She opened the door wide and bowed low before Ezra.

"I'm no longer the Emperor, Agata. There is no need for formality," he said and held out his hand to help her up.

She looked at his hand and considered it before she took it.

He crossed the room and kissed both of my cheeks. "You are absolutely beautiful," he said, his tone proud. "You remind me of your mother on our day."

I smiled at him. "Did you have a big ceremony?"

"We did," he blinked back tears. "We had a grand ceremony, but it will not compare to what we celebrate today. I know your mother would agree if she were here."

"Have the others gone down to the chapel Ezra?" Natasha asked.

"Yes, a few minutes ago, and took the kids."

"Good. Let's head that way and take our places then," Natasha said in an animated tone.

"I'll go ahead and get the kids," Agata said.

"Thank you," Natasha said.

"We should have made this a double wedding, Natasha," I said.

She looked me up and down. "No way am I sharing my day with anyone else, and you shouldn't want to either the way you are glowing."

We made our way through the corridors and to the hall in front of the chapel.

"Take a deep humanlike breath," Natasha said. "I don't want you getting overwhelmed and passing out or something."

"I don't think vampires really have to worry about that," I laughed, even though I had butterflies bouncing around in my belly.

She stared at me. "Well..."

I did as she asked and inhaled what would have been deep for a human. *Rosewater. Ezra. Vampire. Human. Fresh roses. Food. Blood.* I let out the breath and focused on the roses.

"I'm going to grab your bouquet. Wait here."

"She's higher strung than usual," Ezra whispered in my ear.

"Right," I whispered back. "Think how bad she will be when she and Killian get married."

He chuckled. "Indeed."

Agata walked up with the kids.

"Mommy!" Adam yelled.

I held a finger up to my lips. "Sshh. We need to be quiet out here."

"Ok. Pretty Mommy."

"Thank you." I knelt down to kiss the top of his cheek. "I love you."

"I love you too, Mommy." And just like that, his vocabulary had changed.

Emilia stood head and shoulders taller than him. She wore a peach-colored dress. "You look lovely, Emilia."

"Thank you, Aunt Josie," she said. She sounded so much older over the last few days.

Natasha passed me the bouquet and had one for herself. "Hi, sweet pea." She hugged Emilia. "You look so pretty."

Emilia twirled in her dress.

"Are we ready?" Natasha asked.

"Ready," I said. "Let's get me married to that man who has waited far too long for me."

Josie is marrying me. I adjusted the tux in the mirror. Agata altered it yesterday, and it fit better.

"Quit staring at yourself, track ass," Killian chuckled. "Josie isn't marrying you for your good looks." He clasped my shoulder.

"Maybe not," I elbowed him in the gut. "But that might be the only reason she is marrying me."

Killian rubbed his stomach. "Trust me. It's not."

Darius opened the far door. "I thought you could use something for the nerves."

I wasn't a fan of his, but he had thrown his support behind

Josie on several key topics. When I didn't stop him, he entered the room and set the tray on the counter. The glasses were filled with an amber liquid. I need a quick whiff test. *Whiskey. Hard to say no to a good whiskey.*

"Darius, that was thoughtful of you," Killian smirked. "Wasn't it, Vin?"

"Very," I said.

Darius handed each of us a shot glass. "To the next dynasty," he said.

Josie wouldn't approve of that, and I certainly didn't. "To a united people supported by a united government," I said.

"Salut," Killian said.

"Here here," Darius said.

I waited for him to drink first. Then I tilted my head back. The quick burn was replaced by a temporary warm feeling.

Thomas opened the door. "We're ready."

"I'll see you after the ceremony," Darius said.

I nodded to him.

"You'll follow me in and take your places." Thomas held the door like he was afraid to be alone with us. Humans still feared us and who could blame them with people like Darius still part of the ruling body?

Killian moved forward to the doorway near Thomas, and I stood behind him.

"What was that?" Killian asked. "Some kind of peace offering?"

"I have no idea," I said. "He's always been an opportunist."

"Truth," Killian said.

I rolled my shoulders and cleared my head. The only thing I wanted to think about now was making Josie my wife.

We followed Thomas into the chapel and took the positions Natasha assigned us.

"You gave Agata the rings for Adam to carry, right?" I whispered to Killian.

"Yes," he whispered out of the side of his mouth. "And you better shut your mouth when those doors open or Natasha will kick your ass." He chuckled quietly.

"You should marry her," I said. "What are you waiting for?"

Killian froze and swallowed hard. I smirked.

The doors opened. I inhaled, eager for a taste of Josie. Rosewater greeted me. It was my first memory of her from when she rescued me at the gate of this place. The scent was like a trail that led me to her, and it continued to over the last hundred years. Rosewater meant she was near. My shoulders relaxed.

Agata appeared at the doorway of the chapel with the kids. Adam held her right hand and Emilia her left. She whispered to each of them, and they began the walk down. Emilia had silk petals in her free hand and midway down they paused. She held her hand up and blew a vampire breath. The silk petals dispersed like rain over the guests. Gasps came from the crowd. Not a trick for human weddings, but it was a beautiful site. The trio resumed their walk to the end. Agata positioned Emilia and Adam. Then she took her seat in the front row.

"Hi, Daddy," Adam whispered yelled.

The guests giggled.

"Hi, little man," I said.

"Can I come stand with you?"

"Of course," I smiled.

He jumped the edge of the platform and stood between me and Killian.

Natasha crossed the threshold next. Her dress matched the color of Emilia's. She took careful steps.

Killian shifted next to me. I cut my eyes at him. He made kissy lips at Natasha.

Her hand went to her lips, and she blew him a kiss as she made it to the end. She took Emilia's hand and made the step up to the other side of the platform. She gave one nod to the piano player.

His hands phrased the bars of the Wedding March. The guests stood and turned to face the chapel entrance. My gaze followed.

Josie entered on her father's arm. She was breathtaking. I sucked in the rosewater scent. The beauty in front of me came from the inside and radiated out. There was nothing more exquisite than her soul and everything good in her started there. *Gods, I know I haven't prayed much. Looking at Josie, I know we have a soul, and I'm thankful you brought ours together.*

She looked up and our eyes met. Her cheeks reddened, and she smiled. I wanted to sink my hands into her hair and bring our lips together, but that would have to wait for later.

Josie and Ezra reached the end of the aisle. I stared at my lovely bride. She'd made this a priority for me, and I would show her after the ceremony how much that meant to me.

Thomas stepped forward. "Josephine, escorted by your father, Ezra, do you freely give yourself in matrimony to Vincent Cavanaugh?"

She blushed deeper and looked at me, "With my immortality."

Ezra held Josie's hand and passed it to me. I took my place by her side now and forever.

"You may all be seated," Thomas said.

We faced Thomas together, and the rest of the world faded away.

"The bride and groom have prepared vows for each other and will recite those now."

My vows were written and in my pocket, but I'd had them memorized since Josie agreed to marry me.

"Josie, when I proposed to you, I told you how you saved me when I was lost and the moment between each heartbeat, a space I didn't even know needed filled before you. It's true and more. I promise to put our family first and support you in all you do. I promise to be the best father to our son that I can be. My life, undead as it is, will be yours until there is nothing left to give. You are my soul. To you, I pledge my love, my life, and my immortality. " I wiped away the wetness under my eyes.

"Vin, you proposed, and I had the simple task of saying yes. Simple because there was never a life I wanted to imagine without you. Simple because there has never been anyone who reached inside me and made me understand love the way you have. My heart didn't beat until I saw you on the ground at the gate, and it hasn't stopped beating for you since that moment. You are an incredible father, and it made me love you more than I even thought possible. If I have a soul, it is yours. To you, I pledge my love, my life, and my immortality." Pink pooled in her eyes.

"The bride and groom have chosen to exchange rings as part of the ceremony. May I have the rings?"

I tore my eyes away from Josie and held my hand out to

Adam. "Hey, little man, can I have the rings Agata put in your pocket?"

He turned one pocked inside out.

"Maybe try the other one."

He reached into the other one and placed the two rings in my hand. "For you, Daddy."

"Thank you," I said. "And Mommy and I have a surprise at the reception for you."

He beamed.

I handed the rings to Thomas.

"These rings are an expression of the love Vin and Josie have declared for each other. There is no beginning and no end. May that carry them through the end of their days."

I took the ring I'd had engraved for Josie and placed it on her finger. "Josephine, my Josephine. Finally mine. Finally yours."

Josie took my ring and slid it over the knuckle. "Vin, I am eternally yours. Forever and always."

"By the power given to me under our new government, I pronounce you man and wife. You may now kiss the bride," Thomas said, his voice excited like he might be happy for us.

I caressed Josie's cheek and brought her face to mine. My lips pressed against hers, and I fought the urgency building in me. The primal need for my wife grew. I broke the kiss. *My wife. My beautiful, intelligent wife.*

"I present to you Mister and Missus Vincent Cavanaugh," Thomas proclaimed.

Josie is my wife. Finally. I couldn't imagine being happier.

She took my hand and tugged me down the aisle. Everyone clapped their hands and cheered for us.

CHAPTER 31

VIN

Josie and I entered the ballroom Natasha had turned into a reception room. The banquet was excessive, but I wouldn't ruin the day for Natasha's choice. We did leave this up to her. The only request Josie and I had was Adam had his own cake to be part of the day. The miniature version of ours sat on the center table next to the bigger one.

The ground shook under me. My heart pounded in my ears. I looked at Josie. She watched the floor and looked at the wall in front of us. I followed her gaze, and debris flew at us. I pushed Josie to the ground and turned in Adam's direction. Killian and Natasha covered the kids and slid into the hallway. I pressed myself down over Josie and rolled with my back as a shield in the direction of the explosion.

Dust and smoke covered us, I shut off my breath. The weight was stacked on my back. A sharp pain jabbed my neck. Another one pierced my side. *Fuck. That hurts.*

My ears rang and the pain turned to agony. The tie around my neck choked me, and I wanted to rip it off. The rubble on top of me pinned my arms against my side. *My wife.* I couldn't touch her, and she wasn't making any noise.

"Josie, can you hear me? Can you move?"

"Yes, I can," she said, her voice solid but rough. She coughed, and her body shifted against mine.

I shifted to create space for her. The torment in my back was almost unbearable, but the concrete slabs on top shifted. I strained to hold it in place, without the use of my arms.

"I can see some space," Josie said.

The place on my side throbbed. "Ugh."

"We're coming," Killian said, his voice sounded muffled.

"I've got your hand," Natasha said, her voice concerned. She must have Josie's hand.

Some relief came over me despite how excruciating the ache in my neck was.

"Vin, we're coming for you," Josie said, her voice like a worried angel.

Another explosion hit further away. *Mother fucker. Gods be damned.* I knew where they were headed, and I knew it was my mother coming for her prize.

"Go to the lab, Josie," I grunted out. "I'm fine."

"No," she cried out. "I'm not leaving you here." Her hand found its way through the debris, but I couldn't move to touch it." My heart broke. This wasn't how I saw it ending, but I had to be strong for her.

"We've got help," she said.

"No, this is my mother, and she is after your research. You need to go now."

"I'm not leaving you," she said, her voice frantic.

"I'll get out on my own." One way or another, I would. "Killian, take Josie and Ezra to the lab. They have to launch the first reversal this week at low tide. Have Agata and Natasha get the children out of here and to the Southern Compound."

"Are you sure, brother?" Killian asked, his tone incredulous.

"Yes, we don't have time to debate," I said. "Get the fuck out of here." My back was damp with blood. I didn't need to see it to know, and neither did Josie.

"Let go of me, Killian," Josie screamed, her voice wild and unhinged. "I will banish you. Let me fucking go."

Her voice faded away, and I closed my eyes.

"It's bad, isn't it?" Natasha said.

I ground my teeth together. "It's not good. Get our kids out of here, Natasha."

"We'll be back for you, Vin. I promise. We don't leave family behind."

"Just make sure our kids live to see the future we imagined." Tears breached my eyes, and I couldn't move to wipe them away.

"I will, Vin. Hang on. Fight for Josie like she fought for you."

"Always. Now go."

She sobbed once, and her footsteps became distant.

Emilia and Adam's cries were faint in the hallway. "We're going on a trip together. The four of us. Then everyone else will join us there."

"Where?" Adam cried.

My son needed a father. I moved my body, testing the parameters of my prison. Anguish burned through me and the metallic scent of blood bloomed around me.

"The Southern Compound," Agata said.

"I don't want to go," he cried.

"Let me do my thing," Natasha said. "We're going on a little trip, and we'll be patient with each other and understand that some of our family still has work to do here."

"Yes, ma'am," Emilia said.

"Yes, ma'am," Adam repeated.

Natasha would punish herself for using her gift on the children, whether it was a kindness or not. She'd promised Killian she wouldn't use it.

"Let's go," Natasha said, her voice dispassionate. She'd turned her emotions off, and I couldn't blame her for that.

I listened for their footsteps to disappear from my range. "Gods if it is my time, then I accept that, but I'd rather fight for my wife, my family, and my country if you see fit."

Another detonation rocked nearby, and the block on top of me shifted enough to free one arm. *That I can work with.*

My hand moved along the source of agony in my neck. *Rebar.* It penetrated deep where the neck joins the shoulder. I grasped the metal and pushed against it. My muscles and anything else it had damaged, had already started to heal. It ripped it apart as I pushed. The trauma nearly made me pass out, but it freed my other arm. *One down.*

I reached my hand down to the spot on my back. It was another piece of rebar, but there were two pointed ends embedded in me. When I moved, one tip scraped against my spine. If it didn't come out, I'd continue to bleed out until my body stopped and not many came back from that.

"Aagh." I braced myself and reached my hands out as far in front of me as I could. My heart beat fast in my chest. I steadied myself and pulled.

"Fuck." I waited for my body to recover enough to push on the cement chunks. *I need blood.*

"Gods, if you are listening. Give me strength."

I placed both hands on the concrete directly over me and pushed. It moved a little. I mustered power and resolve and heaved into it. The slab shifted to expose a gap sufficient to get my hands through.

The wounds healed at a slow pace, which told me I lost a lot of blood. There hadn't been any more explosions, and I hoped that meant our people were fighting back. Most of them weren't fighters, and that worried me. Many of the humans would take a stand, but they wouldn't last long against Calidora's soldiers, especially if she had Rogues with her.

"Fuck waiting." I spread my hands out the length of the rubble and pushed. It fell away like the lid of a sarcophagus and shattered on the ground. I climbed out of the coffin-like void. The wall where the device detonated opened to the outside. The green was empty. I clamored over the mounds of rubbish and out into the hallway. It was too quiet. I questioned if my hearing was working, but I'd heard remnants slide around as I shuffled through the smaller pieces in the hallway.

A carafe of blood lay on its side in the passage. It still had about half the contents. I picked it up and smelled it. *No sweet gardenia.* I tipped it back and sucked it down. My injuries thanked me by healing faster.

I ran full speed to the lab not knowing if Josie and Ezra would still be there or if they even went, but it was the first place I had to try. The door was locked. I pressed my hand on the keypad unsure if Josie had calibrated it for me. The metal panels groaned and started to move apart. *Faster.* I tried to urge it along.

The door opened. Josie pulled a sword, and Ezra had a sunshine stick. It would have looked funny in other circumstances. "Really? That's how you're planning to defend yourselves?"

Blood covered Josie's white dress. An overwhelming sadness crept up my spine. My mother had ruined a moment and split our family up.

They stared at me like they were in shock. "Do you have everything packed up? We need to get you and your research out of here."

Ezra looked at Josie like he waited for her to answer.

"Close the door, Vin," she said, her voice calm.

I slammed my hand against the button on the inside. It was wet. I glanced at it to see blood. They must have fought their way here, but I hadn't seen any bodies in the hall.

"We're not leaving. We're going to fire the first device tonight."

"Isn't that too early?" I asked. "Where's Killian?"

"We were rerunning the model to see what our success rate will be," she said, her tone matter of fact.

"Josie," I implored her.

"If you are staying, we need your help." She turned back to the computer.

It dinged, and I moved closer.

"Seventy percent," Ezra said, his tone grim.

"Better than zero," Josie said.

"But not the ninety-nine point five if we wait," he said. "Vin, do you think you can get to the roof?"

"Yes, why?"

"We have an old missile launch there that should have

enough power to get the device to the right coordinates," he said.

"What about you two?"

"Josephine will go with you," he paused. "I'm going to face Calidora and buy you both some time."

"What's to say she wouldn't kill you now? I'm the one she wants. I should go, and you should go with Josie."

He pulled his jacket back to reveal a large piece of shrapnel in his side. I noticed the blood pool at the base of his chair. *The blood on the button.*

"Ezra, we can sew you up," I said.

"No, you can't. It's in several organs. I might not be vampire anymore, but I certainly know what it feels like when an organ is damaged. I'm bleeding out inside. I'm a walking dead man."

Josie had turned her emotions off so they could work. It all made sense now. Her shoulders hunched over. It took a toll on her to turn it off.

He rubbed her back. "Keep it off until you finish the mission. Then let it all go in Vin's arms."

"What can I do?" I asked.

"Take this backpack. Everything you need is on the laptop. Plus I put Josie's mother's journals in there for reference." He handed me a smaller case. "The device is in here. Josie knows what to do once you get to the roof. Killian will meet you there."

"We will succeed."

"Don't just succeed," he said. "Survive. Live a thousand years making my daughter happy and raising as many children as you are blessed with."

I hugged him, awkward but gracious. "I hated you once," I said.

"I know," he said.

"Thank you for this," I said.

"Don't thank me. Make me proud." I gave one nod.

Josie stood up. "Can one of you hook the train of my dress up?"

I picked up the edge.

"There is a hook near the bottom of the buttons and loop on the hem," she said.

I found them and secured it on the hook. She was barefoot, her shoes lost somewhere after the explosion. It gripped my heart and squeezed. Our day was ruined and beyond that, her father would not see tomorrow no matter what we did. We could give hope of a future for our children, and we would keep that promise no matter the cost.

She faced Ezra. "I don't know what to say."

"I love you, Josephine, and of all the things I've done in my life, being your father is the only one that mattered."

She leaned against him and wept.

"Sssh," he said. "Shut it all off for now. There will be time for that later. Tonight you must be the strong, fierce warrior you have always been."

"I love you, and I'm so glad I got to know this version of you. The real version. The good version."

"I'm all the versions you remember, so learn from my lessons. Now, go while we have a window. They could show up here any time," he said.

"Don't let them destroy mother's garden," she said.

"I'll do what I can." He pushed her towards me.

I wrapped a protective arm around her. "We'll do this for him and for our son," I whispered in her ear.

She nodded and went rigid. Her emotions were off again as Ezra instructed. The crash after would be awful. I'd been there when she ended things with me decades ago, and yet, I figured this would be a thousand times worse for her.

Ezra opened the door. "Give me one minute, and if you don't hear anything, get to the roof as fast as you can."

"Be well, Ezra," I said.

"Be well, my daughter and my son." He turned and ran.

CHAPTER 32

VIN

I opened the door to the roof and eased out. I inhaled and didn't smell anyone. If Killian was supposed to meet us here, he hadn't made it yet. *He'll be here. Duty first.* I could hear voices over the edge, but I focused on getting Josie set up.

"This has to be the missile launch," I said, keeping my voice low.

Josie walked to it like someone under Natasha's gift. She knelt and examined it in the quarter moonlight. I set the small case with the device in it beside her and opened it.

She went through the steps like she had done it a million practiced times. Her hands maneuvered the pieces of the device together until it looked like a small rocket. She lifted a section of the launch pad and slid the device into place.

"Laptop," she said.

I opened the backpack and pulled the laptop out. She took it from me and placed it on the ground. There was a piece of paper in the case of the device. She entered letters and numbers off of it into the program on the laptop. The delivery device made several clicking noises and a series of red lights blinked to life. My wife moved like a robot, but she and Ezra had done what they set out to do.

She took an earpiece out of the case and put it in her ear. "Killian, we're ready."

"On my way." I heard Killian's voice and let out a breath like a human.

Josie closed the case and handed it to me. "Put it in the backpack. We can't risk Calidora getting any of it."

A whirling noise came in fast from the opposite side of the voices below. I grabbed Josie's arm to run for cover, but she pushed me away.

"It's Killian," she said, her tone restrained.

Blades spun as the transport topped the building. He pulled up next to the roof and the door slid open. Josie held the backpack close to her chest with one arm and took off at a sprint. She leaped into the helio like an expert. I followed suit, my landing less graceful than hers.

Natasha sat in one of the seats. *The kids. Where are they? Are they okay?*

"Later." She mouthed.

I moved to the co-pilot seat and put the headset on. "This was unexpected," I said.

Killian shook his head. "Right, bro." He spun the helio around toward the side where the voices came from. "Madame President?"

I looked over my shoulder at my wife.

She stared at the laptop screen. "I've started the count-down. We need to cover it for thirty seconds and give it time to get into the atmosphere."

"Let me know when it gets to 5 seconds," Killian said.

"Twenty seconds," she said.

Killian flipped a couple of switches on the panel.

"What does that do?" I asked.

"Brings the sun." He smirked.

"Ten seconds," Josie said.

"Everyone buckle in and hold on just in case," Killian said.

I clicked my strap in place.

"5 seconds," Josie said. "Now, Killian."

"Bringing the sun, Madame President." He flipped a couple of switches. The light blinded me.

I covered my eyes with my arm. A distinct zip noise came to life. I looked under my arm.

The small device shot into the air.

"Hold," Josie said. "We need about sixty seconds."

My eyes adjusted to the light. Calidora's forces blasted the same spot Ezra's army had used, widening the hole we had only temporarily patched. I should have pushed to reinforce it after the Rogues showed up last time.

I narrowed my focus to the small group. There was no mistaking my mother and at her side Josie's father. Ezra looked pale for a human or vampire. I unbuckled my belt. My mother wouldn't get away with using him.

Josie kicked her leg out in front of mine. "He made his choice. He was very specific about what we should do. Don't make his sacrifice be in vain. He earned a hero's death, and this is the only way he will have that."

I leaned back against the bulkhead. *Did she know what she was asking? With her emotions off, did she understand what my mother would do down there?*

"Fifteen seconds, Killian. Then, we can head to the rendezvous point."

I watched the events unfold on the ground. My mother looked up into the blinding light.

"We can exit the space whenever you are ready," Josie called over her shoulder to Killian.

Calidora kicked the back of Ezra's legs and forced him to his knees. She forced his head back to look at her.

Josie scooted closer to the open door.

"You don't have to watch this." I slid into the seat beside her.

"No, I want to see. I want to remember what he did for us," Josie said, her tone solemn.

I wrapped an arm around her shoulders. "You can remember without watching."

She trained her eyes on them.

Calidora dropped his head and stared up at the helio. A wicked smile crossed her face.

He looked up at her. His words from a now human voice carried across the wind and over the noise to our vampire ears as if carried by old magic. "We did it. It's done."

She snapped her head back toward him. Her hand extended out, and one of her soldiers placed a knife in it.

"Josie, don't," I said.

Josie didn't look away. I pulled her tighter to me, but she was stiff in my arms.

Ezra sprung up at Calidora and knocked her backward. Her guards grabbed his arms and held him still. She pulled back his coat and saw the shrapnel. Her fingers curled around it, and she twisted it.

To his credit, Ezra remained motionless, and the pain had to be agonizing.

Calidora took the knife and stabbed him in the chest.

Ezra's legs gave slightly, but he stood back up straight. "You lost, Calidora."

She flipped her hand once to the guards.

They pulled Ezra's hands behind his back and pushed him to the ground. A guard with a longsword in his hands walked up. I knew what would happen. Josie knew. We all knew. We'd seen it happen. Killian had done it himself under Ezra's command.

"Madame President?" Killian said, his voice confused.

"He wants this," she said. "We will wait."

The longsword sliced through the air and made one clean swipe. *Small mercy.* Ezra's head rolled to a stop on the ground.

A guard handed a torch to Calidora. No not a guard. Julius. *He will meet his fate at my hands.* She waved the flames up and down Ezra's body until it was engulfed. She picked up his head and threw it on top. *A vampire's death.* There would be no coming back from this. A final death.

Josie slid off the edge of the seat and over to the open door. I moved to pick her up.

"We can't leave his body," she said, her voice quiet and menacing. "She'll parade him around."

"There won't be a body left to parade, Josie," I said, keeping my voice calm and steady. "Killian get us out of here."

I coaxed her away from the door and nodded to Natasha. She closed the door. I held Josie to me, but no tears fell from her. She just stared with her eyes unfocused.

"You can let go. I'm here," I said, running my hand over her hair.

"Not yet," she said. "We're not done."

"We're about twenty seconds away from the muster point,

Jo..." Killian paused. "Madame President." He'd only called her Madame President since we had been in the helio.

"What is going on? You can't launch more until the next neap tide."

"We're going to fight, but we needed time to get the humans far enough away," Natasha said. "And our kids." She swallowed hard.

"Fight? But we just left the perfect opportunity for me to kill my mother," I said, the rage in my voice palpable.

"Vin, we had to make sure the first device got launched and the information open-sourced to our allies," Josie said. Her chin rested on her fingers as she stared at the wall. "My father bought the time for us."

"Touch down in five," Killian called to us.

The bay door started opening before we landed on the ground. A crowd gathered around. A very large crowd. Josie stood and straightened her back. She positioned herself in the center and walked forward as soon as the ramp met the ground.

CHAPTER 33

JOSIE

I tucked my emotions deep like Father told me to do. The time to mourn him and explain to Vin would come later. Tonight I needed to be Madame President for the force we had amassed, and I couldn't do it all with the emotions bubbling under my skin and stabbing at my resolve. I wanted to let it all go and drop into Vin's arms for comfort, but too much was at stake. Our sovereignty. Our future. Our lives.

Gods, if you exist, I pray for our success tonight and in the coming days, and I pray that, if I have a soul, it is still intact when this is over.

The crowd grew quiet as I descended the ramp in front of them. I studied the faces in front of me. Humans and vampires stood together before me, still unified in our goal. Some had blood on them. Some had weapons. Most had fear on their faces, probably from worry our cause would be lost. Or maybe because I stood before them in my bloodied wedding dress.

"Thank you all for staying behind. I know many of you

have families, like me, and it is a sacrifice to remain behind to fight," I said. The memory of my father's head on the ground, eyes wide open, flashed in front of me. I imagined a box to put the memory in and locked it in my mind. "We launched the first reclamation device, and the data will be available in a few hours to measure our success."

The crowd cheered. I wanted to cheer with them, but I couldn't afford to break the thin veil holding back my breakdown. They quieted.

"My father died a warrior's death to ensure our success." The crowd remained silent. I wanted to hear them praise him. "The sequencing and formula to reverse the ice age has been disseminated to our allies in trust they will move forward if we fail," I said. "But we will not fail." I forced a smile across my face.

The crowd roared in support and accolades.

"Tonight we reclaim our home for our families and for our newly formed government. We take our power back, and we eliminate the threat to our children."

The mass of people grew louder around me. They believed in our cause. Father's death would mean something to them.

"Gather your weapons and find the group leader matching your assigned color. If you haven't received an assignment yet, come see a group leader. We will prevail."

I turned back into the tundra. Killian left the helio blades out, in case we needed a getaway. It wasn't an option in my mind. "We need to change clothes." I looked around at the group still in our attire from a happier moment in the day. For a moment I hid back in the trunk of my mind unable to mourn the events of the day.

"There are combat suits like we wore when we repelled into the Chicago Compound." Natasha passed them out along with our armbands.

"That will do." I ducked into the bathroom to change. "Natasha, I need some help with the buttons."

It should have been Vin undoing the buttons, but Calidora made that impossible. I shoved the anger and disappointment into a mental compartment for later.

Natasha appeared at the door. Her dress was marked with blood spatters. Her fingers worked the buttons. "I hate seeing this dress destroyed almost as much as I hate what Calidora did to your day but not near as much as what she did to Ezra."

Natasha babbled when she was nervous. "Later, Natasha. I can't right now."

She hugged me from behind. "When you ready," she said. "All done. I'll go find Vin for you. He looks like a lost puppy dog."

"Thanks," I said over my shoulder. When her steps moved away, I closed the door and let the dress drop to the floor. I didn't want to see myself, but I gazed into the mirror. The woman there wasn't the same one that looked back at me a few hours ago before Vin married me. *Who am I now?* No parent left to turn to for guidance. No grandparent for my child to grow up knowing. A single pink tear rolled down my cheek, and I swiped it away. My friends were still here though, and I was thankful for them, even if I couldn't show it.

A blue thin light glowed behind me in the mirror. I spun around and confirmed it was there. *Am I hallucinating? I haven't called any old magic.* My fingers shook, but I grasped the magic thread.

"Josephine, it's time to claim the blue light," my mother's voice said around me.

"Mother?"

"Open and let the light in," she said.

The sapphire in her ring on my hand twinkled. I peered at it. *I am open to receiving this light.*

Nothing happened. Not a twinge. Father had said it would take old magic to beat Calidora, and here it was in front of me taunting me.

"Mother, I don't know what to do."

"Feel," her voice said in my ear. An intense force thrust into my back and kneaded my heart in a slow beat. All the sentiment and vehemence I'd buried unlocked. The rawness surfaced and agony snaked through my body claiming vengeance for all I denied it. I shuddered, then quaked where I stood. The intense convulsions made my organs ache like they were on the verge of shattering.

I dropped to my knees as my father had, but my hand pulled the blue thread closer to me. My chest heaved. The sobs came with the tortured reminder I was alone. My parents were both gone, and I was alone. Even though I knew there were people who cared for me, I'd never been more alone in my journey.

"Now, you can claim what is yours and rise to save this precious world," my mother's voice whispered in my ear.

A calmness came over me and filled the empty parts of me. My hand felt warm. The sapphire glowed an intense blue. The light covered my hand and traveled up my arm. It wound around me until my entire body bloomed in blueness. It seeped into my skin, and the magic in me awakened. It tingled under my skin ready for the fight ahead.

"I can't give you all the answers, but I can show you where this war started."

Time played in front of me similar to the memories in the library. *Mother and Father met in Europe centuries ago. Their love forbidden by her powerful father. Enter Calidora. Not as old as my mother but older than my father denoted by the hierarchy of introductions to my grandfather. Calidora came from another line. The origin they were not able to determine, but they traced it to another part of the world about the same time. Calidora pursued my grandfather, but he was deep in grief over the loss of my grandmother. It was the reason he refused my father's offer of marriage to my mother. Calidora offered to help my mother convince my grandfather. Grandfather relented and allowed the marriage provided they wait a decade. Calidora tried to use her powers of persuasion on the King, my grandfather, to gain power and he sent her away. She cursed him, his kingdom, and his children.*

"Who carries that around for centuries?" I asked out loud.

"Don't forget you shut Vincent out for decades. How quickly did that time pass?" Mother whispered to me.

"True," I said, my voice full of shame. "I'm not sure what to do with this knowledge or power. How is it going to help me defeat Calidora when I don't even know how to use it?"

"Go to the library and find this book." The image of a hand-tooled brown leather book with gold leafing appeared in front of me. A blue sapphire shone from the center of the cover. "The rest is up to you, my dear special daughter. I love you, Josephine."

"I love you too." The warmth that filled me retreated until it was no more.

I glimpsed my reflection in the mirror and moved closer. My blue eyes reflected a twinkle like the sapphire before them. I held my hand up with the ring facing the mirror for confirmation. The magic in me bolstered my confidence.

My tear-stained face reflected the image of many families if we didn't stop Calidora. I washed the pink residue off and pulled on the tactical suit. We needed to rethink the approach.

I put my unfortunate wedding dress in an empty bin outside the bathroom door and grabbed a pair of boots.

"Next," I said, ticking off tasks to keep myself moving forward. I sat in one of the seats and pulled on the high tops. The laces secured, I looked up to find my husband and friends staring at me.

"There is a change in our plans, and I'll explain. We can't go in wearing formalwear though," I said. "I'm strong right now, but I'm not going to stay that way with you all looking at me like that. The next person needs to get in the bathroom and change clothes. Killian and Vin could go in the cargo hold to change."

"How about Killian and I go change in the bay?" Natasha said. She grabbed his hand and pulled him away.

"Natasha told you the kids, ours and the humans, are on the way to the southern compound in the other helio? Thank Ezra for having his secrets," I said.

"Yes." Vin dropped into the seat next to me. "Josie." He pressed a hand on my knee.

"Don't make me do it twice, Vin. It's taking everything I have to not shatter across this floor," I said, my voice controlled and the direct opposite of the chaos inside me.

"I just want you to know I'm here. However, you need me. Whenever you need me." He wrapped his arm around me and kissed my temple.

"Forever," I whispered and leaned against him.

"Eternally yours, my wife," he whispered back. I closed my eyes and inhaled his scent. *Did I dare tell him how deep his mother's vendetta ran? Would it break him the way I'm broken right now? I couldn't. Wouldn't do that to him.*

CHAPTER 34

JOSIE

"Just the four of us?" Killian asked as he slid into the chair next to Natasha.

"Yes, there are some details we can't share with everyone, so I'll let you share the short version with the group leaders, Killian."

"Your call, Madame President," he said.

"You can drop that for now," I said.

"I'm having whiplash," Killian said. Natasha buried her elbow into his gut. He smiled and raised his hands in a surrender motion. "Fine.

"I'm not sure how, maybe through old magick, but my mother visited me. She awakened it within me." I pointed to my eyes.

"Fuck me," Natasha said.

"That's Killian's job," I said.

"Nice one," Natasha said.

"This happened in the bathroom?" Vin asked.

"Yes, it was like a spiritual thing."

"Well, that's a relief. We thought you were losing your shit and talking to yourself in the bathroom," Natasha said.

Killian's eyes widened, and he turned to Natasha.

"What? You know we all thought it," she said.

"So, what do you need from us, Josie?" Vin asked concern etched across his face in a way I hadn't seen in the century I'd known him.

"I must go to the library and retrieve a specific book Mother showed me. It has whatever it is we need to defeat Calidora for good."

"She's not going to let us walk in without a fight," Killian said. "We'll need a distraction."

"Exactly," I said. "What if we send Rogues into the area Calidora's troops are occupying?"

"Wouldn't she just control them?" Natasha asked, confused.

"Not if someone else is." I looked at Vin. The pit in my stomach ached at the request I made of him.

"Josie, we don't even know if I can. Your father and my mother are the only two we've seen do it," he said.

"If it doesn't work, just lead them in Calidora's direction," I said.

Natasha barked laughter. "You are sending your husband to tame a pack of Rogues? Alone? What the fuck, Josie?"

"You think I want to? He's the only one who can do it, Natasha," I said in a callous tone. "Unless you are volunteering to use your gift on them?"

"That's enough," Vin said, his voice quiet but forceful. "I'll do it. The sun will be up soon. Are we just going to let them burn once it does?"

"There should be enough cloud cover today to offer them protection. A new storm is moving in on the jet stream."

"Vin's leading an army of mass killers. What are Killian and I doing?"

"Guarding our President on her mission," Killian answered.

I nodded. "Yes, you'll infiltrate our home with me."

"And where will the group leaders be with their forces?" Natasha asked.

"They will be stationed at a distance. We will only call them up if the Rogue army fails at the distraction," I said. "Vin, won't let it fail though. No more than I'll let Calidora have our home."

"I'm in, Josie. When I married you, I pledged my love, my life, and my immortality to you. That applies as much now as it did a few hours ago," Vin said.

My heart ached for the task I asked of him. If there were Gods watching us, that would surely cost me something. "And I you. We'll meet you in the courtyard when I have the book."

"Killian, can you and Natasha prep the group leaders? I need to chat with Vin alone," I said.

"Of course," he said. His turn to tug Natasha out of the room. She dug her heels and narrowed her eyes at me. She didn't like secrets, and she didn't like my plan.

"You don't have to explain to me," Vin said. "This is what we signed up for as husband and wife."

"It's not just that, Vin," I said. "I want to tell you this alone, and you can decide how important it is."

He sat down and pulled me into his lap. "I'm listening."

"There is a reason your mother was after my family, and it goes back centuries. About five."

"She is from another very powerful line, possibly another original line from a different part of the world than mine," I said. "She can't wield magic like mine, but she does have some very special gifts."

"Like Natasha's," he said.

"Yes," I said. "Only stronger, but not strong enough for my grandfather. And you certainly are more gifted at tracking than anyone else. You have power in your blood too."

"How does this relate to your family?"

"She wanted to marry my grandfather after my grandmother died. I don't know all the detail, but he banished her from the kingdom. Then she followed them here when they came to America in the eighteen hundreds. She's had five centuries of hate building in her veins." I rested my hand against his face and braced for the conflict this would cause in his moral compass.

"Josie, you and Adam are my family. Killian, Natasha, and Emilia are part of our family. Calidora has never been my mother. If you are worried about making me choose, the choice is already made. I choose my family. My real family," Vin said, his tone sincere.

I leaned my forehead to his. "You surprise me every day my dear husband."

"And you me," I pressed my lips to his forehead.

His mouth sought out mine. "When we win this today, I'm taking you to bed for a week," he whispered against my cheek.

"Our son might take issue with that," I laughed.

Vin chuckled. "You're right. We'll figure it out," he said. "Like we always do."

He stood up and supported me as I slid down his body. "We better find some supplies and power up."

"Let me check the deployment status of the device." I retrieved the laptop from the backpack and connected it to the tundra's system. The radar popped up on the bigger screen. I ran my fingers along the path and read the numbers captured on the side. "These look good. The future calculations look better than expected."

I smiled at Vin. "We should start seeing some thawing in the next day or so. Coastal areas will probably see it first, but we can expect it here soon."

Vin picked me up at the waist. I wrapped my arms around his neck. He swung me around in a circle. "You did it," he said.

"We did it. You, Ezra, me, Killian, Natasha. We all did it," I said.

"I'm so proud of you," he said.

"Let's find Natasha and Killian and share the news with the others. We have success to give the army confidence and inspiration."

I took his hand, and we walked down the platform into the sea of supporters.

CHAPTER 35

JOSIE - VIN

Killian entered the library first, even though we smelled nothing in the air except leather and paper. He waved us into the room. "Close the door."

Natasha kicked it with her foot but caught it before it slammed. She shut it with a near-soundless click.

"Where should we start, Josie?" Killian asked.

Mother's ring sparked to life the closer I got to the shelf with her books. If the brown leather book with gold leafing was here, it was with them. I ran my hand along the spines, but there weren't any vibrations.

"I'll check this shelf over here," Natasha said. "Old brown leather with gold on it, right?"

"Right," I pulled one of the books off. *Not it.* "Is there a step stool in here?"

"There's one." Killian carried it over and placed it in front of the shelf for me.

I climbed it and moved the books from side to side. The ring brightened near one. I opened it, but the ring dimmed again. The book didn't have brown leather or gold leaf on it. I sat it back on the shelf, and the ring intensified like a compass pointed in a direction. *Hmm.*

"Killian, can you shine a sunshine stick under here?" I pushed the books aside from the area the ring directed.

"Sure," Killian said, his tone skeptical. He pushed the button, and the light illuminated the underside of the top panel.

"Look," I pointed. "Doesn't that section look like another color?"

"It does," Killian said.

"Let me see," Natasha said. "Shit, it does." She pulled out a knife and handed it to me. "Better open it before I do."

I slid the edge of the knife around the rectangle shape. It loosened and fell out in my hand with the book.

"Well, fuck me," Natasha said.

"Later," Killian retorted.

I giggled. "We found it." I flipped it around to show them.

"Your eyes are starry looking," Natasha said. "Is that a good sign or a bad sign? If you're going to erupt or something, I'd like to get out of the way."

"I have no idea, but I think I'd know if there was a pending eruption." I climbed off the stool and carried the book to the desk. "How do you think Vin is doing?" I set the book on the desk but didn't open it.

"He's fine, Josie. He'll be fine," Natasha said.

"I'm going to check the corridor while you two look at the book," Killian crossed the room.

"He needs to feel useful, and standing around doesn't cut it," Natasha said.

"I know the feeling," I said, thankful for some normal conversation.

"Yeah, I'm not much for sitting or waiting. Emilia is like that too," she said. "She's so damn bossy. I don't know where she gets that."

I laughed. "Really? Does she babble when she's nervous too?"

"Just open the damn book, Josie," Natasha said, but she smiled.

My hand slid over the lock, but there wasn't a release. Just a depression in the middle.

"I know what this is," I said.

"Doesn't it have a button to open it?" She leaned over to examine it.

"No, it's a blood lock," I said in an abrupt tone.

"That's a bit barbaric," she said.

"Is it really? We are vampires," I said. "Calidora left one on the puzzle box for Vin in the cabin above her lair."

"She is so fucked up," Natasha flipped her hair over her shoulder.

"You have no idea how bad." I regretted it when it left my mouth. Natasha, out of all of us, had experienced the worst Calidora had in her arsenal. "When Vin engaged the one on the puzzle box, it put him in a trance-like state for quite some time. If that happens to me and trouble comes, you and Killian save yourselves. She won't kill me until she has what she wants."

"That's possibly the stupidest thing that has ever come out of your mouth, Madame President. I might revoke my vote for you. Now, open the damn book." Natasha's eyes grew wider with each word. I thought her eyes might bug right out of her head.

"Here I go." I positioned my thumb in the small well and

pressed down against the needle. The small jab was barely a prick. A mechanism clicked, and the strap fell open.

I lifted my thumb and flipped the book open to the first page. Red ink appeared across the page like my blood uncovered each letter.

"Are all the pages blank?" Natasha asked in an exasperated tone.

"What do you mean? Do you not see the red letters?"

She narrowed her eyes on me. "Did it mess up your eyes? There is nothing on that page."

"There is. You can't see it, Natasha. There must be an incantation protecting it from being visible to anyone other than someone with my bloodline," I said.

She ran her hand over the page. "You can really see something on there?"

"Yes, but it's in a script I don't recognize. Something ancient."

"Of course, it fucking is, because nothing can ever be easy for us." Natasha rolled her eyes. "Are there any translations or ancient language books here?" She looked around.

"I think there were some short references in one of Mother's books." I walked over to the table where I left them. "This one." I brought it back over to the desk and sat it next to the brown leather book.

"I know some of these. Calidora had me learn several," she said in disbelief.

"Do you know this one?" I pointed to one that looked similar to what was on the pages of our new book.

"Yes," she said. "Is that what is on the page?"

"It looks like it. The letters on the page are a little more ornate," I said.

"That language hasn't been used in about a thousand years," she said. "I questioned why she'd want me to learn a dead language, but I believe we have the answer why."

"Should I write them down?" I asked. "Or you could bite me and see the memories of it. That would be quicker."

We looked at each other. "Bite," we said in unison.

I jutted my wrist out toward her. "Be careful and stay in the present," I said like we didn't both know exactly how dangerous this was.

Natasha cradled my wrist with one hand and bared her fangs over the other. Her free hand slipped into mine.

I squinted my eyes and peered through a slit. My mother's ring illuminated.

The door opened, and I jerked my head. "Natasha, no!" Killian shouted.

"He's right. Don't." I yanked my arm back. The ring dimmed.

"What is going on?"

"Oh, you know. We were bored and decided to try a little blood play kink," Natasha said. "We're trying to read this damn book. What did you think we were doing?"

"And biting each other helps you read?"

"It's an ancient language I can see but Natasha can't, but she knows the language. Can we move on now?" I said. "Take my hand again, Natasha. Let's see if maybe you can read it if we are touching."

"Hmm. We probably should have tried that first."

Killian rubbed his forehead.

I held my palm up for Natasha, and she took it. The ring glowed like a blue sun.

"Can you see the writing on the paper?" I asked.

"No, " she said, exasperated. "It's still blank." She loosened her grip.

"Wait," I said. The words started to unscramble for me. I tightened my grip on her. "It's working for me. I can read it." My heart raced in excitement. "This is an incantation to relive memories. It's the same meditation my mother had in her book."

"We don't need to relive memories. Find something more useful," Natasha said. "Your palm is getting sweaty."

I flipped the pages. "Maybe this one. It makes someone believe they are burning alive."

"Boring. Try again," Natasha said.

"I have to agree with her on that one," Killian said.

I thumbed through a few more. "This has to be the one mother wanted me to find."

"Spill it," Natasha said.

"It turns the recipient into stone or maybe it means freezes? It says stone cold." I looked up at them.

"Either way, that sounds like a winner to me," Natasha said. "Do you need to write the incantation down? I'm not sure how much longer I can hold your hand with all this perspiration."

"I can't write with my left hand," I said. "I can remember it for a minute." I pulled back my hand and wiped it on the leg of my tactical suit.

"So gross. Who knew a vampire could sweat so much?" Natasha wiped her hand too.

"The ring generates a small amount of heat." I laughed.

"That was more than a little heat from a ring," she said.

"Let me concentrate." I ripped a blank page from the back of a more modern book and wrote down the short incantation. The desperation grew in me as I finished. "What if it doesn't work? What if old magic doesn't answer me when I read it?"

"I don't think you have to worry about that," Natasha said.

"I'm going to check to see if Calidora is still in the courtyard. You two stay here until I get back. Then we'll go down together," Killian said.

JOSIE PREDICTED THE RESPONSE. The Rogues responded to my command. There were at least three dozen who listened to me and followed me to the breach in the wall. I had no way of knowing if they belonged to the same hoard Calidora controlled, but it's not like I could ask.

I waited. They waited. I walked. They walked. I ran. They ran. It disgusted me that my mother engaged in the experiments to create these creatures. She did all vampires a disservice that could not be righted. Her actions stole the humanity from them, and it couldn't be returned. Maybe we could add reversing it to the list of things Josie had going. She had the weight of the world literally, and I thought of saving the creatures no one thought were savable.

A short light flashed from the window closest to the library. *Killian.* Calidora and Julius both had their back to me. I shot the briefest flash back.

Where was the rest of Calidora's army?

I inhaled and scented nothing beyond the Rogues with me, the guards in the courtyard, Julius and Calidora... and another familiar odor. *Death.* Ezra's charred body lay at Calidora's feet.

She used his body to set a trap for Josie. Her confidence exceeded my assessment with minimal guards by her side.

There wasn't a way to get a message to Killian. I steadied my mind and strengthened my connection with the Rogues. They shifted behind me. I sensed the desire for blood in their very nature. Nothing else mattered to them. It overpowered me and made me hungry. I pulled back. *Horrible existence.*

I commanded them into formation around me, and we flooded into the courtyard.

"Attack," I shouted, praying they wouldn't attack me since I controlled them. They ran past me towards Calidora and her guards.

"Leave her for me," I whispered into their minds. The small hoard slaughtered her guards in the same way they had Ann.

Josie, Natasha, and Killian burst out the backdoor toward me. The urge to tuck her against my side was hard to fight. She didn't need my protection. Josie's strength blossomed as President of our new world.

"We have it," she said. "We can stop her."

"What do you need?" I asked.

"To get close enough to her to use an incantation," she said.

No part of me wanted her that close to my mother, but my formidable wife didn't need my permission. "We can use the Rogues to make a path."

"Are you insane?" Natasha said.

"They are under my control. If that makes me insane, then yes," I said.

"Always with you, tracker ass," Killian said.

I smirked. "You'd be lost without me." I moved forward and the hoard parted at my whisper. "Let's go."

CHAPTER 36

JOSIE

Vin managed us through the dozens of Rogues. The sounds deafening as they devoured Calidora's guards. They had her and Julius surrounded. *And my father's body.* I knew it would be there. A pawn she planned to use against me in some way.

I held up my hand for us to stop. Calidora stood stone-faced. Either she accepted what was to come, or there was more to the trap than she exposed with my father. We'd missed our chance more than once. I had to take it this time.

The Rogues parted, and I stepped through the opening flanked by my husband and my family.

I held up the piece of paper and began to read.

"This enemy before me stands in dishonor
Make them live in an eternal memory
Stone cold and frozen for eternity."

Nothing happened.

Calidora cackled. Her wretched laughter bounced off the walls. "You thought you could wield old magic?" She laughed harder. "You weak water-downed version of an original line."

She struck a thread of anger in me, and my ring fired blue light out. Wind blew the snow up around us. I let the paper fly from my hand into the swirl around us and held my palm up in her direction. My soul tapped into the power of the words. The old magick radiated out from me, and the incantation floated through my mind.

This enemy before me stands in dishonor
Make them live in an eternal memory
Stone cold and frozen for eternity.

A blue thread shot from my hand to Calidora's chest. Her hands spread out wide. The magick started with her feet, planting her in place like a tree. Her legs cemented in place. She tried to speak but only grunts came out.

"Stop," Julius yelled.

"Step back," Vin said. "Or you will be next."

Calidora's body was solid to her waist.

"You don't understand," Julius said. "She has your children."

I tried to sever the connection, but it refused to let go. Old magic required an end once there was a beginning. It would finish what it started with or without me. I cut the thread mentally, and it recoiled on me with a sharp snap. The force knocked me backward, but strong arms caught me before I hit the ground. *Vin.*

He righted me.

"I couldn't stop it, and I don't know if it can be reversed." My voice shook.

Killian had Julius by the collar and pushed him toward us on his tippy toes.

"Talk," Killian said. "Or I feed you to the Rogues."

"She intercepted the transport with them and routed it to the Chicago Compound."

"All of the kids? Ours and human kids too?" The alternative was too much to even think about.

"Yes, all of them," he said. "I told her it was a bad idea."

"You're coming with us," Vin said. "Unless you would rather stay with our statuesque mother."

Julius shuddered. "No, I'll go. I'll go."

"If one child is harmed, you will pay for your mother's sins," Natasha bared her fangs at him.

He flinched back against Killian, who tightened his grip on the collar.

"Killian, can you have someone take my father's remains inside? I can't do it, and I can't leave him here while we are gone. He will receive a hero's burial when we return."

Killian shoved Julius to Vin and jogged off.

"Hello brother," Vin said., his tone low and menacing. "For every horror my son faces, you will face ten. For every one Emilia faces, you will face another ten."

"What else can you tell us, Julius?" Natasha touched his temple.

"The Rogue army is surrounding the Chicago Compound waiting on you. If you don't surrender, they will force you by killing you from least important to most important."

"Tell me more," Natasha whispered in his ear.

"Darius can command them too."

"Darius?" I repeated.

"Yes, he and Calidora had an alliance to restore vampire aristocracy."

"She was still chasing a crown after five centuries," I said. "A fucking crown."

"No tundras," Vin said. "We need to go in silent."

"Then the humans will have to stay here. They can't keep

up with us on foot, and it would slow us down to carry them," Natasha said in her normal voice.

"Agree. They stay here. This is a vampire fight," I said.

Killian returned with five citizens, three vampires and two humans. "These kind souls have volunteered to care for Ezra's remains."

"Thank you," I said. "Please treat him with the respect and honor of a hero."

One man stepped forward, "I heard you say he assisted in deciphering the formula and delivery system that will return our lands to the greenness they once were. I'm honored to care for his remains as that is a debt we cannot repay."

"He would be honored to have you take care of him." I shook the man's hand. "Thank you."

JULIUS' description of the Chicago Compound being surrounded by Rogues was an understatement. Double the numbers stood like sentries around the compound and along the cliff, we repelled down last time. Our vampire army and three dozen rogues were outnumbered times three at least.

"We could have airdropped in from a helio tundra," Natasha said.

"But it couldn't carry all of us, and it would have announced our arrival," I said.

"Can you turn all of them to stone like you did Calidora?" Killian asked.

"Did you not see the number of blood bags she downed on our way here?" Natasha cut her eyes at him. "And that was one person."

"Julius, is there a way in that isn't guarded?" Vin asked.

He shook his head. "No, not unless you can pole-vault onto the roof unseen."

"And you can't control them, Vin?" I asked.

"No, if what we learned here before is true, it looks like they can only bond with one of us at a time. If we could break Darius' connection, then maybe, but I'm not sure."

I skewered Julius with my eyes. "Do you know?"

"I wasn't allowed in on those discussions. You know more than I do," Julius leaned back.

Old magick are you the answer? Can I tap into you to get us through this moat of death? I scrutinized my ring and channeled my thoughts to the passage. A blue thread appeared, and I grasped it in my mind. My hand warmed as the sapphire glowed with power. I jutted my palm out. The Rogues parted.

"Go now," I gritted out. "I'm not sure how long I can hold it."

"I'll stay with her," Natasha said.

"No," I grunted. "I'll follow last. Go."

Killian whistled and Natasha went to his side. Together they led the troops across.

"Go, Vin. Take your Rogues."

"They're not mine." He looked at them and pack at me. "Fuck. Promise me you're right behind us."

"Promise," I ground the word.

He moved forward, but the Rogues didn't. "They're not responding."

"Go without them."

He ran across where Killian and Natasha held the door. I stood up and made my way toward the passage. It flickered like my strength. Vin's Rogues followed me. They wouldn't walk in the blue light, but they filled in the space behind me. The light formed a barrier in front of me, and Vin's Rogues formed one the other way.

Natasha and Killian stepped back out of sight, but Vin held the door open. I stumbled into his arms. His Rogues wouldn't follow inside. No Rogue wanted in this horrible building, and our kids were here somewhere. My stomach flipped in fits.

Vin scooped me into his arms.

Natasha slammed the door shut.

Killian stood over me with a blood bag.

I severed the blue thread in my mind as I had with the incantation for Calidora.

"Drink it, Josie. We need to find the kids," Natasha said. She took the blood bag from Killian and ripped it open. Her hand squeezed my face, and liquid dripped into my throat. *Blood.* I swallowed in gulps.

"One more, my love," Vin said.

"I can sit up," I said

Vin knelt to make a chair with his leg.

Natasha handed me another open bag. I let it slide down my throat. My foggy brain cleared, and I stood.

"Let's go get our kids," I said.

"And refrain from using old magic the rest of the trip," Vin said.

"We'll have to see on the second point," I said. If it meant the difference in bringing our children home or not, I'd use it until my immortality bled dry.

"Julius, you're up," Vin said.

Killian grabbed his collar like the scruff of a cat's neck.

"This way," Julius pointed.

Killian forced Julius out front. If any of us died, he'd be

first. He led us down a long corridor into a smaller one. There were no signs of guards or Darius. The compound seemed vacant.

Julius led us through a narrow set of stairs down to the next level where we could only pass single file. The steps were metal with gaps and crisscrossed back and forth on the way down. The path was slow. It made us easy targets. I inhaled the air, and I heard others do the same. I didn't catch the scent of Darius.

Natasha met my gaze. Julius might have played us. I maneuvered to get closer to him. Laughter drifted up.

I glanced at Natasha, and she smiled. The kids were safe.

Julius guided us to an old maintenance room. *Who's idea was it to put kids in a room with a bunch of old tools?*

"Open the door," Killian shoved Julius.

Julius complied and stepped back. Killian nodded to one of our soldiers, and he pinned Julius against the wall.

There were more kids inside than I expected. I exchanged a look of confusion with Natasha.

"Adam?" I called out.

"Emilia?" Natasha followed.

They came running to us.

"Mommy." Adam jumped in my arms. "We went adventure."

"I know. Were you scared?" I smoothed his wild hair down and kissed his cheek.

"No, I not scared."

I laughed. Of course, he wasn't. My amazing boy wasn't scared of anything.

"Mom, I'm fine," Emilia said. "Where's Dad?"

"Here," Killian called from the door.

Emilia made her way to him and wrapped her arms around his waist.

"Want to see Daddy?" I asked Adam.

"Yes, where?"

"Right there." I pointed to Vin in the hallway

Adam leaned toward him. Vin walked in the room and took him. "Hey, little man. Ready to go home?"

"Yes, play with Pop Pop," Adam said.

Vin reached out and rubbed my arm. I held back tears, but the grief settled in my chest. I'd figure out how to tell him when we got back to Dallas. That conversation would not be tonight

"Who are all these kids?" Vin asked.

"I have no idea," I said.

"They went venture too. New York. Chicago. Dallas," Adam said.

"They told you that?" I asked him.

He nodded. "Yep, Mommy."

I scanned the crowd of kids, and in the corner, there was a little girl about Emilia's size. Her head rested on her knees. I knelt in front of her. "Luna?"

She looked up with eyes I recognized even if she'd grown so much. "Luna, do you remember me?"

She nodded.

"Does your mom know where you are?"

She shrugged.

"Do you want to come with us to Dallas and we'll try to find her?" I held my hand out for her.

Luna's hand squeezed mine with a tight grip like I was her last lifeline. This poor girl had been separated from her mother multiple times now in her short life. Darius and anyone else involved would pay for this.

"Where is Livia?" Natasha whispered to me.

"Losing her mind wherever she is," I said. "Let's get these kids upstairs. The sun is due out in about an hour. If we time it right, we should have a Rogue free window."

I counted the number of children. "We'll need thirty volunteers to carry kids provided their parents aren't here."

"I'm going to check our path," Killian said.

We sorted out the children and prepped for the trip. Each one had an assigned adult for the trip. Killian met us at the top level.

"The Rogues are gone except for the ones under Vin's control," he said.

"I better send them for cover before the sun breaks through." Vin passed Adam to me. Adam invented his own game and bounced back and forth between us every few minutes.

Natasha leaned over to me. "Where do you think they went?"

"Wherever Darius is I'm sure," I said. "Let's get the kids to safety and then worry about the rest."

"Do we need to get the devices while we are here?"

I shook my head. "Not with the kids. I took a quick look while Adam was with Vin, but I didn't find them. We'll make a trip up here before we need them. We still have a few in Dallas to use."

"All clear and the sun is out bright. Time to go," Vin said.

"Daddy," Adam squirmed in my arms. Vin took him.

"I'll take Luna," I said. I squatted in front of her. "Can you climb on my back?"

She nodded and climbed on wrapping her arms around my neck. I secured her legs by looping my arms around them. "Ready?" I asked over my shoulder.

"Yes," she whispered.

I looked down the hallway and got thumbs up all the way.

"We're ready," I said to Vin.

Our group trekked out into the snow with the sun warming the air.

CHAPTER 37

JOSIE

One week later

Natasha walked into my office. "Any luck reaching Livia?" She dropped down in the chair in front of my desk.

"No, none of the contacts in New York seem to know her," I said. "At least not as Livia."

"The parents of the twins are supposed to be here today. Other than Luna, they are the last of the kids from other compounds."

"Adam misses having the kids around," I said. "Speaking of kids, how are you feeling?"

"I'm feeling great. Lots less puking this time around. Em misses having the other kids too, but she is excited to have a little brother or sister." Natasha caressed her belly.

I smiled at her. "That's great, Natasha. She's going to make the best big sister."

"I know right," she said. "Have you decided what to do with Julius?"

"No, Vin and Killian have him on trash duty for now, and he's in the cell when he's not working."

"What about Darius? I know you wanted to catch him before you had Ezra's services, but it's been a week."

"No sign of him." I paused. "I picked a date for Ezra's memorial."

She nodded. "Killian told me. I'm here for you, Josie. I know you have a lot to do, but I'm here to help or listen to you complain or for a shoulder to cry on," she said. "As long as you don't leave stains on my shirts."

I laughed. "I'm good, Natasha, but thank you. My two priorities are filling the empty spots on the council and getting everything ready to launch the next device."

"My hands are yours however you need them."

I knew what she was saying. Ezra left a hole, and she wanted to help fill the void he left.

"Would you ever consider running for President?" I asked her.

"Hell no," she said without hesitation.

A knock at my door had Natasha on her feet.

Vin stuck his head in and smiled. "Am I interrupting?"

"I was on my way out," Natasha said. "Before Josie passes all her duties off to me."

Vin laughed. "Bye Natasha."

She turned at the door. "We all know you two have sex on that desk." She smirked and shut the door.

"Oh, my gods." I sunk down in the chair. "Do you think she was guessing or do you think they know?"

"Well, you can be pretty loud sometimes." Vin grinned.

"Me? What about you shoving papers in the floor?" I threw my pen at him.

He caught it and tossed it onto the desk. "More serious subject. Everything you asked for is set for the memorial services."

I walked around the desk and sat on the edge. I leaned forward and rested my hands on his shoulder. "Thank you for helping me through the last week."

He pulled me into his lap and wrapped his arms around me. "There will be good days and bad days, but the good ones will start to outnumber the bad."

"Today has been a pretty good one. I haven't broken down once," I said.

Vin kissed my cheek.

A rumble came from outside. The blood in my glass sloshed but didn't spill. "What was that?"

"I don't know." He stood up and sat me on my feet.

I opened my office door and the head guard met us. "The ..." he stopped. "Calidora exploded.

"What do you mean she exploded?" I asked.

"The stone blew apart," he said.

Vin and I rushed down to see, and there on the ground were more than a dozen pieces of Calidora. My personal guards fanned out around us.

"Do you think it was the old magic?" I asked.

"Maybe," Vin said.

It claimed death for the Vampire Rite when I enacted it with Ezra, so could it have claimed Calidora in a similar way? I picked up one of the pieces and turned it over in my hand. The inside appeared hollowed out instead of solid as I expected.

"Could she have escaped?" Vin flipped a large piece around and studied it.

Killian came out the back door. "Julius is in his cell, so it wasn't him. I have the guards sweeping the perimeter."

Natasha was right behind him. "The kids are fine. What happened?"

"We don't know," I said.

Natasha examined the pieces. "She's old and powerful. Maybe it took her this long to build up the strength to break free."

I considered it, and that would make sense. When I used magic, I needed extra blood.

"Are we going after her?" Natasha asked.

"Not until after Ezra's ceremony," Vin said.

I wrapped my arm around his waist and leaned against him.

"Did I read the temperature right in the dining hall?" Natasha asked.

"The highest in almost a century," I said. "We can start planting outside soon."

"I haven't seen the humans this excited since we offered them shelter. It's nice to see. One of the little girls said she played outside without a coat for a whole five minutes." Natasha laughed. "She was so cute."

A guard jogged up to Killian and turned to me. "Madam President."

I nodded to him. "Please tell us what you found."

"We noted a single set of footprints leading away from the compound to the clearing. Then they disappeared," he said. "I'm sorry we don't have better news."

"Thank you," I said.

"Increase the patrols to every fifteen minutes," Killian's said.

"Yes, sir." He jogged back in the direction he came.

"Helio," we all four said at the same time.

"I'll send some scouts to known areas. We'll find her and Darius," Killian said.

"My only ask is that nothing disrupts Ezra's services," I said. After his death, a peaceful memorial was the last dignified act I could give him. "I'll ask someone to clean up the pieces and lock them up in one of the labs."

"I'll do it," Vin said. "She was my mother."

I RAN to the lab Vin was in to tell him the good news. "Guess what?"

He locked the drawer where he stored the stone pieces from Calidora. "What is it, my beautiful wife?"

"We heard from Livia," I said. "She's on her way to get Luna now."

"Where did you find her?"

"I didn't. One of her family members told her we were looking for her, and she hoped it was because of Luna. I already let Luna talk to her, and they are both excited."

"Do you think Livia will stay once she gets here?" Vin asked.

"I hadn't thought about it, but I'll ask when she arrives." I smiled. "We still have so much to do and another set of capable hands would be welcome."

Vin took my hand and led me out of the lab. "Let's take a walk."

"Sure," I said.

We got to the familiar doors, now with two guards posted out front. "The garden?" I smiled.

"Yes." He guided me through the doors into the center of

the room. A small table was set up with a picture of Ezra. Some flowers were on the table with it. Mother's flesh-colored roses were in an arrangement on the floor in front of it. Six chairs sat in front of it.

"What's this?" I whispered.

"We thought you might need a private service for Ezra where you could be a daughter mourning her father versus the President celebrating her predecessor," he squeezed my hand.

Natasha carried Adam and Killian held Emilia's hand as they entered. They filed into the row of chairs and waited. I looked up into Vin's eyes. His forehead was wrinkled in concern.

"Thank you." I leaned against him.

He guided me to the two seats vacant at the end. "We can sit as long as you want, or if you want to speak you can."

I took the few steps next to the table.

"Pop Pop," Adam shouted.

I smiled. "Yes, Pop Pop," I said, my voice barely above a whisper.

"He died, Mommy," Adam looked at me with tears in his eyes. "But he's still with us."

My words to him echoed back at me. Tears pooled in my eyes. "Yes, he did, little man, and I loved him."

Adam climbed off his chair and came to hug me. "He wouldn't want us to be sad."

I brushed his messy hair out of his face. "It's okay to be sad sometimes, Adam, especially when people like Pop Pop, leave us."

Little pink tears ran down my son's face, and it yanked all of my grief forward. It broke like a fractured dam inside me.

I buried my face in my hands and sobbed. Adam patted the top of my head. "It's okay, Mommy," he said. "He knows."

"Knows what, Adam?" I raised my head.

"He knows how much you love him," he said, a matter of fact like I should have known what he meant.

Vin sat on the ground next to me and encircled me with his arms. Adam hopped in his lap. Natasha and Killian perched on the seats in front of us and leaned forward. Emilia sat in front of Adam and took his hands.

"We will finish this for him," I said. "In Ezra's honor, we will complete the task of reversing the ice age and restoring the world. He warned we will have to go back into the shadows eventually. That we will be forgotten to tales of lore like our ancestors, and to that I say, I'm fine with sinking into the background. I don't know about you, but I'm ready for a time of peace where we can just be a family."

Natasha glided down to the floor to sit face-to-face with me. Killian slid in behind her.

"Well, you might want to be behind the scenes, but this face deserves a spotlight," she smiled and looked up at the ceiling in a fake pose.

"Mom," Emilia said. "Good grief."

Our group erupted in laughter.

"I'm joking, Em," she said. Then she turned to me and took my hand. "And my sister knows this. We are family, Josie. I'm not sure exactly when it happened, but this is a family unit. We are here for you, and we support you no matter where you lead us as head of the family or head of the country."

My throat thickened. "Thank you, Natasha." I cleared my throat. "And thank you for always calling me out on my bullshit."

She laughed. "It's what I'm here for. And we all know Killian would jump on a flaming stake for you."

"And for you and your daughter." I squeezed her hand.

"I don't do this mushy stuff, but you have always been my family, Josie. And my family grew when I fell in love with Natasha and had Em."

"Look at my man all up in his feelings." Natasha leaned back and kissed him.

"Gross." Emilia gagged.

I stifled a laugh and centered myself.

"Thank you all for accepting me and always having my back. I couldn't have made it through this past week without you." I fixed my gaze on Vin. "And thank you for loving me and always knowing what I need, even when I don't know for myself."

"I'm always here for you." He pressed his lips to my temple.

Calidora's fate loomed over us as did Darius's whereabouts, but today, we immersed ourselves in our family. As I regarded each of them with affection, happiness and joy slinked into the broken crevices of my heart and mended them. Each laugh, smile, and touch healed my heart and my soul. I peered at Vin, and his eyes met mine. A smile spread across his face. Old magick wasn't his thing, but he was gifted. Warmth in my hand drew my attention. My family ring glimmered as oft blue like it confirmed what was already in my heart.

The path we chose wasn't easy We could face a century or more of battles, but we would win the war. Our efforts would reverse the ice age and restore the environment for humans. I refused a future where we failed, and with old magic on our side and the plan Ezra and I made it could be done.

The reclamation of this world from ice waited only for us to stay on this track. A route that brought each of us into the same orbit and made us a family. If we were lucky, we would have at least five centuries together like my mother and father, but I hoped for more. I'd never have enough of this family. They completed my life and reminded me that vampires could foster humanity. If I understand our history, we were once part of it, and that gave us responsibility.

"I thought Ezra had changed, and I realized, after seeing some memories from when he met my mother, he found himself again. When he and Mother met, he was ambitious, but he was kind, like her. He loved her with a fierceness that I know well because I love you with that same fierceness."

"I love you, Josie. Forever," he said.

"Eternally yours," I said.

To be continued...

ACKNOWLEDGMENTS

This book was finished after my biggest cheerleader, my mom, passed away. Writing through grief was the biggest struggle I've faced in my writing career, and I am beyond thankful for those who continued to encourage me when I didn't think I could do it.

Thanks to the family and friends that cheered me on through this process, and to the readers who loved *In Blood & Ice* and got me excited about writing *Reclamation In Ice*.

To my incredible editor, Dawn Alexander, you make me a better writer with every book. Thank you for always pushing me along the writer's journey so that my characters and story evolve into something special.

Love and thanks to you all!

ABOUT THE AUTHOR

Susan Person is a multi-contest finalist in the paranormal and dark paranormal categories with five published books. Recently, she returned to college to pursue a degree in anthropology and graduated in May 2021. Susan enjoys meeting writers and readers alike at conferences. She knew at an early age she wanted to write powerful heroines and fulfills that dream by writing badass empowered heroines who take charge in their paranormal worlds.

Susan grew up on a thoroughbred horse farm before moving to the big city of Dallas. She considers herself a Texan but is loyal to her home state of Arkansas. A lover of travel, she has visited several countries with many more to go on her list. She particularly loved dowsing at Stonehenge. The outdoors are a place Susan finds inspiration and can often be found in a park, at the lake, or on a road trip. She especially loves the mountains. Furry animals hold a special place in her heart, and dogs tend to seek her out as a friend. A friendship she happily returns.

Connect with her at susanperson.com

facebook.com/therealsusanperson

instagram.com/susanwritespnr

tiktok.com/@susanpersonauthor

amazon.com/author/susanperson

goodreads.com/susanperson

twitter.com/susanwritespnr

ALSO BY SUSAN PERSON